"How about loosening up a bit, Major?"

"What do you mean?"

"Come off it," Carraciola said roughly. "You know damn well what he means. It's our lives. Why do we have to go down into that damned village? If we're to commit suicide, tell us why. You owe us that."

"I owe you nothing," Smith said flatly. "I'll tell you nothing. And if you know nothing you can't talk. You'll be told when the time comes."

"You, Smith, are a cold-blooded devil."

"It's been said before," Smith said indifferently.

FAWCETT CREST BOOKS
by Alistair MacLean:

Alistair MacLean

WHERE
EAGLES DARE

FAWCETT CREST • NEW YORK

A Fawcett Crest Book
Published by Ballantine Books

Copyright © 1967 by Cymbeline Productions Ltd.

ISBN 0-449-20707-2

This edition published by arrangement with
Doubleday & Company, Inc.

Printed in Canada

First Fawcett Crest Edition: November 1968
First Ballantine Books Edition: January 1985

ONE

THE VIBRATING clangour from the four great piston engines set teeth on edge and made an intolerable assault on cringing eardrums. The decibel-level, Smith calculated, must have been about that found in a boiler factory, and one, moreover, that was working on overtime rates, while the shaking cold in that cramped, instrument-crowded flight deck was positively Siberian. On balance, he reflected, he would have gone for the Siberian boiler factory any time because, whatever its drawbacks, it wasn't liable to fall out of the sky or crash into a mountainside which, in his present circumstances, seemed a likely enough, if not imminent, contingency for all that the pilot of their Lancaster bomber appeared to care to the contrary. Smith looked away from the darkly opaque world beyond the windscreens where the wipers fought a useless battle with the driving snow and looked again at the man in the left-hand captain's seat.

Wing Commander Cecil Carpenter was as completely at home in his environment as the most contented oyster in his shell in Whitstable Bay. Any comparison with a Siberian boiler factory he would have regarded as the ravings of an unhinged mind. Quite clearly, he found the shuddering vibration as soothing as the ministrations of the gentlest of masseurs, the roar of the engines positively soporific and the ambient temperature just right for a man of his leisured literary tastes. Before him, at a comfortable reading distance, a book rested on a hinged contraption which he had swung out from the cabin's side. From what little Smith could occasionally see of the lurid cover, depicting a bloodstained knife plunged into the back of a girl who didn't seem to have any clothes

5

on, the wing commander held the more serious contemporary novelists in a fine contempt. He turned a page.

"Magnificent," he said admiringly. He puffed deeply on an ancient briar that smelt like a fumigating plant. "By heavens, this feller can write. Banned, of course, young Tremayne"—this to the fresh-faced youngster in the co-pilot's seat—"so I can't let you have it till you grow up." He broke off, fanned the smoke-laden air to improve the visibility, and peered accusingly at his co-pilot. "Flying Officer Tremayne, you have that look of pained apprehension on your face again."

"Yes, sir. That's to say, no, sir."

"Part of the malaise of our time," Carpenter said sorrowfully. "The young lack so many things, like appreciation of a fine pipe tobacco or faith in their commanding officers." He sighed heavily, carefully marked the place in his book, folded the rest away and straightened in his seat. "You'd think a man would be entitled to some peace and quiet on his own flight deck."

He slid open his side screen. An icy gust of snow-laden wind blew into the flight deck, carrying with it the suddenly deepened roar from the engines. Carpenter grimaced and thrust his head outside, shielding his eyes with a gauntleted right hand. Five seconds later he shook his head dispiritedly, screwed his eyes shut as he winced in what appeared to be considerable pain, withdrew his head, closed the screen, brushed the snow away from his flaming red hair and magnificent handlebar moustache, and twisted round to look at Smith.

"It is no small thing, Major, to be lost in a blizzard in the night skies over war-torn Europe."

"Not again, sir," Tremayne said protestingly.

"No man is infallible, my son."

Smith smiled politely. "You mean you don't know where we are, sir?"

"How should I?" Carpenter slid down in his seat, half-closed his eyes and yawned vastly. "I'm only the driver. We have a navigator and the navigator has a radar set and I've no faith in either of them."

"Well, well." Smith shook his head. "To think that they lied to me at the Air Ministry. They told me you'd flown some three hundred missions and knew the Continent better than any taxi driver knows his London."

"A foul canard put about by unfriendly elements who are trying to prevent me from getting a nice safe job behind a desk in London." Carpenter glanced at his watch. "I'll give you exactly thirty minutes' warning before we shove you out over the dropping zone." A second glance at his watch and a heavy frown. "Flying Officer Tremayne, your gross dereliction of duty is endangering the entire mission."

"Sir?" An even deeper apprehension in Tremayne's face.

"I should have had my coffee exactly three minutes ago."

"Yes, sir. Right away, sir."

Smith smiled again, straightened from his cramped position behind the pilots' seats, left the flight deck and moved aft into the Lancaster's fuselage. Here in this cold, bleak, and forbidding compartment, which resembled nothing so much as an iron tomb, the impression of the Siberian boiler factory was redoubled. The noise level was so high as to be almost intolerable, the cold was intense and metal-ribbed metal walls, dripping with condensation, made no concessions whatsoever to creature comfort. Nor did the six metal-framed canvas seats bolted to the floor, functionalism gone mad. Any attempt to introduce those sadistically designed instruments of torture in H.M. penitentiaries would have caused a national outcry.

Huddled in those six chairs sat six men, probably, Smith reflected, the six most miserable men he'd ever seen. Like himself, each of the six was dressed in the uniform of the German Alpine Corps. Like himself, each man wore two parachutes. All were shivering constantly, stamping their feet and beating their arms, and their frozen breath hung heavy in the icechill air. Facing them, along the upper starboard side of the fuselage, ran a taut metal wire which passed over the top of the doorway. On to this wire were clipped snap catches, wires from which led down to folded parachutes resting on top of an assortment of variously shaped bundles, the contents of only one of which could be identified by the protruding ends of several pairs of skis.

The nearest parachutist, a dark intense man with Latin features, looked up at Smith's arrival. He had never, Smith thought, seen Edward Carraciola look quite so unhappy.

"Well?" Carraciola's voice was just as unhappy as his face. "I'll bet he's no more bloody idea where we are than I have."

"He does seem to navigate his way across Europe by opening his window and sniffing the air from time to time," Smith admitted. "But I wouldn't worry—"

He broke off as a sergeant air-gunner entered from the rear, carrying a can of steaming coffee and enamel mugs.

"Neither would I, sir." The sergeant smiled tolerantly. "The wing commander has his little ways. Coffee, gentlemen? Back at base he claims that he reads detective novels all the time and depends upon one of the gunners telling him from time to time where we are."

Smith cradled frozen hands round the coffee mug. "Do *you* know where we are?"

"Of course, sir." He seemed genuinely surprised, then nodded to the metal rungs leading to the upper machine-gun turret. "Just nip up there, sir, and look down to your right."

Smith lifted an enquiring eyebrow, handed over his mug, climbed the ladder and peered down to his right through the Perspex dome of the turret cupola. For a few seconds only the darkness filled his eyes then gradually, far below and seen dimly through the driving snow, he could make out a ghostly luminescence in the night, a luminescence which gradually resolved itself into a criss-cross pattern of illuminated streets. For a brief moment only Smith's face registered total disbelief then quickly returned to its normal dark stillness.

"Well, well." He retrieved his coffee. "Somebody should tell them down there. The lights are supposed to be out all over Europe."

"Not in Switzerland, sir," the sergeant explained patiently. "That's Basle."

"Basle?" Smith stared at him. "Basle! Good God, he's gone seventy or eighty miles off course. The flight plan routed us north of Strasbourg."

"Yes, sir." The sergeant air-gunner was unabashed. "The wing commander says he doesn't understand flight plans." He grinned, half apologetically. "To tell the truth, sir, this is our milk run into the Voralberg. We fly east along the Swiss frontier, then south of Schaffhausen—"

"But that's over Swiss territory!"

"Is it? On a clear night you can see the lights of Zurich. They say Wing Commander Carpenter has a room permanently reserved for him there in the Baur-au-Lac."

"What?"

"He says if it's a choice between a prisoner-of-war camp in Germany and internment in Switzerland he knows which side of the frontier he's coming down on . . . After that we fly down the Swiss side of Lake Constance, turn east at Lindau, climb to eight thousand to clear the mountains and it's only a hop, skip, and jump to the Weissspitze."

"I see," Smith said weakly. "But—don't the Swiss object?"

"Frequently, sir. Their complaints always seem to coincide with the nights we're around those parts. Wing Commander Carpenter claims it's some ill-intentioned Luftwaffe pilot trying to discredit him."

"What else?" Smith asked, but the sergeant was already on his way to the flight deck. The Lancaster lurched as it hit an infrequent air pocket, Smith grabbed a rail to steady himself and Lieutenant Morris Schaffer, of the American Office of Strategic Services and Smith's second-in-command, cursed fluently as the better part of a cup of scalding coffee emptied itself over his thigh.

"That's all I need," he said bitterly. "I've no morale left. I wish to God we *would* crash-land in Switzerland. Think of all those lovely *Wiener schnitzels* and *Apfel strudels*. After a couple of years living among you Limeys, spam and powdered eggs and an ounce of margarine a day, that's what Mama Schaffer's little boy requires. Building up."

"You'd also live a damn sight longer, friend," Carraciola observed morosely. He transferred his gaze to Smith, gave him a long considering look. "The whole setup stinks, Major."

"I don't think I understand," Smith said quietly.

"Suicidal, is what I mean. What a bunch. Just look at us." He gestured to the three men sitting nearest to him on his left: Olaf Christiansen, a flaxen-haired first cousin of Leif Ericsson, Lee Thomas, a short dark Welshman—both those men seemed slightly amused—and Torrance-Smythe, as languidly aristocratic-looking as any *ci-devant* French count that ever rode a tumbril, a doleful ex-Oxford don who clearly wished he were back among the University cloisters. "Christiansen, Thomas, old Smithy, and myself. We're just a bunch of civil servants, filing clerks—"

"I know very well what you are," Smith said quietly.

"Or yourself." In the de-synchronised thunder of the engines the soft-voiced interruption had gone unnoticed. "A major in the Black Watch. No doubt you cut quite a dash playing the bagpipes at El Alamein, but why the hell *you* to command us? No offence. But this is no more in your line than it is in ours. Or Lieutenant Schaffer here. An airborne cowboy—"

"I hate horses," Schaffer said loudly. "That's why I had to leave Montana."

"Or take George here." Carraciola jerked a thumb in the direction of the last member of the party, George Harrod, a stocky Army sergeant radio operator with an expression of profound resignation on his face. "I'll bet he's never as much as made a parachute jump in his life before."

"I have news for you," Harrod said stoically. "I've never even been in a plane before."

"He's never even been in a plane before," Carraciola said despairingly. "My God, what a bunch of no-hopers! All we need is a team composed of specialist Alpinists, commandos, mountaineers, and safe-breakers and what do we have?" He shook his head slowly. "We have us."

Smith said gently: "We were all the colonel could get. Be fair. He told us yesterday that the one thing in the world that he didn't have was time."

Carraciola made no reply, none of the others spoke, but Smith didn't have to be any clairvoyant to know what was in the minds of all of them. They were thinking what he was thinking, like himself they were back several hours in time and several hundred miles in space in that Admiralty Operations Room in London where Vice-Admiral Rolland, ostensibly Assistant Director of Naval Operations but, in fact, the long-serving head of M.I.6, the counter-espionage branch of the British Secret Service and his deputy, Colonel Wyatt-Turner, had gravely and reluctantly briefed them on what they had as gravely and reluctantly admitted to be a mission born from the sheerest desperation.

"Deucedly sorry and all that, chaps, but time is of the essence." Wyatt-Turner, a big, red-faced, heavily moustached colonel, tapped his cane against a wall map of Germany, pointing to a spot just north of the Austrian border and a little west of Garmisch-Partenkirchen. "Our man was brought down here at 2 A.M. this morning but SHAEF, in their all-knowing wisdom, didn't let us know until 10 A.M. Damned idiots! Damned idiots for not letting us know until so late and double-damned idiots for ignoring our advice in the first place. Gad, will they never learn to listen to us?" He shook his head in anger, tapped the map again. "Anyway, he's here. Schloss Adler. The castle of the eagle. Believe me, it's well named, only an eagle could get there. Our job——"

Smith said: "How are you so sure he's there, sir?"

"We're sure. Mosquito he was in crash-landed only ten miles away. The pilot got off a radio message just before a

German patrol closed in." He paused, smiled grimly, continued: "Schloss Adler, Major Smith, is the combined HQ of the German Secret Service and the Gestapo in South Germany. Where else would they take him?"

"Where indeed? How was he brought down, sir?"

"Through the most damnable ill-luck. We carried out a saturation raid on Nürnberg last night and there shouldn't have been a German fighter within a hundred miles of the Austrian border. But a wandering Messerschmitt patrol got him. That's unimportant. What's important is getting him out before he talks."

"He'll talk," Thomas said sombrely. "They all do. *Why* did they disregard our advice, sir? We told them two days ago."

"The whys don't matter," Wyatt-Turner said tiredly. "Not any more. The fact that he'll talk does. So we get him out. *You* get him out."

Torrance-Smythe cleared his throat delicately. "There are paratroops, sir."

"Scared, Smithy?"

"Naturally, sir."

"The Schloss Adler is inaccessible and impregnable. It would require a battalion of paratroops to take it."

"Of course," Christiansen said, "the fact that there's no time to mount a massed paratroop attack has no bearing on the matter." Christiansen appeared positively cheerful, the proposed operation obviously appealed vastly to him.

Wyatt-Turner gave him the benefit of his icy blue stare, then decided to ignore him.

"Secrecy and stealth are the only hope," he went on. "And you gentlemen are—I trust—secretive and stealthy. You are experts at that and experts at survival behind enemy lines where all of you have spent considerable periods of time, Major Smith, Lieutenant Schaffer and Sergeant Harrod here in their professional capacities, the rest of you in—um—other duties. With the—"

"That was a damned long time ago, sir," Carraciola interrupted. "At least for Smithy, Thomas, Christiansen, and myself. We're out of touch now. We don't know the latest developments in weapons and combat techniques. And God only knows we're out of training. After a couple of years behind a desk it takes me all my time to run fifty yards after a bus."

"You'll have to get fit fast, won't you?" Wyatt-Turner said coldly. "Besides, what matters most is, that with the exception of Major Smith, you all have an extensive knowledge of

Western Europe. You all speak fluent German. You'll find your combat training—on the level you'll be engaged in—as relevant today as it was five years ago. You are men with exceptional records of resourcefulness, ability, and ingenuity. If anyone has a chance, you have. You're all volunteers, of course."

"Of course," Carraciola echoed, his face carefully deadpan. Then he looked speculatively at Wyatt-Turner. "There is, of course, another way, sir." He paused, then went on very quietly indeed. "A way with a hundred percent guarantee of success."

"Neither Admiral Rolland nor I claim to be infallible," Wyatt-Turner said slowly. "We have missed an alternative? You have the answer to our problems?"

"Yes. Whistle up a Pathfinder squadron of Lancasters with ten-ton blockbuster bombs. Do *you* think *anyone* in the Schloss Adler would ever talk again?"

"I don't think so." Admiral Rolland spoke gently and for the first time, moving from the wall map to join the group. Admiral Rolland always spoke gently; when you wielded the almost incredible range of power that he did, you didn't have to talk loudly to make yourself heard. He was a short, grey-haired man, with a deeply trenched face and an air of immense authority. "No," he repeated, "I don't think so. Nor do I think that your grasp of the realities of the situation is any match for your total ruthlessness. The captured man, Lieutenant General Carnaby, is an American. If we were to destroy him General Eisenhower would probably launch his Second Front against us instead of against the Germans." He smiled deprecatingly, as though to remove rebuke from his voice. "There are certain—um—niceties to be observed in our relationships with our Allies. Wouldn't you agree?"

Carraciola didn't agree or disagree. He had, apparently, nothing to say. Neither did anyone else. Colonel Wyatt-Turner cleared his throat.

"That's it then, gentlemen. Ten o'clock tonight at the airfield. No more questions, I take it?"

"Yes, sir, there bloody well is, begging the colonel's pardon, sir." Sergeant George Harrod not only sounded heated, he looked it, too. "What's all this about? Why's this geezer so bloody important? Why the hell do we have to risk our necks—"

"That'll do, Sergeant." Wyatt-Turner's voice was sharp, authoritative. "You know all you require to know—"

12

"If we're sending a man to what may be his death, Colonel, I think he has the right to know why," Admiral Rolland interrupted gently, almost apologetically. "The rest know. He should too. It's painfully simple, Sergeant. General Carnaby is the overall coordinator of planning for the exercise known as Operation Overlord—the Second Front. It would be absolutely true to say that he knows more about the Allied preparations for the Second Front than any man alive.

"He set off last night to meet his opposite numbers in the Middle East, Russia, and the Italian Front to coordinate final plans for the invasion of Europe. The rendezvous was in Crete—the only meeting point the Russians would accept. They haven't a plane fast enough to outrun the German fighters. The British Mosquito can—but it didn't last night."

Silence lay heavy in the austere operations rooms. Harrod rubbed his hand across his eyes, then shook his head slowly, as if to clear it. When he spoke again all the truculence, all the anger had vanished from his voice. His words came very slowly.

"And if the general talks—"

"He'll talk," Rolland said. The voice was soft, but it carried total conviction. "As Mr. Thomas has just said, they all talk. He won't be able to help himself. A mixture of mescaline and scopolamine."

"And he'll tell them all the plans for the Second Front." The words came as from a man in a dream. "When, where, how . . . Good God, sir, we'll have to call the whole thing off!"

"Precisely. We call it off. No Second Front this year. Another nine months on the war, another million lives needlessly lost. You understand the urgency, Sergeant, the sheer desperate urgency of it all?"

"I understand, sir. Now I understand." Harrod turned to Wyatt-Turner. "Sorry I spoke like that, sir. I'm afraid—well, I'm a bit edgy, sir."

"We're all a bit edgy, Sergeant. Well, the airfield at ten o'clock and we'll check the equipment." He smiled without humour. "I'm afraid the uniforms may not fit too well. This is early closing day in Savile Row."

Sergeant Harrod huddled more closely into his bucket seat, beat freezing hands against freezing shoulders, morosely surveyed his uniform, wrinkled like an elephant's legs and about

13

three sizes too big for him, then raised his voice above the clamour of the Lancaster's engines.

"Well," he said bitterly, "he was right about the bloody uniforms, anyway."

"And wrong about everything else," Carraciola said heavily. "I still say we should have sent in the Lancasters."

Smith, still standing against the starboard fuselage, lit a cigarette and eyed him speculatively. He opened his mouth to speak when it occurred to him that he had seen men in more receptive mood. He looked away without saying anything.

In the flight deck, now slid so impossibly far forward in his seat that the back of his head rested on the back of his seat, Wing Commander Carpenter was still deeply and contentedly preoccupied with pipe, coffee and literature. Beside him, Flying Officer Tremayne was obviously failing to share his mood of pleasurable relaxation. He was, in fact, keeping a most anxious watch, his eyes constantly shifting from the instrument panel to the opaque darkness beyond the windscreen to the recumbent figure of his superior officer who appeared to be in danger of dropping off to sleep at any moment. Suddenly Tremayne sat far forward in his seat, stared for long seconds through the windscreen ahead of him then turned excitedly to Carpenter.

"There's Schaffhausen down there, sir!"

Carpenter groaned heavily, closed his book, swung back the hinged bookrest, finished his coffee, levered himself upright with another groan, slid open his side screen and made an elaborate pretense of examining the loom of light far below, without, however, actually going to the lengths of exposing his face to the wind and the driving snow outside. He closed the screen and looked at Tremayne.

"By heavens," he said admiringly, "I believe you're right. It's a great comfort to have you along, my boy, a great comfort." He switched on the intercom while Tremayne looked suitably abashed. "Major Smith? Yes. Thirty minutes to go." He switched off and turned again to Tremayne. "Right. Southeast down the old Bodensee. And for God's sake keep to the Swiss side."

Smith hung up the headphones and looked quizzically at the six seated men.

"That's it, then. Half an hour. Let's hope it's warmer down there than it is up here."

No one had any comment to make on that. No one seemed

to have any hope either. Soundlessly, wordlessly, they looked without expression at one another, then pulled themselves stiffly to their frozen feet. Then very slowly, very awkwardly, their numbed hands and cramped conditions making things almost impossibly awkward for them, they prepared themselves for the drop. They helped each other strap loads on their backs, beneath the high-mounted parachutes, then struggled into their white waterproof snow trousers. Sergeant Harrod went one better. He pulled a voluminous snow smock over his head, zipped it up with difficulty and drew the hood over his head. He turned round questioningly as a hand tapped the hummocked outline below his white smock.

"I hardly like to say this," Schaffer said diffidently, "but I really don't reckon your radio is going to stand the shock of landing, Sergeant."

"Why not?" Harrod looked more lugubrious than ever. "It's been done before."

"Not by you it hasn't. By my reckoning you're going to hit the ground with a terminal velocity of 180 miles an hour. Not to put too fine a point on it, I think you're going to experience some difficulty in opening your chute."

Harrod looked at him, looked at his other five smockless companions, then nodded slowly and touched his own smock. "You mean I put this on *after* we reach the ground?"

"Well," Schaffer said consideringly, "I really think it would help." He grinned at Harrod, who grinned back almost cheerfully. Even Carraciola's lips twitched in the beginnings of a smile. The release of tension within that frozen fuselage was almost palpable.

"Well, well, time I earned my wing commander's pay while you stripling pilots sit and gaze in rapt admiration." Carpenter studied his watch. "Two fifteen. Time we changed places."

Both men unhooked their safety belts and awkwardly changed over. Carpenter fastidiously adjusted the right-hand seat's back rest until it was exactly right for him, maneuvered his parachute to its position of maximum comfort, fastened his seatbelt, unhooked and adjusted on his head a combined earphones and microphone set and made a switch.

"Sergeant Johnson?" Carpenter never bothered with the regulation call-up formalities. "Are you awake?"

Back in the navigator's tiny and extremely uncomfortable recess, Sergeant Johnson was very much awake. He had been awake for hours. He was bent over a glowing greenish radar

15

screen, his eyes leaving it only to make rapid reference to the charts, an Ordnance map, a picture and a duplicate compass, altimeter and air-speed indicator. He reached for the switch by his side.

"I'm awake, sir."

"If you fly us into the side of the Weissspitze," Carpenter said threateningly, "I'll have you reduced to aircraftman. Aircraftman second class, Johnson."

"I wouldn't like that. I make it nine minutes, sir."

"For once we're agreed on something. So do I." Carpenter switched off, slid open the starboard screen and peered out. Although there was just the faintest wash of moonlight in the night sky, visibility might as well have been zero. It was a greyly opaque world, a blind world, with nothing to be seen but the thinly driving snow. He withdrew his head, brushed away the snow from his huge moustache, closed the screen, looked regretfully at his pipe and carefully put it away in his pocket.

For Tremayne, the stowage of the pipe was the final proof that the wing commander was clearing the decks for action. He said, unhappily: "A bit dicey, isn't it, sir? Locating the Weissspitze in this lot, I mean?"

"Dicey?" Carpenter sounded almost jovial. "Dicey? I don't see why? It's as big as a mountain. In fact, it *is* a mountain. We can't miss it, my dear boy."

"That's what I mean." He paused, a pause with more meaning in it. "And this plateau on the Weissspitze that we have to drop them on. Only three hundred yards wide, sir. Mountain above it, cliff below it. And those adiabatic mountain winds, or whatever you call them, blowing in any old unpredictable direction. A fraction to the south and we'll hit the mountain, a fraction to the north and they'll fall down that whacking great cliff and like as not break all their necks. Three hundred yards!"

"What do you want?" Carpenter demanded expansively. "Heathrow Airport? Three hundred yards? All the room in the world, my boy. We land this old crate on runways a tenth of that width."

"Yes, sir. I've always found runway landing lights a great help, sir. At seven thousand feet up the side of the Weissspitze—"

He broke off as a buzzer rang. Carpenter made a switch.

"Johnson?"

"Yes, sir." Johnson was huddled more closely than ever

16

over his radar screen where the revolving scanner-line had picked up a white spot immediately to the right of centre of the screen. "I have it, sir. Right where it should be." He looked away from the screen and made a quick check on the compass. "Course oh-nine-three, sir."

"Good lad." Carpenter smiled at Tremayne, made a tiny course alteration and began to whistle softly to himself. "Have a look out your window, laddie. My moustache is beginning to get all waterlogged."

Tremayne opened his window, strained his head as far as possible, but still there was only this grey and featureless opacity. He withdrew his head, silently shook it.

"No matter. It must be there somewhere," Carpenter said reasonably. He spoke into the intercom. "Sergeant? Five minutes. Hook up."

"Hook up!" The sergeant air-gunner repeated the order to the seven men standing in line along the starboard side of the fuselage. "Five minutes."

Silently they clipped their parachute snap catches on to the overhead wire, the sergeant air-gunner carefully checking each catch. Nearest the door and first man to jump was Sergeant Harrod. Behind him stood Lieutenant Schaffer whose experiences with the OSS had made him by far the most experienced parachutist of the group and whose unenviable task it was to keep an eye on Harrod. He was followed by Carraciola, then Smith—as leader he preferred to be in the middle of the group—then Christiansen, Thomas and Torrance-Smythe. Behind Torrance-Smythe two young aircraftmen stood ready to slide packaged equipment and parachutes along the wire and heave them out as swiftly as possible after the last man had jumped. The sergeant air-gunner took up position by the door. The tension was back in the air again.

Twenty-five feet forward of where they were standing, Carpenter slid open his side screen for the fifth time in as many minutes. The now downward drooping moustache had lost much of its splendid panache but the wing commander had obviously decided that there were more urgent considerations in life than waterlogged moustaches. He was wearing goggles now, continuously brushing away snow and moisture with a chamois leather, but the view ahead—or lack of view —remained obstinately the same, still that greyly driving snow looming out of and vanishing into that greyly impenetrable opacity, still nothingness. He closed the screen.

17

A callup buzzer rang. Carpenter made a switch, listened, nodded.

"Three minutes," he said to Tremayne. "Oh-nine-two."

Tremayne made the necessary minute course adjustment. He no longer looked through the side screen, he no longer even looked at the screen ahead of him. His whole being was concentrated upon flying that big bomber, his all-exclusive attention, his total concentration, on three things only: the compass, the altimeter, and Carpenter. A degree too far to the south and the Lancaster would crash into the side of the Weissspitze: a couple of hundred feet too low and the same thing would happen: a missed signal from Carpenter and the mission was over before it had begun. The young, the absurdly young face was expressionless, the body immobile as he piloted the Lancaster with a hair-trigger precision that he had never before achieved. Only his eyes moved, in a regular, rhythmic, unvarying pattern: the compass, the altimeter, Carpenter, the compass, the altimeter, Carpenter: and never longer than a second on each.

Again Carpenter slid open his side screen and peered out. Again he had the same reward, the opacity, the grey nothingness. With his head still outside he lifted his left hand, palm downwards and made a forward motion. Instantly Tremayne's hand fell on the throttle levers and eased them forward. The roar of the big engines died away to a more muted thunder.

Carpenter withdrew his head. If he was concerned, no trace of it showed in his face. He resumed his soft whistling, calmly, almost leisurely, scanned the instrument panel, then turned his head to Tremayne. He said conversationally:

"When you were in flying school, ever hear tell of a strange phenomenon known as stalling speed?"

Tremayne started, glanced hurriedly at the instrument panel and quickly gave a fraction more power to the engines. Carpenter smiled, looked at his watch and pressed a buzzer twice.

The bell rang above the head of the sergeant air-gunner standing by the fuselage door. He looked at the tense, expectant faces before him and nodded.

"Two minutes, gentlemen."

He eased the door a few inches to test whether it was moving freely. With the door only fractionally open the suddenly deepened roar from the engines was startling but nowhere nearly as dismaying as the snow-laden gust of icy wind that whistled into the fuselage. The parachutists exchanged carefully expressionless glances, glances correctly interpreted by the sergeant who closed the door and nodded again.

"I agree, gentlemen. No night for man nor beast."

Wing Commander Carpenter, his head once again poked through the side screen, didn't think so either. Five seconds' exposure to that arctic wind and driving snow and your face was full of porcupine quills: fifteen seconds and the totally numbed skin conveyed no sensation at all, it was when you withdrew your head and waited for the exquisite pain of returning circulation that the fun really started: but this time Carpenter was determined not to withdraw his head until he had complete justification for doing so: and the only justification would be the sighting of the Weissspitze. Mechanically, industriously, he rubbed the chamois leather across his goggles, stared unblinkingly into the greyly swirling gloom and hoped that he saw the Weissspitze before the Weissspitze saw him.

Inside, Tremayne's eyes continued on their rhythmic, unvarying pattern of movement, the compass, the altimeter, Carpenter, the compass, the altimeter, Carpenter. But now his gaze was resting fractionally on Carpenter each time, waiting for the sudden signal that would galvanise him into throwing the big Lancaster into a violent bank to port, the only avoiding action they could possibly take. Carpenter's left hand was moving, but he wasn't giving any signal, the fingers of his left hand were drumming gently on his knee. This, Tremayne suddenly and incredulously realised, was probably the highest state of excitement that Carpenter was capable of achieving.

Ten seconds passed. Five. And another five. Tremayne was conscious that, even in that ice-cold cabin, the sweat was pouring down his face. The urge to pull the bomber away to the left, to avoid the shattering, annihilating collision that could be only seconds away now, was almost overpowering. He was aware of a fear, a fear bordering on a reason-abdicating panic, such as he had never previously guessed at, let alone experienced. And then he became aware of something else. The drumming of Carpenter's left fingers had abruptly ceased.

Carpenter had it now. It was more imagined than real, more guessed at than seen, but he had it now. Then gradually, almost imperceptibly, ahead and a little to the right of the direction of flight, he became aware of something more

19

solidly tangible than wishful thinking beginning to materialise out of the nothingness. And then, suddenly, it wasn't materialising any more, it was solidly, unmistakably there, the smooth, unbroken side of an almost vertically towering mountain soaring up at a dizzy 80° until it vanished in the grey darkness above. Carpenter withdrew his head, leaving the screen open this time, and pressed his head switch.

"Sergeant Johnson?" The words came out stiffly, mechanically, not because of any crisis of emotion that the wing commander was passing through but because his entire face, lips included, was so frozen that he could no longer articulate properly.

"Sir?" Johnson's voice over the intercom was disembodied, empty, but even the metallic impersonality of that single word could not disguise the bow-taut tension behind it.

Carpenter said: "I think Flying Officer Johnson a much nicer name."

"Sir?"

"Relax. I have it. You can go back to sleep." He switched off, took a quick look through the side screen, reached up and touched an overhead switch.

Above the starboard door in the fuselage, a red light came on. The sergeant air-gunner laid his hand on the door.

"One minute, gentlemen." He jerked the door wide open, securing it on its standing latch, and a miniature blizzard howled into the belly of the Lancaster. "When the red light turns green—"

He left the sentence unfinished, partly because those few words were crystal clear in themselves, partly because he had to shout so loudly to make himself heard over the combined roar of wind and engines that any superfluity of words was only that much wasted effort.

No one else said anything, mainly because of the near impossibility of making one's self heard. In any event, the parachutists' silently exchanged glances conveyed more eloquently than words the very obvious thought that was in the minds of all of them: if it was like that inside, what the hell was it like outside? At a gesture from the sergeant, they moved up in line to the open door, Sergeant Harrod in the lead. On his face was the expression of a Christian martyr meeting his first and last lion.

The Lancaster, like some great black pterodactyl from out of the primeval past, roared on through the driving snow alongside the smoothly precipitous side of the Weissspitze.

That sheer wall of ice-encrusted rock seemed very close indeed. Tremayne was convinced that it was impossibly close. He stared through the still open screen by Carpenter's head and would have sworn that the starboard wingtip must be brushing the side of the mountain. Tremayne could still feel the sweat that bathed his face but his lips were as dry as ashes. He licked them, surreptitiously, so that Carpenter would not see him, but it didn't do any good at all: as dry as ashes they remained.

Sergeant Harrod's lips weren't dry, but that was only because his face was taking the full brunt of the horizontally driving snowstorm that lashed along the bomber's fuselage. Otherwise, he shared Tremayne's sentiments and apprehensions to a very marked degree. He stood in the doorway, gripping the fuselage on each side to hold him in position against the gale of wind, his storm-lashed face showing no fear, just a peculiarly resigned expression. His eyes were turned to the left, looking forward with an almost hypnotised fixity at that point in space where it seemed that at any second now the starboard wingtip must strike against the Weissspitze.

Inside the fuselage, the red lamp still burned. The sergeant air gunner's hand fell on Harrod's shoulder in an encouraging gesture. It took Harrod all of three seconds to free himself from his thrall-like fixation with that starboard wingtip and take a half step back inside. He reached up and firmly removed the sergeant's hand.

"Don't shove, mate." He had to shout to make himself heard. "If I'm to commit suicide, let me do it in the old-fashioned way. By my own hand." He again took up position by the open door.

At the same instant Carpenter took a last quick look through the side screen and made the gesture that Tremayne had been waiting for, been praying for, a slight turning motion of the left hand. Quickly Tremayne banked the big bomber, as quickly straightened up again.

Slowly, the mountainside fell away, the mountain-brushing episode had been no mere bravado or folly, Carpenter had been deliberately lining up for his predetermined course across the narrow plateau. Once again, and for the last time, he had his head outside, while his left hand slowly—interminably slowly, it seemed to Tremayne—reached up for the button on the bulkhead above the screen, located it, paused, then pressed it.

Sergeant Harrod, head craned back at a neck-straining angle, saw the red light turn green, brought his head down, screwed shut his eyes and, with a convulsive jerk of his arms, launched himself out into the snow and the darkness, not a very expert launching for, instead of jumping out he had stepped out and was already twisting in midair as the parachute opened. Schaffer was the next to go, smoothly, cleanly, feet and knees together, then Carraciola followed by Smith.

Smith glanced down below him and his lips tightened. Just dimly visible in the greyness beneath, Harrod, a very erratic human pendulum, was swinging wildly across the sky. The parachute cords were already badly twisted and his clumsily desperate attempts to untwist them resulted only in their becoming more entangled than ever. His left-hand cords were pulled too far down, air was spilling from the parachute, and, still swaying madly, he was side-slipping to his left faster than any man Smith had ever seen side-slip a parachute before. Smith stared after the rapidly disappearing figure and hoped to God that he didn't side-slip his way right over the edge of the precipice.

Grim-faced, he stared upwards to see how the others had fared. Thank God, there was no worry there. Christiansen, Thomas, and Smithy all there, so close as to be almost touching, all making perfectly normal descents.

Even before the last of the parachutists, Torrance-Smythe, had cleared the doorway, the sergeant air-gunner was running towards the after end of the fuselage. Swiftly he flung aside a packing case, dragged a tarpaulin away, reached down and pulled a huddled figure upright. A girl, quite small, with wide dark eyes and delicate features. One would have looked for the figure below to be as petite as the features, but it was enveloped in bulky clothes over which had been drawn a snow suit. Over the snow suit she wore a parachute. She was almost numb with cold and cramp but the sergeant had his orders.

"Come on, Miss Ellison." His arm round her waist, he moved quickly towards the doorway. "Not a second to lose."

He half-led, half-carried her there, where an air-craftsman was just heaving the second last parachute and container through the doorway. The sergeant snapped the parachute catch onto the wire. Mary Ellison half-turned as if to speak to him, then turned away abruptly and dropped out into the darkness. The last parachute and container followed at once.

For a long moment the sergeant stared down into the darkness. Then he rubbed his chin with the palm of his hand, shook his head in disbelief, stepped back and pulled the heavy door to. The Lancaster, its four engines still on reduced power, droned on into the snow and the night. Almost immediately, it was lost to sight and, bare seconds later, the last faint throb of its engines died away in the darkness.

TWO

SMITH REACHED his hands far up into the parachute shrouds, hauled himself sharply upwards and made a perfect knees-bent, feet-together landing in about two feet of snow. The wind tugged fiercely at his parachute. He struck the quick release harness clasp, collapsed the parachute, pulled it in, rolled it up and pressed it deeply into the snow using for weight the pack he had just shrugged off his shoulders.

Down there at ground level—if seven thousand feet up on the Weissspitze could be called ground level—the snowfall was comparatively slight compared to that blizzard they'd experienced jumping from the Lancaster but, even so, visibility was almost as bad as it had been up above, for there was a twenty knot wind blowing and the dry powdery snow was drifting quite heavily. Smith made a swift 360° sweep of his horizon but there was nothing to be seen, nobody to be seen.

With fumbling frozen hands Smith clumsily extracted a flashlight and whistle from his tunic. Facing alternately east and west, he bleeped on the whistle and flashed his flashlight. The first to appear was Thomas, then Schaffer, then, within two minutes altogether, all of the others with the exception of Sergeant Harrod.

"Pile your chutes there and weight them," Smith ordered. "Yes, bed them deep. Anyone seen Sergeant Harrod?" A shaking of heads. "Nobody? No sight of him at all?"

"Last I saw of him," Schaffer said, "he was going across my bows like a destroyer in a heavy sea."

"I saw a bit of that," Smith nodded. "The shrouds were twisted?"

"Put a corkscrew to shame. But I'd have said there was no

danger of the chute collapsing. Not enough time. We were almost on the ground before I lost sight of him."

"Any idea where he landed then?"

"Roughly. He'll be all right, Major. A twisted ankle, a bump on the head. Not to worry."

"Use your flashlights," Smith said abruptly. "Spread out. Find him."

With two men on one side of him, three on the other, all within interlocking distance of their torch beams, Smith searched through the snow, his flashlight raking the ground ahead of him. If he shared Schaffer's optimism about Harrod, his face didn't show it. It was a set and grim. Three minutes passed and then came a shout from the right. Smith broke into a run.

Carraciola it was who had called and was now standing at the further edge of a windswept outcrop of bare rock, his flashlight shining downwards and slightly ahead. Beyond the rock the ground fell away abruptly to a depth of several feet and in this lee a deep drift had formed. Half-buried in its white depths, Sergeant Harrod lay spread-eagled on his back, his feet almost touching the rock, his face upturned to the falling snow, his eyes open. He did not seem to notice the snow falling on his eyes.

They were all there now, staring down at the motionless man. Smith jumped down into the drift, dropped to his knees, slid an arm under Harrod's shoulders and began to lift him to a sitting position. Harrod's head lolled back like that of a broken rag doll. Smith lowered him back into the snow and felt for the pulse in the throat. Still kneeling, Smith straightened, paused for a moment with bent head then climbed wearily to his feet.

"Dead?" Carraciola asked.

"He's dead. His neck is broken." Smith's face was without expression. "He must have got caught up in the shrouds and made a bad landing."

"It happens," Schaffer said. "I've known it happen." A long pause, then: "Shall I take the radio, sir?"

Smith nodded. Schaffer dropped to his knees and began to fumble for the buckle of the strap securing the radio to Harrod's back.

Smith said: "Sorry, no, not that way. There's a key around his neck, under his tunic. It fits the lock under the flat of the breast buckle."

Schaffer located the key, unlocked the buckle after some difficulty, eased the straps off the dead man's shoulders and finally managed to work the radio clear. He rose to his feet, the radio dangling from his hand, and looked at Smith.

"Second thoughts, what's the point. Any fall hard enough to break his neck wouldn't have done the innards of this radio any good."

Wordlessly, Smith took the radio, set it on the rock, extended the antenna, set the switch to Transmit, and cranked the callup handle. The red telltale glowed, showing the transmission circuit to be in order. Smith turned the switch to Receive, turned up the volume, moved the tuning knob, listened briefly to some static-laden music, closed up the radio set and handed it back to Schaffer.

"It made a better landing than Sergeant Harrod," Smith said briefly. "Come on."

"We bury him, Major?" Carraciola asked.

"No need." Smith shook his head and gestured with his flashlight at the drifting snow. "He'll be buried within the hour. Let's find the supplies."

"Now, for God's sake don't lose your grip!" Thomas said urgently.

"That's the trouble with you Celts," Schaffer said reprovingly. "No faith in anyone. There is no cause for alarm. Your life is in the safe hands of Schaffer and Christiansen. So don't worry."

"What else do you think I'm worrying about?"

"If we all start sliding," Schaffer said encouragingly, "we won't let you go until the last possible minute."

Thomas gave a last baleful glance over his shoulder and then began to edge himself out over the black lip of the precipice, Schaffer and Christiansen with an ankle apiece, and they in turn anchored by the others. As far as the beam of Thomas's flashlight could reach the cliff stretching down into the darkness was absolutely vertical, black naked rock with the only fissures in sight blocked with ice and with otherwise never a hand- or foothold in sight.

"I've seen all I want to," he said over his shoulder. They pulled him back and he edged his way carefully up to their supply pile before getting to his feet. He prodded the pack with the skis protruding from one end.

"Very handy," he said morosely. "Oh, very handy for this lot indeed."

"As steep as that?" Smith asked.

"Vertical. Smooth as glass and you can't see the bottom. How deep do you reckon it is, Major?"

"Who knows?" Smith shrugged. "We're seven thousand feet up. Maps never give details at this altitude. Break out that nylon."

The proper supply pack was located and the nylon produced, one thousand feet of it coiled inside a canvas bag as it had come from the makers. It had very little more diameter than a clothes rope but its wire core made it immensely strong and every yard of it had been fully tested to its rated breaking strain—its actual breaking strain was much higher —before leaving the factory. Smith tied a hammer to one end and, with two of the men holding him securely, paid it out over the edge, counting his arm spans as he let it go. Several times the hammer snagged on some unseen obstruction but each time Smith managed to swing it free. Finally the rope went completely slack and, despite all Smith's efforts, it remained that way.

"Well." Smith moved back from the edge. "That seems to be about it."

"And if it isn't, hey?" Christiansen asked. "If it's caught on a teensy-weensy ledge a thousand feet above damn all?"

"I'll let you know," Smith said shortly.

"You measured it off," Carraciola said. "How deep?"

"Two hundred feet."

"Eight hundred feet left, eh?" Thomas grinned. "We'll need it all to tie up the garrison of the Schloss Adler."

No one was amused. Smith said: "I'll need a piton and two walkie-talkies."

Fifteen feet back from the edge of the cliff they cleared away the snow and hammered an angled piton securely into the bare rock. Smith made a double bowline at one end of the nylon, slipped his legs through the loops, unclasped his belt then fastened it tightly round both himself and the rope and slipped a walkie-talkie over his shoulder. The rope was then passed round the piton and three men, backs to the cliff, wrapped it round their hands and prepared to take the weight. Schaffer stood by with the other walkie-talkie.

Smith checked that there were no sharp or abrasive edges on the clifftop, wriggled cautiously over and gave the signal to be lowered. The descent itself was simple. As Thomas had said, it was a vertical drop and all he had to do was to fend himself off from the face as the men above paid out the rope. Once only, passing an overhang, he spun wildly in

27

space, but within ten seconds regained contact with the rock face again. Mountaineering made easy, Smith thought. Or it seemed easy: perhaps, he thought wryly, it was as well that he couldn't see what stretched beneath him.

His feet passed through eighteen inches of snow and rested on solid ground. He moved his flashlight in a semicircle, from cliff wall to cliff wall. If it was a ledge, it was a very big one for, as far as his eye and flashlight could reach, it appeared to be a smooth plateau sloping gently outwards from the cliff. The cliff wall itself was smooth, unbroken, except for one shallow fissure, a few feet wide, close by to where he stood. He climbed out of the double bowline and made the switch on the walkie-talkie.

"O.K. so far. Haul up the rope. Supplies first, then yourselves."

The rope snaked upwards into the darkness. Within five minutes all the equipment had been lowered in two separate loads. Christiansen appeared soon afterwards.

"What's all the fuss about this Alpine stuff, then?" he asked cheerfully. "My grandmother could do it."

"Maybe we should have brought your grandmother along instead," Smith said sourly. "We're not down yet. Take your flashlight and find out how big this ledge is and the best way down and for God's sake don't go falling over any precipices."

Christiansen grinned and moved off. Life was for the living and Christiansen gave the impression of a man thoroughly enjoying himself. While he was away reconnoitering, all the others came down in turn until only Schaffer was left. His plaintive voice came over the walkie-talkie.

"And how am I supposed to get down? Hand over hand for two hundred feet? Frozen hand over frozen hand for two hundred feet on a rope this size? You'd better stand clear. Somebody should have thought of this."

"Somebody did," Smith said patiently. "Make sure the rope is still round the piton, then kick the other eight hundred feet over the edge."

"There's always an answer." Schaffer sounded relieved.

They had just lowered him to the ground when Christiansen returned.

"It's not so bad," he reported. "There's another cliff ahead of us, maybe fifty yards away, curving around to the east. At least I think it's a cliff. I didn't try to find out how deep or how steep. I'm married. But the plateau falls away gently to the west there. Seems it might go on a fair way. Trees, too. I followed the line of them for two hundred yards."

"Trees? At this altitude?"

"Well, no masts for a tall ship. Scrub pine. They'll give shelter, hiding."

"Fair enough," Smith nodded. "We'll bivouac there."

"So close?" The surprised tone in Schaffer's voice showed that he didn't think much of the idea. "Shouldn't we get as far down this mountain as possible tonight, Major?"

"No need. If we start at first light we'll be well below the main tree line by dawn."

"I agree with Schaffer," Carraciola said reasonably. "Let's get as much as we can behind us. What do you think, Olaf?" This to Christiansen.

"It doesn't matter what Christiansen thinks." Smith's voice was quiet but cold as the mountain air itself. "Nor you, Carraciola. This isn't a round-table seminar, it's a military operation. Military operations have leaders. Like it or not, Admiral Rolland put me in charge. We stay here tonight. Get the stuff across."

The five men looked speculatively at one another, then stopped to lift the supplies. There was no longer any question as to who was in charge.

"We pitch the tents right away, boss?" Schaffer asked.

"Yes." In Schaffer's book, Smith reflected, "boss" was probably a higher mark of respect than either "Major" or "Sir." "Then hot food, hot coffee, and a try for London on the radio. Haul that rope down, Christiansen. Come the dawn, we don't want to start giving heart attacks to any binocular-toting characters in the Schloss Adler."

Christiansen nodded, began to haul on the rope. As the free end rose into the air, Smith gave a shout, jumped towards Christiansen and caught his arm. Christiansen, startled, stopped pulling and looked round.

"Jesus!" Smith drew the back of his hand across his forehead. "That was a close one."

"What's up?" Schaffer asked quickly.

"Two of you. Hoist me up. Quickly! Before that damn rope disappears."

Two of them hoisted him into the air. Smith reached up and caught the dangling end of the rope, dropped to earth, taking the rope with him and then very carefully, very securely, tied it to the other end of the rope.

"Now that you've *quite* finished—" Torrance-Smythe said politely.

"The radio." Smith let out a long sigh of relief. "There's only one list of frequencies, call signs and code. Security. And that one list is inside Sergeant Harrod's tunic."

"Mind if I mop my brow, too, boss?" Schaffer enquired.

"I'll go get it for you if you like," Christiansen volunteered.

"Thanks. But it's my fault and I'll get it. Besides, I'm the only person here who's done any climbing—or so I believe from Colonel Wyatt-Turner—and I think you'd find the cliff rather more awkward to climb than descend. No hurry. Let's bivouac and eat first."

"If you can't do better than this, Smithy," Schaffer said to Torrance-Smythe, "you can have a week's notice. Starting from a week ago." He scraped the bottom of his metal plate and shuddered. "I was brought up in a Christian home, so I won't tell you what this reminds me of."

"It's not my fault," Torrance-Smythe complained. "They packed the wrong size can openers." He stirred the indeterminate-looking goulash in the pot on top of the butane stove and looked hopefully at the men seated in a rough semicircle in the dimly lit tent. "Anyone for any more?"

"That's not funny," Schaffer said severely.

"Wait till you try his coffee," Smith advised, "and you'll be wondering what you were complaining about." He rose, poked his head through the door to take a look at the weather, looked inside again. "May take me an hour. But if it's been drifting up there . . ."

The seated men, suddenly serious, nodded. If it had been drifting up there it might take Smith a very long time indeed to locate Sergeant Harrod.

"It's a bad night," Schaffer said. "I'll come and give you a hand."

"Thanks. No need. I'll haul myself up and lower myself down. A rope around a piton is no elevator, but it'll get me there and back and two are no better than one for that job. But I'll tell you what you can do." He moved out and reappeared shortly afterwards carrying the radio which he placed in front of Schaffer. "I don't want to go all the way up there to get the code book just to find that some hobnailed idiot has fallen over this and given it a heart attack. Guard it with your life, Lieutenant Schaffer."

"Aye, aye, sir," Schaffer said solemnly.

With a hammer and a couple of spare pitons hanging from his waist, Smith secured himself to the rope, with double bowline and belt as before, grabbed the free end of the rope and began to haul himself up. Smith's statement to the others that this was a job for a mountaineer seemed hardly accurate for the amount of mountaineering skill required was minimal. It was gruelling physical labour, no more. Most of the time, with his legs almost at right angles to his body, he walked up the vertical cliff face: on the stretch of the overhang, with no assistance for his arms, he twice had to take a turn of the free end of the rope and rest until the strength came back to aching shoulder and forearms muscles: and by the time he finally dragged himself, gasping painfully and sweating like a man in a sauna bath, over the edge of the cliff, exhaustion was very close indeed. He had overlooked the crippling effect of altitude to a man unaccustomed to it.

He lay face down for several minutes until breathing and pulse returned to something like normal—or what was normal for seven thousand feet—rose and examined the piton round which the nylon passed. It seemed firm enough but, for good measure, he gave it another few heavy blows with the hammer, undid the double bowline around his legs and secured the end of the rope to the piton with a round turn and two half-hitches, hauling on the rope until the knot locked tight.

He moved a few feet further away from the cliff edge, cleared away the snow and lightly hammered in one of the spare pitons he had brought with him. He tested it with his hand to see if it broke clear easily. It did. He tapped it in lightly a second time and led round it the part of the rope that was secured to the firmly anchored first piton. Then he walked away, moving up the gently sloping plateau, whistling "Lorelei." It was, as Smith himself would have been the first to admit, a far from tuneful whistle, but recognisable for all that. A figure appeared out of the night and came running towards him, stumbling and slipping in the deep snow. It was Mary Ellison. She stopped a short yard away and put her hands on her hips.

"Well!" He could hear her teeth chattering uncontrollably with the cold. "You took your time about it, didn't you?"

"Never wasted a minute," Smith said defensively. "I had to have a hot meal and coffee first."

"You had to have—you beast, you selfish beast!" She took

31

a quick step forward and flung her arms around his neck. "I hate you."

"I know." He pulled off a gauntlet and gently touched her disengaged cheek. "You're frozen."

"You're frozen, he says! Of course I'm frozen. I almost *died* in that plane. Why couldn't you have supplied some hot water bottles or—or an electrically heated suit or—or something? I thought you loved me!"

"I can't help what you think," Smith said kindly, patting her on the back. "Where's your gear?"

"Fifty yards. And *stop* patting me in that—that avuncular fashion."

"Language, language," Smith said severely. "Come on, let's fetch it."

They trudged upwards through the deep snow, Mary holding his arm tightly. She said curiously: "What on earth excuse did you give for coming back up here? Lost a cuff link?"

"There was something I had to come for, something apart from you, although I gave a song-and-dance act of having forgotten about it until the last moment, until it was almost too late. The radio code book inside Sergeant Harrod's tunic."

"He—he lost it? He dropped it? How—how could he have been so criminally careless!" She stopped, puzzled. "Besides, it's chained—"

"It's still inside Sergeant Harrod's tunic," Smith said sombrely. "He's up here, dead."

"Dead?" She stopped and clutched him by the arms. After a long pause, she repeated: "He's dead! That—that nice man. I heard him saying he'd never jumped before. A bad landing?"

"So it seems."

They located the kit bag in silence and Smith carried it back to the edge of the cliff. Mary said: "And now? The code book?"

"Let's wait a minute. I want to watch this rope."

"Why the rope?"

"Why not?"

"Don't tell me," Mary said resignedly. "I'm only a little girl. I suppose you know what you're doing."

"I wish to God I did," Smith said feelingly.

They waited, again in silence, side by side on the kit bag. Both stared at the rope in solemn concentration as if nylon ropes at seven thousand feet had taken on a special meaningfulness denied nylon ropes elsewhere. Twice Smith tried to light a cigarette and twice it sputtered to extinction in the drifting snow. The minutes passed, three, maybe four: they felt more like thirty or forty. He became conscious that the girl beside him was shivering violently—he guessed that she had her teeth clamped tight to prevent their chattering—and was even more acutely conscious that his entire left side—he was trying to shelter her from the wind and snow—was becoming numb. He rose to leave when suddenly the rope gave a violent jerk and the piton further from the cliff edge was torn free. The loop of the rope slid quickly down past the piton to which it was anchored and kept on going till it was brought up short by its anchor. Whatever pressure was on the rope increased until the nylon bit deeply into the fresh snow on the cliff edge. Smith moved across and tested the pressure on the rope, at first gingerly and tentatively then with all his strength. The rope was bar-taut and remained bar-taut. But the piton held.

"What—what on earth—" Mary began, then broke off. Her voice was an unconscious whisper.

"If—if that spike hadn't held we'd never have got down again." The tremor in her voice wasn't all due to the cold.

"It's a fair old jump," Smith conceded.

He took her arm and they moved off. The snow was heavier now and even with the aid of their flashlights visibility was no more than six feet, but, by using the rocky outcrop as a bearing it took Smith no more than two minutes to locate Sergeant Harrod, now no more than a featureless mound buried in the depths of the snowdrift. Smith brushed aside the covering shroud of white, undid the dead man's tunic, recovered the code book, hung the chain round his neck and buttoned the book securely inside his own Alpenkorps uniform.

Then came the task of turning Sergeant Harrod over on his side. Unpleasant Smith had expected it to be, and it was: impossible he hadn't expected it to be, and it wasn't—not quite. But the effort all but defeated him, the dead man was stiff as a board, literally frozen solid into the arms-outflung position into which he had fallen. For the second time that night Smith could feel the sweat mingling with the melted snow on his face. But by and by he had him over, the frozen right arm pointing up into the snow-filled sky. Smith knelt, brought his flashlight close and carefully examined the back of the dead man's head.

"What are you trying to do?" Mary asked. "What are you looking for?" Again her voice was a whisper.

"His neck is broken. I want to find out just *how* it was broken." He glanced up at the girl. "You don't have to look."

"Don't worry." She turned away. "I'm not going to.

The clothes, like the man, were frozen stiff. The hood covering Harrod's head crackled and splintered in Smith's gauntleted hands as he pulled it down, exposing the back of the head and neck. Finally, just below the collar of the snow smock, Smith found what he was searching for—a red mark at the base of the neck where the skin was broken. He rose, caught the dead man's ankles and dragged him a foot or two down the slope.

"What now?" In spite of herself Mary was watching again, in reluctant and horrified fascination. "What are you looking for now?"

"A rock," Smith said briefly. There was a cold edge to the words and although Mary knew it wasn't intended for her, it was an effective discouragement to any further questioning.

Smith cleared the snow for two feet around where Harrod's head had lain. With hand and eyes he examined the ground with meticulous care, rose slowly to his feet, took Mary's arm and began to walk away. After a few steps he hesitated, stopped, turned back to the dead man and turned him over again so that the right arm was no longer pointing towards the sky.

Halfway back to the cliff edge, Smith said abruptly:

"Something struck Harrod on the back of the neck. I thought it might have been a rock. But there was no rock where he lay, only turf."

"There was a rocky outcrop nearby."

"You don't break your neck on a rocky outcrop, then stand up and jump out into a snowdrift. Even had he rolled over into the drift, he could never have finished with his head seven feet out from the rock. He was struck by some hard metallic object, either the butt of a gun or the haft of a knife. The skin is broken but there is no bruising for the neck was broken immediately afterwards. When he was unconscious. To make us think it was an accident. It must have happened on the rock—there was no disturbance in the snow round Harrod—and it must have happened while he was upright. A tap on the neck, a quick neck twist, then he fell or was pushed over the edge of the outcrop. Wonderful stuff, stone," Smith finished bitterly. "It leaves no footprints."

Mary stopped and stared at him.

"Do you realise what you're saying?" She caught his speculative and very old-fashioned look, took his arm and went on quickly: "No, I mean the implications. I'm sorry, I'm sorry, of course you do. John, I—I'm scared. Even all those months with you in Italy—well, you know, nothing like this—" She broke off, then continued: "Couldn't there—couldn't there be some other explanation?"

"Like he hit himself on the back of the head or the abominable snowman got him?"

She looked at him steadily, her dark eyes far too large in what could be seen of her hooded face. "I don't deserve that, John. I *am* frightened."

"Me, too."

"I don't believe you."

"Well, if I'm not, it's damn well time I started to be."

Smith checked his descent when he estimated he was about forty feet from the foot of the cliff. He took two turns of the nylon round his left leg, clamped it with his right, took a turn round his left arm, pulled off his right gauntlet with his teeth, stuffed it inside his tunic, eased out his Luger, slid the safety catch and went on his way again, checking his speed of descent with his gauntleted left hand. It was a reasonable enough expectation that whoever had tried to pull down the rope would be waiting there to finish off the job.

But there was no reception committee waiting, not, at least, at the spot where he touched down. He traversed a quick circle with his flashlight. There was nobody there and nothing there and the footprints that there must have been there were long obscured by the drifting snow. Gun in one hand, flashlight in the other, he moved along the cliff face for thirty yards then moved out in a semicircle until he arrived back at the cliff face. The rope-puller had evidently opted for discretion. Smith returned to the rope and jerked it. In two minutes he had Mary's kit bag down and, a few minutes later, Mary herself. As soon as she had stepped out of the double bowline, Smith undid the knot, pulled the rope down from the top of the cliff and coiled it. So numbed and frozen were his hands by this time that the operation took him nearly fifteen minutes.

Rope over one shoulder, her kit bag in the other, Smith led Mary to the fissure in the cliffside.

"Don't pitch the tent," Smith said. "Unroll it, put your sleeping bag on one half, get into it and pull the other half of the tent over you. Half an hour and you'll be covered with drifting snow. The snow will not only keep you warm, it'll hide you from any somnambulists. I'll be along in the morning before we leave."

He walked away, stopped, looked back. Mary was still standing where he had left her, looking after him. There was no sag to her shoulders, no particular expression to her face, but for all that she looked oddly defenceless, lonely and forlorn, a quality as undefinable as it was unmistakable. Smith hesitated, then went back to her, unrolled her tent and sleeping bag, waited until she had climbed in, zipped up the bag and pulled the other half of the tent up to her chin. She smiled at him. He fixed the sleeping bag hood, pulled a corner of the tent over it and left, all without saying a word.

Locating his own tent was simple enough, a steady light burnt inside it. Smith beat the snow from his clothes, stooped and entered. Christiansen, Thomas and Carraciola were in their sleeping bags and were asleep or appeared to be. Torrance-Smythe was checking over their store of plastic explosives, fuses, detonators, and grenades while Schaffer was reading a paperback—in German—smoking a cigarette—also German—and faithfully guarding the radio. He put down the book and looked at Smith.

"O.K.?"

"O.K." Smith produced the code book from his tunic. "Sorry I was so long, but I thought I'd never find him. Drifting pretty badly up there."

"We've arranged to take turns on watch," Schaffer said. "Half an hour each. It'll be dawn in three hours."

Smith smiled. "What are you guarding against in these parts?"

"The abominable snowman."

The smile left Smith's face as quickly as it had come. He turned his attention to Harrod's code book and spent about ten minutes in memorising callup signals and wave frequencies and writing a message out in code. Before he had finished Schaffer had turned into his sleeping bag, leaving Torrance-Smythe on watch. Smith folded the message, tucked it in a pocket, rose, took the radio and a rubber ground sheet to protect it from the snow.

"I'm going to move out a bit," he said to Torrance-Smythe. "Reception is lousy among trees. Besides, I don't want to wake everyone up. Won't be long."

Two hundred yards from the tent, after having stopped twice and changed direction twice, Smith knelt with his back—and the rubber ground sheet—to the drifting snow. He extended a fourteen foot telescopic aerial, adjusted a preselected callup and cranked a handle. Four times he cranked the handle and on the fifth he got results. Someone was keeping a very close radio watch indeed.

"This is Danny Boy," the set speaker crackled. The signal was faint and intermittent, but just comprehensible. "Danny Boy replying to you. Over."

Smith spoke into the mouth microphone. "This is Broadsword. Can I speak to Father Machree or Mother Machree? Over."

"Sorry. Unavailable. Over."

"Code," Smith said. "Over."

"Ready."

Smith extracted the paper from his pocket and shone his flashlight on it. There were two lines containing meaningless jumbles of letters and, below that, the plain language translation, which read: "SAFE LANDING HARROD DEAD WEATHER FINE PLEASE AWAIT MESSAGE 0800 G.M.T. Smith read off the corresponding code figures and finished off: "Have that delivered to Father Machree by 0700. Without fail."

Torrance-Smythe looked up at Smith's return.

"Back already?" Surprise in his voice. "You got through?"

"Not a chance," Smith said disgustedly. "Too many bloody mountains around."

"Didn't try for very long, did you?"

"Two and a half minutes." It was Smith's turn to look surprised. "Surely you know that's the safe maximum?"

"You think there may be radio monitoring stations hereabouts?"

"Oh, no, not at all." Smith's voice was heavy with sarcasm. "You wouldn't expect to find radio monitors in the Schloss Adler, would you now?"

"Well, now." Torrance-Smythe smiled tiredly. "I believe someone did mention it was the southern HQ of the German Secret Service. Sorry, Major. It's not that I'm growing old, though there's that, too. It's just that what passes for my mind is so gummed up by cold and lack of sleep that I think it's stopped altogether."

Smith pulled off his boots and snow suit, climbed into his sleeping bag and pulled the radio close to him.

"Then it's time you had some sleep. My explosives expert is going to be no good to me if he can't tell a detonator from a doorknob. Go on. Turn in, I'll keep watch."

"But we had arranged—"

"Arguments, arguments," Smith sighed. "Insubordination on every hand." He smiled. "Straight up, Smithy, I'm wide awake. I know I won't sleep tonight."

One downright lie, Smith thought, and one statement of incontrovertible truth. He wasn't wide awake, he was physically and mentally exhausted and on the slightest relaxation of will power oblivion would have overtaken him in seconds. But that he wouldn't sleep that night was beyond doubt: no power on earth would have let him sleep that night but, in the circumstances, it was perhaps wiser not to say so to Torrance-Smythe.

THREE

THE PREDAWN greyness was in the sky. Smith and his men had broken camp. Tent and sleeping bags were stowed away and the cooking utensils—after a very sketchy breakfast scarcely deserving of the name—were being thrust into haversacks. There was no conversation, none at all: it wasn't a morning for speaking. All of them, Smith thought, looked more drawn, more exhausted, than they had done three hours ago: he wondered how he himself, who had had no sleep at all, must look. It was as well, he reflected, that mirrors were not part of their Commando equipment. He looked at his watch.

"We'll leave in ten minutes," he announced. "Should give us plenty of time to be down in the tree line before sunup. Assuming there are no more cliffs. Back in a moment. Visibility is improving and I think I'll go recce along the cliff edge. With any luck, maybe I can see the best way down."

"And if you haven't any luck?" Carraciola asked sourly.

"We've still that thousand feet of nylon rope," Smith said shortly.

He pulled on his snow suit and left, angling off in the direction of the cliff. As soon as he was beyond the belt of the scrub pines and out of sight of the camp he changed direction uphill and broke into a run.

A single eye appeared under a lifted corner of snow-covered canvas as Mary Ellison heard the soft crunch of running footsteps in the snow. She heard the first two bars of a tuneless whistling of "Lorelei," unzipped her sleeping bag and sat up. Smith was standing above her.

"Not already!" she said protestingly.

"Yes already. Come on. Up!"

"I haven't slept a wink."

"Neither have I. I've been watching that damned radio all night—and watching to check that no somnambulists took a stroll in this direction."

"You kept awake. You did that for me?"

"I kept awake. We're off. Start in five minutes. Leave your tent and kit bag here, you won't be requiring them again. Take some food, something to drink, that's all. And for God's sake, don't get too close to us." He glanced at his watch. "We'll stop at 7 A.M. Check your watch. Exactly 7 A.M. And *don't* bump into us."

"What do you think I am?" But Smith didn't tell her what he thought she was. He had already gone.

A thousand feet farther down the side of the Weissspitze the trees were something worth calling trees, towering conifers that soared sixty and seventy feet up into the sky. Into the clear sky, for the snow had stopped falling now. It was dawn.

The slope of the Weissspitze was still very steep, perhaps one in four or five. Smith, with his five men strung out behind him in single file, slipped and stumbled almost constantly: but the deep snow, Smith reflected, at least cushioned their frequent falls and as a mode of progress it was a damn sight preferable to shinning down vertical cliff faces on an impossibly thin clothesline. The curses of his bruised companions were almost continuous but serious complaints were marked by their total absence: there was no danger, they were making excellent time and they were now completely hidden in the deep belt of pines.

Two hundred yards behind them Mary Ellison carefully picked her way down the tracks made by the men below her. She slipped and fell only very occasionally for, unlike the men, she was carrying no overbalancing gear on her back. Nor had she any fear of being observed, of coming too close to Smith and the others: in still, frosty air on a mountain sound carries with a preternatural clarity and from the sound of the voices farther down the slope she could judge her distance from them to a nicety. For the twentieth time she looked at her watch: it was twenty minutes to seven.

Sometime later, for much more than the twentieth time, Smith checked his watch again. It was exactly seven o'clock. The dawn had gone and the light of full daytime filtered down through the snow-bent boughs of the conifers. Smith stopped and held up his hand, waiting until the other five had caught up with him.

"We must be halfway down now." He shrugged off the heavy pack on his back and lowered it gratefully into the snow. "I think it's time we had a look at the scenery."

They piled their gear and moved off to their right. Within a minute the pines started to thin out and at a signal from Smith they all dropped to hands and knees and crawled forward the last few yards towards the edge of the belt of pines. Smith carried a telescope in his hand: Christiansen and Thomas both wore binoculars. Zeiss binoculars. Admiral Rolland had left nothing to chance. Beyond the last of the pines a mound of snow obstructed their view of the valley below. Shrouded from top to toe in the all-enveloping white of their snow smocks, they completed the last few feet on their elbows and knees.

What lay below them was something out of a fairy tale, an impossibly beautiful scene from an impossibly beautiful fairy tale, a fairy tale set aeons back in the never-never land of the age of dreams, a kindlier land, a nobler land than man had ever known since first he had set his hand against his brother. A land that never was, Smith thought, a land that never was: but there it lay before them, the golden land that never was, the home of that most dreaded organisation in the entire world, the German Gestapo. The impeccable incongruity of it all, Smith reflected, passed all belief.

The valley was bowl-shaped, open to the north, hemmed in by steeply rising hills to the east and west, closed off by the towering bulk of the Weissspitze to the south.

A scene of fantastic beauty. Nine thousand, seven hundred and ten feet in height, the second highest mountain in Germany, the Weissspitze soared up menacingly like another north wall of the Eiger, its dazzling whiteness caught in the morning sun, its starkly lovely outline sharply etched against the now cloudless blue of the sky. High up near the cone-shaped summit could be seen the line of black rock marking the cliff Smith and his men had descended during the night with, just below it, a much greater cliff face on the plateau above which they had spent the night.

Directly opposite where they lay, and almost exactly on the same level, was the Schloss Adler itself. The castle of the eagle had been aptly named, an impregnable fortress, an inaccessible eyrie between mountain and sky.

Just below the spot where the steep-sided slopes of the

Weissspitze began to flatten out northwards into the head of the valley, a geological freak, known as a volcanic plug, jutted two hundred vertical feet up into the sparkling, ice-cold air. It was on this that the Schloss Adler had been built. The northern, western, and eastern sides of this volcanic plug were sheer, perpendicular walls of rock, walls that swept up smoothly, without intermission or break, into the structure of the castle itself: from where they lay, it was impossible to say where the one ended and the other began. To the south, a steeply sloping ridgeback connected the plug to the equally sloping ramparts of the Weissspitze.

The castle itself was another dream, the dream of the apotheosis of medievalism. This dream, Smith was aware, was as illusory as the golden age of its setting. It wasn't medieval at all, it had been built as late as the mid-nineteenth century to the express order of one of the madder of the Bavarian monarchs who had suffered from a comprehensive list of delusions, of which grandeur had not been the least. But, delusions or not, he had had, as the deluded so often had—to the dismay and consternation of their allegedly saner brethren—impeccable taste. The castle was perfect for the valley, the valley for the castle. Any other combination would have been inconceivable.

The Schloss Adler was built in the form of a hollow square. It was towered, battlemented and crenellated, its most imposing aspects, two perfectly circular towers, the one to the east higher than that to the west, facing down the valley towards the north. Two smaller but still magnificent towers lay at the southern corners, facing the looming bulk of the Weissspitze. From where Smith lay, at some slight level above that of the castle, he could just see into the open square in its middle, outside access to which was obtained by a pair of huge iron gates at the rear. The sun had not yet climbed sufficiently high above the eastern hills for its rays to strike the castle directly, but, for all that, its incredibly white walls gleamed and glittered as if made of the most iridescent marble.

Below the soaring northern ramparts of the castle the valley fell away steeply to the Blau See, a beautiful pine-fringed jewel of a lake of the deepest and most sparkling blue, a colour which with the green of the pines, the white dazzle of the snow and the brilliant, lighter blue of the sky above formed a combination of breath-taking loveliness. Impossibly lovely,

Smith thought, a completely faithful colour reproduction of the scene would have had everybody shouting "fake."

From where they lay they could see that the belt of pines in which they lay hidden extended almost all the way down to the lake. Getting down there unobserved would be no problem at all. An almost exactly matching line of pines swept down the opposite—the eastern—side of the valley. From the lakes those two long sweeps of pines, climbing steadily upwards as they marched to the south, must have appeared like a pair of great curving horns almost meeting at the top of the lower of the two cliff faces on the Weissspitze.

A small village lay at the head of the lake. Basically it consisted of a single wide street, perhaps two hundred yards in length, a railway station, two inevitable churches perched on two inevitable knolls and a thin scattering of houses climbing up the steep slopes on either side of the village. From the southern end of the village a road curved up the far side of the valley till it reached the ridgeback to the south of the castle: this ridgeback it ascended by a series of hairpin bends, the last of which led to the great doors guarding the forecourt at the back of the castle. The road, just then, was completely blocked by snow and sole access to the castle was obviously by means of the *Luftseilbahn,* an aerial cableway. Two cables stretched from the village straight up to the castle, crossing three supporting pylons en route. Even as they watched, a cable car was completing the last section of its journey up to the castle. At a distance of not much more than a hundred feet from the glittering walls of the Schloss Adler it appeared to be climbing almost vertically.

On the Blau See, about a mile beyond the village, lay a very large group of regularly spaced huts, arranged in rectangular patterns. It bore an uncommonly close resemblance to a military encampment.

"Well, I'll be damned!" With an almost physical effort of will, Schaffer forced himself to look away and Smith could see the wonder reflected in his eyes. "Is this for real, boss?"

It wasn't a question that called for an answer. Schaffer had summed up their collective feeling pretty well and there was nothing that anyone could add that wouldn't seem and sound superfluous. Prone in the snow, they watched in silence as the cable car climbed agonisingly slowly up the last fifty feet towards the castle. It seemed as if it would never make it and Smith could almost palpably sense the empathy of his companions and himself as they willed that little car on the last few

43

feet of its journey. But make it it did and it disappeared from sight under the roof of the cable header station that had been built into the western foot of the castle. The tension relaxed and Schaffer cleared his throat.

"Boss," he said diffidently, "there are a couple of minor points that occur to me. Requiring elucidation, one might say. First of all, if I didn't know better I'd say that was a military barracks down by that little old lake there."

"You don't know better. That *is* a military barracks down by that little old lake there. And no ordinary military barracks either, I might say. That's the training HQ of the Jaeger battalions of the Wehrmacht's Alpenkorps."

"Oh, my gosh! The Alpine Corps! If I'd known this I'd never have come along. The Alpine Corps! Why didn't someone tell Ma Schaffer's nearest and dearest?"

"I thought you knew," Smith said mildly. "Why do you think we're not dressed as German sailors or Red Cross nurses?"

Schaffer unzipped his snow smock, minutely examined his Alpenkorps uniform as if seeing it for the first time, then zipped it up again. He said carefully: "You mean to say we're going to mingle, careless like, with the German Army." He paused, looked wide-eyed at Smith's smiling nod, then went on incredulously: "But—but we'll be recognised as strangers!"

"Training troops come and go all the time," Smith said offhandedly. "What's six new faces among six hundred new faces?"

"This is terrible," Schaffer said gloomily.

"Worse than horses?" Smith smiled. "After all, the Alpenkorps don't buck and trample all over you."

"Horses don't carry machine guns," Schaffer said morosely. "And your second point?"

"Ah, yes. The second point. There's the little matter of the old Schloss itself. Kinda forgotten our helicopter, haven't we? How do we get in?"

"A good point," Smith conceded. "We'll have to think about it. But I'll tell you this. If Colonel Wyatt-Turner can penetrate the German High Command and, more important, get away again, this should be a piece of cake for us."

"He did what?" Schaffer demanded.

"Didn't you know?"

"How should I know?" Schaffer was irritated. "Never met the guy till yesterday."

"He spent the years '40 to '43 inside Germany. Served in the Wehrmacht for part of the time. Ended up in the GHQ in Berlin. Says he knows Hitler quite well."

"Well, I'll be damned." Schaffer poised for a long moment, finally arrived at a conclusion. "The guy," he said moodily, "must be nuts."

"Maybe. But if he can do it, we can. We'll figure a way. Let's get back among the trees."

They inched their way back into cover, leaving Christiansen behind with Smith's telescope to keep watch. After they'd made a temporary camp, heated and drunk some coffee, Smith announced his intention of trying to contact London again.

He unpacked the radio and sat down on a kit bag a few feet distant from the others. The switch that cut in the transmitter circuit was on the left-hand side of the radio, the side remote from where the other four men were sitting. Smith switched on with a loud positive click, cranked the callup handle with his left hand. With the very first crank his left hand moved the transmitting switch from "On" to "Off," the whirring of the callup blanketing the sound. Smith cranked away diligently at intervals, stopping from time to time to make minute adjustments to the controls, then finally gave up and sat back, shaking his head in disgust.

"You'll never make it with all those trees around," Torrance-Smythe observed.

"That must be it," Smith agreed. "I'll try the other side of the wood. Might have better luck there."

He slung the transmitter over his shoulder and trudged off through the deep snow, cutting straight across to the other side of the belt of pines. When he thought he was safely out of eyeshot of the men at the camp, he checked with a quick look over his shoulder. They were out of sight. He turned more than ninety degrees left and hurried up the hill until he cut the tracks that he and his men had made on the way down. He followed the tracks uphill, whistling "Lorelei," but whistling softly: in that frosty air, sound travelled dangerously far. He stopped whistling when Mary appeared from where she had been hiding behind a fallen pine.

"Hullo, darling," she said brightly.

"We'll have less of the 'darlings,' " Smith said briskly. "It's 8 A.M. Father Machree awaits. And keep your voice down."

He sat on the fallen tree, cranked the handle and established contact almost immediately. The transmission from

London was still very faint but clearer than it had been in the earlier hours of the morning.

"Father Machree is waiting," the radio crackled. "Hold. Hold."

Smith held and the unmistakable voice of Admiral Rolland took over from the London operator.

"Position please, Broadsword."

Smith consulted the piece of paper in his hand, again in code and plain language. The message read: WOODS DUE WEST CASTLE DESCENDING W.H. THIS EVENING. Smith read out the corresponding code letters.

There was a pause, presumably while Rolland was having the message decoded, then his voice came again.

"Understood. Proceed. Harrod killed accidentally?"

"No. Over."

"By the enemy? Over."

"No. What is the weather report? Over."

"Deteriorating. Freshening winds, strong later. Snow. Over."

Smith looked up at the still and cloudless sky above. He assumed that Rolland hadn't got his forecasts mixed up. He said: "Time of next broadcast uncertain. Can you stand by? Over."

"Am remaining HQ until operation complete," Rolland said. "Good luck. Good-bye."

Smith closed up the radio and said thoughtfully to Mary: "I didn't much care for the way he said good-bye there."

In the Naval Operations room in Whitehall, Admiral Rolland and Colonel Wyatt-Turner, one on either side of the radio operator manning a huge transceiver, looked at each other with heavy faces.

"So the poor devil was murdered," Wyatt-Turner said flatly.

"A high price to pay for confirmation that we were right," Rolland said sombrely. "Poor devil, as you say. The moment we gave him that radio to carry we signed a death warrant. I wonder who's next. Smith himself?"

"Not Smith." Wyatt-Turner shook his head positively. "Some people have a sixth sense. Smith has a seventh, eighth, and ninth, and a built-in radar set for danger. Smith can survive under any circumstances I can conceive of. I didn't pick him with a pin, sir. He's the best agent in Europe."

"Except possibly yourself. And don't forget, Colonel, there

may possibly be circumstances that even you can't conceive of."

"Yes, that's so." He looked directly at Rolland. "What do you reckon his chances are, sir?"

"Chances?" Rolland's eyes were remote, unseeing. "What do you mean chances? He doesn't have any."

Almost precisely the same thought was in Smith's mind as he lit a cigarette and looked at the girl beside him, careful not to let his thoughts show in his face. Not until that first sight he'd just had of the castle had the full realisation of the apparent impossibility of their task struck him. Had he known what the precise physical situation had been, he doubted very much whether he would have come. Deep in the farthest recesses of his mind, he knew, although he would not admit it to himself, that there really was no room for the element of doubt. He wouldn't have come. But he had come. He was here and he had better do something about it.

He said to Mary: "Have you had a squint at the old schloss yet?"

"It's a fantastic place. How on earth do we ever get General Carnaby out of there?"

"Easy. We'll take a walk up there tonight, get inside and take him away."

Mary stared at him in disbelief and waited for him to amplify his statement. He didn't. Finally, she said: "That's all?"

"That's all."

"The simplicity of true genius. You must have spent a lot of time working that one out." When he still didn't reply, she went on, elaborately sarcastic: "In the first place, of course, there'll be no trouble about getting in. You just go up to the main door and knock."

"More or less. Then the door—or window—opens, I smile at you, say thank you and pass inside."

"You what?"

"I smile and say thank you. Even in wartime, there's no reason why the little courtesies—"

"Please!" She was thoroughly exasperated now. "If you can't talk sense—"

"*You* are going to open the door for *me*," Smith explained patiently.

"Are you feeling all right?"

"The staff shortage in Germany is acute. The Schloss Adler is no exception. You're just the type they're looking for.

Young, intelligent, good-looking, you can cook, polish, sew on Colonel Kramer's buttons—"

"Who's Colonel Kramer?" Her tone as much as her face showed the bewilderment in her mind.

"Deputy Chief of the German Secret Service."

Mary said with conviction: "You must be mad."

"If I wasn't I wouldn't be doing this job." He glanced at his watch. "I've been gone too long and I fear that I'm surrounded by the odd suspicious mind. We move off at five. Exactly five. Down in the village there's a *Gasthaus* on the east side of the main street called Zum Wilden Hirsch. The Wild Deer. Remember it, Zum Wilden Hirsch. We don't want you wandering into the wrong pub. Behind it there's a shed used as a beer cellar. It's always kept locked but there will be a key in the door tonight. I'll meet you there at exactly eight o'clock."

He turned to go, but she caught him by the arm.

"How do you know all this?" she asked tensely. "About the *Gasthaus* and the bottle store and the key being there and about Colonel Kramer and—"

"Ah, ah!" Smith shook his head admonishingly and touched her lips with his forefinger.

"Handbook for spies, golden rule number one." She drew away from him and stared down at the snow-covered ground, her voice low and bitter. "Never ever ever tell anyone anything unless you have to." She paused and looked up. "Not even me?"

"Especially not you, poppet." He patted her lightly on the cheek. "Don't be late."

He walked away down the slope leaving her looking after him with an expressionless face.

Lieutenant Schaffer lay stretched out and almost buried in the deep snow, half-hidden behind the bole of a pine, with a telescope to his eye. He twisted as he heard the soft crunch of snow behind him and saw Smith approaching on his hands and knees.

"Couldn't you knock or something?" Schaffer asked irritably.

"Sorry. Something you wanted to show me, so the boys say."

"Yeah." Schaffer handed Smith the telescope. "Take a gander at this. Thought it might interest you."

Smith took the telescope and fingered the very precise adjustment until he achieved maximum definition.

"Lower down," Schaffer said. "At the foot of the rock."

Smith traversed the telescope down the sides of the Schloss Adler and the sheer walls of the volcanic plug until the fine crosshairs came to rest on the snow-covered slopes at the foot. Moving across the slope he could see two soldiers with slung machine carbines and, not on leashes, four dogs.

"My, my," Smith murmured thoughtfully. "I see what you mean."

"Those are Doberman pinschers, boss."

"Well, they aren't toy poodles and that's a fact," Smith agreed. He moved the telescope a little way up the walls of the volcanic plug, held it there.

"*And* floodlights?" he added softly.

He lowered the telescope again, past the patrolling soldiers and dogs, till it came to rest on a high wire fence that appeared to go all the way around the base of the volcanic plug.

"*And* a dinky little fence."

"Fences," Schaffer said pontifically, "are made to be cut or climbed."

"You try cutting or climbing this one, laddie, and you'll be cooked to a turn in nothing flat. A standard design, using a standard current of 2300 volt, single-phase, 60 cycle AC. All the best electric chairs have it."

Schaffer shook his head. "Amazing the lengths some folks will go to protect their privacy."

"Fences, floods and Dobermans," Smith said. "I don't think that combination will stop us, do you, Lieutenant?"

"Of course not. Stop us? Of course not!" He paused for some moments, then burst out: "How in God's name do you propose—"

"We'll decide when the time comes." Smith said easily.

"You mean you'll decide," Schaffer said complainingly. "Play it pretty close to the chest, don't you?"

"That's because I'm too young to die."

"Why me, for God's sake?" Schaffer demanded after a long pause. "Why pick me for this job? This isn't my game, Major."

"God knows," Smith said frankly. "Come to that, why me?"

Schaffer was in the middle of giving him a long and pointedly disbelieving look when he suddenly stiffened and cocked his head up to the sky in the direction of the unmistakably rackety whir of a helicopter engine. Both men picked it up at once. It was coming from the north, over the Blau See, and heading directly towards them. It was a big military version and, even at that distance, the swastika markings were clearly distinguishable. Schaffer started to move backwards towards the line of pines.

"Exit Schaffer," he announced hurriedly. "The bloodhounds are out for us."

"I don't think so," Smith said. "Stay where you are and pull your smock over your head."

Quickly they pulled their white smocks over their heads until only their eyes, and Smith's telescope, partly buried in the snow, could be seen. From thirty yards in any direction, including straight up, they must have been quite invisible.

The helicopter swept up the valley still maintaining a course directly towards the spot where the two men lay hidden. When it was only a few hundred yards away even Smith began to feel uneasy and wondered if by some evil mischance the enemy knew or suspected their presence. They were bound to have heard the engines of the Lancaster, muted though they had been, during the night. Had some suspicious and intelligent character—and there would be no lack of those in the Schloss Adler—come up with the right answer to the question of the presence of this errant bomber in one of the most unlikely places in all Germany? Could picked members of the Alpenkorps be combing the pine woods even at that moment—and he, Smith, had been so confident that he hadn't even bothered to post a guard. Then, abruptly, when the helicopter was almost directly overhead, it side-slipped sharply to its left, sank down over the castle courtyard, hovered for a few moments and slowly descended. Smith surreptitiously mopped his forehead and applied his eye to the telescope.

The helicopter had landed. The rotor stopped, steps descended and a man climbed down to the courtyard floor. From his uniform, Smith decided a very senior officer. Then he suddenly realised that it was a very very senior officer indeed. His face tightened as he pushed the telescope across to Schaffer. "Take a good look," he advised.

Schaffer took a good look, lowered the telescope as the man passed through a doorway. "Pal of yours, boss?"

"I know him. Reichsmarschal Julius Rosemeyer. The Wehrmacht Chief of Staff."

"My very first Reichsmarschal and me without my telescopic rifle," Schaffer said regretfully. "I wonder what his highness wants."

"Same as us," Smith said briefly.

"General Carnaby?"

"When you're going to ask the Allies' over-all coordinator of planning a few questions about the second front you don't send just the corporal of the guard to interview him."

"You don't think they might have come to take old Carnaby away?" Schaffer asked anxiously.

"Not a chance. The Gestapo never gives up its prisoners. In this country the Wehrmacht does what the Gestapo says."

"Or else?"

"Or else. Off you go—they've more coffee on the brew back there. Send someone to relieve me in an hour."

Admiral Rolland's weather forecast for the area turned out to be perfectly correct. As the endless shivering hours dragged slowly by the weather steadily deteriorated. By noon the sun was gone and a keen wind sprung up from the east. By early afternoon snow had begun to fall from the darkened sky, slowly at first then with increasing severity as the east wind steadily increased in strength and became bitingly cold. It looked like being a bad night, Smith thought. But a bad night that reduced visibility to near-zero and kept people indoors was what they wanted: it would have been difficult for them to saunter up to the Schloss Adler bathed in the warm light of a harvest moon. Smith checked his watch.

"Time to go." He climbed stiffly to his feet and beat his arms to restore circulation. "Call Thomas, will you."

Rucksacks and kit bags were slung and shouldered. Thomas, who had been keeping watch, appeared carrying Smith's telescope. Thomas was very far from being his usual cheerful self, and it wasn't just the fact that he'd spent the last hour exposed to the full force of wind and snow that had left him in such ill-humour.

"Is that damned radio working yet?" he asked Smith.

"Not a hope. Six tries, six failures. Why?"

"I'll tell you why," Thomas said bitterly. "Pity we couldn't get the admiral to change his mind about the paratroops. A full troop train just got in, that's all."

"Well, that's fine," Smith said equably. "The old hands will

51

think we're new boys and the new boys will think we're old hands. Very convenient."

Thomas looked thoughtfully at Smith.

"Very, *very* convenient." He hesitated, then went on: "How about loosening up a bit, Major?"

"What do you mean?"

"Come off it," Carraciola said roughly. "You know damn well what he means. It's our lives. Why do we have to go down into that damned village? And how do you intend to get Carnaby out? If we're to commit suicide, tell us why. You owe us that."

"I owe you nothing," Smith said flatly. "I'll tell you nothing. And if you know nothing you can't talk. You'll be told when the time comes."

"You, Smith," Torrance-Smythe said precisely, "are a cold-blooded devil."

"It's been said before," Smith said indifferently.

The village railway station was a small, two-track, end-of-the-line depot. Like all end-of-the-line depots it was characterised by rust, dilapidation, the barest functionalism of design and an odd pessimistically expectant air of waiting for someone to come along and finish it off properly. At any time, its air of desolation was total. That night, completely deserted, with a high, gusting wind driving snow through pools of light cast by dim and swaying electric lamps, the ghostly impression of a place abandoned by man and by the world was almost overwhelming. It suited Smith's purpose perfectly.

He led his five snow-smock clad men quickly across the tracks and into the comparative shelter of the station buildings. They filed silently past the closed bookstall, the freight office, the ticket office, flitted quickly into the shadows beyond and stopped.

Smith lowered the radio, shrugged off his rucksack, removed snow smock and trousers and sauntered casually alongside the tracks—the thrifty Bavarians regarded platforms as a wasteful luxury. He stopped outside a door next to a bolted hatch which bore above it the legend *GEPACK AB-NAHME*. He tried the door. It was locked. He made a quick survey to check that he was unobserved, stooped, examined the keyhole with a pencil flash, took a bunch of oddly shaped keys from his pockets and had the door open in seconds. He whistled softly and was almost at once joined by the others, who filed quickly inside, already slipping off their packs as they went. Schaffer, bringing up the rear, paused and glanced up at the sign above the hatch.

"My God!" He shook his head. "The left baggage room!"

"Where else?" Smith asked reasonably. He ushered Schaffer in, closed and locked the door behind him. Hooding his pencil flash until only a finger-width beam emerged, he passed by the baggage racks till he came to the far end of the room where a bay window was set in the wall. It was a perfectly ordinary sash window and he examined it very minutely, careful that at no time the pinpoint of light touched the glass to shine through to the street beyond. He turned his attention to the vertical wooden planking at the side of the window, took out his sheath knife and levered a plank away to expose a length of twin-cored flex stapled vertically to the wall. He split the cores, sliced through each in turn, replaced the plank and tested the lower sash of the window. It moved easily up and down.

"An interesting performance," Schaffer observed. "What was all that supposed to do?"

"It's not always convenient to enter by the front door. Or, come to that, leave by it either."

"A youth misspent in philandering or burgling," Schaffer said sadly. "How did you know it was wired for sound?"

"Even a small country station will have valuables stored in its left baggage room from time to time," Smith said patiently. "But it will *not* have a fulltime baggage attendant. The attendant, ticket clerk, ticket collector, porter, and stationmaster are probably all one and the same man. So it's kept locked. But there's no point in barring the front door if your bag-snatcher can climb in through the back window. So your back window is grilled or wired. No grill—and a badly fitting plank. Obvious."

"Obvious to you, maybe," Carraciola said sourly. "All this —ah—expertise with skeleton keys and burglar alarms. The Black Watch you said you were in?"

"That's right."

"Very odd training they give you in these Scottish regiments. Very odd indeed."

" 'Thorough' is the word you're searching for," Smith said kindly. "Let's go and have a drink."

"Let's do that," Carraciola said heavily. "Remind me to get mine down in one go or ten gets you one that I'll never live to finish it."

"It would be a shame to waste good beer," Smith agreed. He waited until the last man was out, locked the door behind him and rejoined them as they walked out of the main station entrance under the BAHNHOF sign. They were now no longer carrying rucksacks or wearing snow smocks. All were dressed in the uniforms of soldiers of a Jaeger battalion, Smith as a major, Schaffer as a lieutenant, and the other four as sergeants. Their uniforms were no longer as immaculately crease-free as they might have been nor for that matter, as Sergeant Harrod had observed, did they fit as well as they might have done. But in a village street or crowded bar, at nighttime, they should pass muster. Or so Smith devoutly hoped.

It was a typical main street in a typically high Alpine village. The buildings lining either side of the street, solid, rugged, four-square buildings, looked as if they had been defying the bitter Bavarian winters for a long time and intended going on doing so for as long again. Nearly all the houses were of the wooden chalet type, with great sweeping eaves and balconies running the full width of the front of the houses. A few were of comparatively modern construction, with shingled walls, large double-glazed windows and fancy wrought-iron grillwork, but most were very old and low, planked with rough adze-cut wood, and having the interlocking wall beams projecting at corners.

There were no streetlamps but neither was there any attempt at a blackout. Elongated rectangles of light from uncurtained windows patterned the snow-packed streets. Beyond the far or southern end of the street, intermittently seen through the sweeping curtains of snow, a cluster of bright lights seemed to hang suspended in the sky. Instinctively, almost, Smith stopped to gaze at this distant constellation and his men stopped with him. The lights of the Schloss Adler, the castle of the eagle, seemed impossibly remote, as unattainable as the mountains of the moon. The men looked at them in long silence, then at one another, then, by mutual and still silent consent, moved on their way again, their boots crunching crisply in the beaten snow, their frozen breaths wisping away in the chill night wind.

The main street—the only street—was deserted, quite empty of life. Inevitably so, on so bitter a night. But if the street was deserted, the village was anything but: the sounds of laughter and singing and the babel of voices filled the night air and the nose-to-tail row of parked German trucks along one side of the street showed clearly enough just who was responsible for the singing and the laughter. For the training troops in the military barracks on the Blau See there was only one centre of entertainment for twenty miles around and this village was it: the *Gasthausen* and *Weinstuben* were jammed to the doors with soldiers of the Alpenkorps, probably the most highly trained combat troops in Europe.

Schaffer said plaintively: "I don't really feel like a drink, boss."

"Nonsense," Smith said encouragingly. "You're just shy at the thought of meeting strangers." He stopped in front of a *Gasthaus* with the legend DREI KÖNIGEN above the door. "Here's a likely looking place, now. Hang on a minute."

He climbed the steps, opened the door and looked inside. Down in the street the other five looked at one another, the same mingled apprehension and expectancy mirrored in every eye. Austrian *Schrammel* music, hauntingly and nostalgically evocative of a kindlier and happier age, flooded through the open doorway. The expressions on the faces of the men below didn't change. There was a time and a place for *Schrammel* music and this wasn't it.

Smith shook his head, closed the door and rejoined his men.

"Packed," he said. "Not even standing room." He nodded across the street to another hostelry, the Eichhof, a small, squat, beetle-browed building with adze-cut corner beams and an air of advanced dilapidation. "Let's see what this has to offer."

But the Eichhof had nothing to offer. Regretfully but firmly Smith closed its front door and turned away.

"Jammed," he announced. "Besides, a low-class dump unsuitable for officers and NCOs of the Wehrmacht. But this next place looks more promising, don't you think?"

From the pointed silence it was apparent that the other five didn't think anything of the kind, and, in fact, apart from the factor of size, the third *Weinstube* looked remarkably like the one Smith had just passed up. Zum Wilden Hirsch, it was called, and above the sign was a snow-shrouded wooden carving of a wild deer.

Smith walked up the half-dozen steps to the front door and opened it. He winced as the blast of sound reached him, an almost physical assault upon the eardrums. Heaven knew the last two *Weinstuben* had been clamorous enough but compared to this place they now seemed, in retrospect, to have been invested in a cathedral silence. To the blaring accompaniment of a battery of discordant accordions what appeared, from the sheer volume of sound, to be an entire regiment were giving "Lili Marlene" all they had. Smith glanced at his men, nodded and passed inside.

As the others followed, Schaffer paused in the doorway as Christiansen took his arm and said wonderingly: "You think he thinks this *isn't* packed?"

"They must," Schaffer conceded, "have had them stacked six deep in the other joints."

FOUR

THEY WEREN'T exactly stacked six deep inside Zum Wilden Hirsch but they might well have been if the music-swaying crowd of elbow-jostling customers had assumed the horizontal instead of the perpendicular. He had never, Smith thought, seen so many people in one bar before. There must have been at least four hundred of them. To accommodate a number of that order called for a room of no ordinary dimensions, and this one wasn't. It was a very big room indeed. It was also a very very old room.

The floor of knotted pine sagged, the walls sagged and the massive smoke-blackened beams on the roof seemed about to be ready to fall down at any moment. In the middle of the room stood a huge black wood-burning stove, a stove stoked with such ferocious purpose that the cast-iron top cover glowed dull red. From just below the cover two six-inch twenty-foot long black-enamelled stove pipes led off to points high up on opposite sides of the room—a primitive but extremely efficient form of central heating. The three-sided settees—half booths—lining three walls of the room were of oak darkened by age and smoke and unknown centuries of customers, each booth having recessed holes for stowing newspapers rolled round slats of wood. The twenty or so tables scattered across the floor had hand-cut wooden tops of not less than three inches in thickness with chairs to match. Most of the back of the room was taken up by a solid oaken bar with a coffee-machine at one end, and, behind the bar, swing doors that presumably led to the kitchen. What little illumination there was in the room came from ceiling-suspended and very sooty oil lamps each one with its generations-old patch of coal-black charred wood in the roof above.

Smith transferred his attention from the room to the customers in the room, a clientele of a composition such as one might expect to find in a high Alpine village with a military encampment at its back door. In one corner were a group of obvious locals, men with still, lean, aquiline, weather-beaten faces, unmistakably men of the mountains, many of them in intricately embroidered leather jackets and Tyrolean hats. They spoke little and drank quietly, as did another small group at the back of the room, perhaps a dozen or so nondescript civilians, clearly not locals, who drank sparingly from small schnapps glasses. But ninety percent of the customers were soldiers of the German Alpenkorps, some seated, many more standing, but all giving of their very best with "Lili Marlene," and nearly all of them enthusiastically waving their pewter-capped litre *Steinbechers* in the air, happily oblivious, in that moment of tearfully nostalgic romanticism, of the fact that the amount of beer finding its way to comrades' uniforms and the floor was about the equivalent of a moderately heavy rainstorm.

Behind the bar was the obvious proprietor, a gargantuan three-hundred-pounder with an impassive moonlike face and several girls busy filling trays with *Steinbechers*. Several others moved about the room, collecting or serving beer mugs. One of them approaching in his direction caught Smith's eye.

It would have been surprising if she hadn't. It would have been surprising if she hadn't caught the attention of every man there. But there was no surprise. She did. She would have won any Miss Europe contest hands down if she had had a face other than her own which though pleasant and plump, was rather plain. But any possible lack of attraction in that cheerfully smiling face was more than over-compensated for elsewhere. She was dressed in a gaily patterned dirndl and Tyrolean blouse, had a hand-span waist, an hour-and-a-half-glass figure and an obvious predilection for low-cut blouses that, in terms of attracting local custom, must have been worth a fortune to the gigantic proprietor behind the bar. She drew a great deal of attention from the assembled soldiery, not all of it just consisting of admiring glances: if she weren't wearing armour-plating, Smith reflected, she must be permanently black and blue. She approached Smith, brushed back her blond hair and smiled, the gesture as provocative as the smile.

"Can I help you, sir?"

"Dark beer, please," Smith said politely. "Six."

"With pleasure, sir." Again the provocative smile, this time accompanied by a half-appraising, half-lingering look from cornflower blue eyes, then she turned and walked her way, if her method of locomotion could strictly be described as walking. Schaffer, a slightly dazed expression on his face, stared after her, then caught Smith by the arm.

"*Now* I know why I left Montana, boss." His voice held something of the dazed quality on his face. "It wasn't because of the horses after all."

"Your mind on the job if you don't mind, Lieutenant." Smith looked thoughtfully after the girl, rubbed his chin and said slowly: "Barmaids know more about what's going on in their own manor than any chief of police—and that one looks as if she might know more than most. Yes, I'll do that."

"Do what?" Schaffer asked suspiciously.

"Try to get next to her."

"I saw her first," Schaffer said plaintively.

"You can have the next dance," Smith promised. The levity of the words were belied by the cool watchful expression on his face as his eyes constantly travelled the room. "When you get your drinks, circulate. See if you can hear any mention of Carnaby or Reichsmarschal Rosemeyer."

He caught sight of an empty chair by a corner table, moved across and sat on it, nodding politely to a rather bleary-eyed Alpenkorps captain deep in what appeared to be rather patronising conversation with two lieutenants. The captain showed no more than a brief recognition of his presence and, as far as Smith could tell, no other person present was showing the slightest interest in either himself or his companions. The accordion band finished its stint more or less on the same note and more or less at the same time and the singing of "Lili Marlene" died away. For long seconds there was a profound and nostalgic silence, four hundred men alone with Lili Marlene under the barrack gate lantern, then, as if on cue, a babel of voices broke out all over the room: four hundred men with unfinished litre mugs do not remain sentimental for overly long.

He caught sight of the girl returning with six *Steinbechers* on a tray, pushing her way through the crowd and fending off admirers with a practised hand. She gave drinks to Smith's men who immediately but unostentatiously broke up and began to wander away into different parts of the room. The girl looked around, located Smith, smiled brightly, crossed to his table and put the *Steinbecher* on it. Before she

59

could straighten, Smith put his arm around her waist and pulled her onto his knee. The Jaeger captain across the table broke off his conversation, stared across in startled disapproval, opened his mouth as if to speak, caught Smith's discouraging glance, decided to mind his own business and resumed his conversation. Smith, in his turn, looked away, squeezed the girl's waist, patted her knee and smiled what he hoped was a winning smile.

"And what might your name be, my Alpine rose?" His voice had a slightly slurred edge to it.

"Heidi." She struggled to rise, but didn't really put her heart into it. "Please, Major. I have work to do."

"There is no more important work than entertaining soldiers of the Fatherland," Smith said loudly. Holding Heidi firmly to forestall any attempt at escape, he took a long pull at his beer, then continued, quietly now, the mug still in front of his face: "Shall I sing you a song?"

"What song?" Heidi asked warily. "I hear too much singing."

"I whistle better than I sing. Listen." He whistled, very softly, the first two bars of "Lorelei." "Do you like that?"

Heidi stiffened and stared but immediately relaxed and smiled at him coquettishly.

"It's very nice, Major. And I'm sure you have a beautiful singing voice, too."

Smith put his *Steinbecher* down with an unsteady bang that brought more disapproval from the other side of the table, then lifted his hand to wipe the froth from his lips. Heidi smiled down at him, but the wary eyes weren't smiling.

Smith said from behind his hand: "The men at the bar? The civilians? *Don't* turn round."

"Gestapo." She made another apparently futile attempt to free herself. "From the castle."

"One's a lip reader." Smith had the *Steinbecher* in front of his face again. "I can tell. They're watching. Your room in five minutes. Hit me good and hard."

Heidi stared at him in bewilderment, then yelped in pain as he pinched her, far from gently. She drew back, her right hand came over in a roundhouse swing and the sound of the slap could be heard clear across the crowded room, cutting sharply through the deep buzz of conversation. The voices died away, *Steinbechers* remained poised halfway toward lips, and every eye in the room turned until it was focussed on the scene of the disturbance. Smith now had the exclusive and undivided attention of close on four hundred German soldiers which was exactly how he wanted it: no man anxious to avoid attention at all costs would ever do anything to incur the slightest risk of drawing that unwanted attention.

Heidi pushed herself to her feet, rubbed herself tenderly, snatched up the note which Smith had earlier placed on the table and stalked haughtily away. Smith, his already reddening face discomfited and tight in anger, rose, made to leave the table then halted when confronted by the Jaeger who had already risen from his side of the table. He was a spruce, erect youngster, very much of the Hitler Jugend type, punctilious and correct but at that moment rather suffering from the effect of too many *Steinbechers*. Beneath the redly dulled eyes lay a gleam which bespoke the not uncommon combination of self-importance and officious self-righteousness.

"Your conduct does not become an officer of the Wehrmacht," he said loudly.

Smith did not reply at once. The embarrassed anger faded from his face to be replaced by an expressionlessly penetrating stare. He gazed unwinkingly into the captain's eyes for so long that the other finally looked away. When Smith's voice came it was too quiet to be heard even at the next table.

"*Herr* Major, when you talk to me, little man." The tone was glacial: so now were also the eyes. "Major Bernd Himmler. You may have heard of me?"

He paused significantly and the young captain seemed to shrink perceptibly before his eyes. Himmler, head of the Gestapo, was the most feared man in Germany. Smith could have been any relative of Himmler, possibly even his son.

"Report to me at eight tomorrow morning," Smith said curtly. He swung away without waiting for an answer. The Alpenkorps captain, suddenly very sober indeed, nodded wordlessly and sank wearily into his chair. As Smith strode towards the door the hubbub of conversation resumed. For the soldiers stationed in that remote military outpost, drinking beer, very large quantities of beer, was the only pastime: such incidents were no sooner seen than forgotten.

On his way to the door Smith stopped briefly by Schaffer and said: "Well, I fouled that one up."

"You could have handled it differently," Schaffer conceded, then went on curiously: "What did you say to him? The young Alpine Corps captain, I mean."

"I gave him to understand that I was Himmler's son."

"The Gestapo boss?" Schaffer asked incredulously. "God above, you took a chance."

"I couldn't afford to take a chance," Smith said cryptically. "I'll go try the Eichhof. Better luck there, maybe. Back in ten minutes. Less."

He left Schaffer looking uncertainly after him, made an urgent negative move of his hand towards Carraciola, who was approaching him, and passed outside. He moved a few paces along the wooden boardwalk, stopped and glanced briefly up and down the snow-filled street. It was deserted in both directions. He turned and walked quickly up a narrow alleyway which paralleled the side of Zum Wilden Hirsch. At the rear stood a small wooden hut. Smith checked again that he was unobserved, opened the door quietly.

"Eight o'clock," he said into the darkness. "Come on."

There was a rustle of clothes and Mary appeared in the doorway. She was shivering violently, her face blue-tinged with the extreme cold. She looked questioningly at Smith but he took her arm without a word and led her quickly to the back door of the *Gasthaus*. They entered into a small hallway, dimly lit by a small oil lamp, crossed it, climbed a flight of stairs, moved along a corridor and stopped at the second door on the right. They passed swiftly inside, Smith closing the door behind him.

It was a small room, plainly furnished, but from the chintz soft furnishings and toilet articles on a dressing table, very obviously a feminine room. Mary sat down on the bed, hugging herself tightly to try to restore some warmth and looked up at Smith without any admiration in her face.

"I hope you're enjoying your little game," she said bitterly. "Seem to know your way around, don't you?"

"Instinct," Smith explained. He stooped over the low-burning oil lamp by the bed, turned up the flame, glanced briefly about the room, located a battered leather case in one corner, swung it to the bed and snapped open the lid. The case contained women's clothing. He pulled Mary to her feet and said: "Don't waste time. Take off your clothes. And when I say that, I mean your clothes. Every last stitch. Then get into that top outfit there. You'll find everything you need."

Mary stared at him.

"Those clothes? Why on earth must I—"

"Don't *argue*. Now!"

"Now it is," she said resignedly. "You might at least turn your back."

"Relax," Smith said wearily. "I have other things on my mind." He crossed to the window, stood peering out through a crack in the chintz curtains and went on: "Now, hurry. You're supposed to be coming off the bus from Steingaden that arrives in twenty minutes' time. You'll be carrying that case, which contains the rest of your clothes. Your name is Maria Schenk, you're from the Rhineland, a cousin of a barmaid that works here, and you've had TB and been forced to give up your factory job and go to the mountains for your health. So you've got this new job, through this barmaid, in the Schloss Adler. And you have identity papers, travel permit, references and letters in appropriately postmarked envelopes to prove all of it. They're in that handbag in the case. Think you got all that?"

"I—I think so," she said uncertainly. "But if you'd only tell me—"

"For God's sake!" Smith said impatiently. "Time, girl, time! Got it or not?"

"Maria Schenk, Rhineland, factory, TB, cousin here, Steingaden—yes, I have it." She broke off to pull a ribbed blue wool dress over her head, smoothed it down and said wonderingly: "It's a perfect fit! You'd think this dress was made for me!"

"It *was* made for you." Smith turned round to inspect her. "It's a 36-26-36 or whatever. We—um—broke into your flat and borrowed a dress to use as a model. Thorough, that's us."

"You broke into my flat?" she asked slowly.

"Well, now, you wouldn't want to go around like a refugee from a jumble sale," Smith said reasonably. He looked at the dress with an approving eye. "Does something for you."

"I'd like to do something for you," she said feelingly. Her eyes mirrored her bafflement, her total lack of understanding. "But—but it must have taken *weeks* to prepare those clothes —and those papers!"

"Like enough," Smith agreed. "Our Forgery Section did a very special job on those papers. Had to, to get you into the lion's den."

"Weeks," Mary said incredulously. "Weeks! But General Carnaby's plane crashed only yesterday morning." She stared at him, registering successive expressions of confusion, accusation and, finally, downright anger. "You *knew* it was going to crash!"

"Right first time, my poppet," Smith said cheerfully. He gave her an affectionate pat. "We rigged it."

"Don't do that," she snapped, then went on carefully, her face still tight with anger: "There really *was* a plane crash?"

"Guaranteed. The plane crash-landed on the airfield HQ of the Bavarian Mountain Rescue pilots. Place called Oberhausen, about five miles from here. The place we'll be leaving from, incidentally."

"The place we'll be leaving—" She broke off, gazed at him a long moment then shook her head almost in despair. "But —but in the plane I overheard you telling the men that if the mission failed or you had to split up that you were all to make a rendezvous at Frauenfeld, over the Swiss border."

"Did you now?" There was mild interest in Smith's voice. "I must be getting confused. Anyway, this Mosquito put down on the Oberhausen airfield riddled with machine-gun bullet holes. British machine-gun bullet holes, but what the hell, holes are holes."

"And you'd risk the life of an American general—and all the plans for the second front—"

"Well, now, that's why I'm in such a hurry to get inside the Schloss Adler." Smith cleared his throat. "Not before they get his secrets out of him but before they find out that he's *not* an American general and knows no more about the second front than I do about the back of the moon."

"What! He's a plant?"

"Name of Jones," Smith nodded. "Cartwright Jones. American actor. As a thespian he's pretty second rate but he's a dead ringer for Carnaby."

She looked at him with something like horror in her eyes.

"You'd risk an innocent—"

"He's getting plenty," Smith interrupted. "Twenty-five thousand dollars for a one-night stand. The peak of his professional career."

There came a soft double knock on the door. A swift sliding movement of Smith's hand and a gun was suddenly there, a Mauser automatic, cocked and ready to go. Another swift movement and he was silently by the door, jerking it open. Smith put his gun away. Heidi came in, Smith shutting the door behind her.

"Well, cousins, here we are," he announced. "Mary—now Maria—and Heidi. I'm off."

"You're off!" Mary said dazedly. "But—but what am I supposed to *do?*"

"Heidi will tell you."

Mary looked uncertainly at the other girl. "Heidi?"

64

"Heidi. Our top secret agent in Bavaria since 1941."

"Our—top—" Mary slowly shook her head. "I don't believe it!"

"Nobody would." Smith surveyed Heidi's opulent charms with an admiring eye. "Brother, what a disguise!"

Smith opened the back door of the *Gasthaus* with a cautious hand, moved swiftly outside and remained stock-still in the almost total darkness, waiting for his eyes to become accustomed to the change of light. The snow, he thought, was heavier than when they had first entered Zum Wilden Hirsch and the wind had certainly freshened. It was bitingly cold.

Satisfied that he was unobserved, Smith turned to the left, took two steps and bit off an exclamation as he tripped over some unseen object and fell his length in the snow. He rolled over three times in the snow just in case any bystander might have a knife or gun and homicidal ideas about using them, then got to his feet with catlike speed, his Mauser in one hand, his pencil flash in the other. He snapped on the flash and swung round in a 360° turn. He was alone.

Alone, that was, but for the crumpled form over which he had tripped, an Alpenkorps sergeant lying face-down in the snow, a form lying still and curiously relaxed in that huddled shapelessness of death.

Smith stooped and rolled the figure over to expose the great red stain in the snow where the body had been lying. The pencil flash rested briefly on the front of the tunic, a tunic gashed and soaked in blood. The beam of the light moved up to the face. No more cloisters for this don, Smith thought in irrational emptiness, no more honey still for tea, and the fault is all mine and I can see it in his face. The already dulled and faded eyes of Torrance-Smythe stared up at him in the sightless reproach of death.

Smith straightened to his feet, his face remote and withdrawn, and quartered the immediate ground area with his light. There were no signs of a struggle but struggle there must have been, for some tunic buttons had been ripped off and the high collar torn open. Smithy had not died easily. Flash still in hand, Smith walked slowly along to the mouth of the narrow alleyway, then stopped. A confusion of footprints, dark smears of blood in the trodden snow, dark bare patches on the wooden walls of the *Gasthaus* where struggling men had staggered heavily against it—here was where the struggle had been. Smith switched off the light, returned both flash and gun to their hiding places and stepped out into the street. On the one side was Zum Wilden Hirsch with the sound of singing once again emanating from it, on the other side a brightly-lit telephone kiosk outside a post office. In the kiosk, talking animatedly on the telephone, was a uniformed figure, a soldier Smith had never seen before. The street itself was deserted.

Schaffer leaned negligently against the bar, the picture of complete and careless relaxation. His face belied him. It was grim and shocked and he was savagely shredding a cigarette between his fingers.

"Smithy!" Schaffer's voice was a low and vicious whisper. "Not Smithy! You *sure*, boss?"

"I'm sure." Smith's face still held the same remote and withdrawn expression, almost as if all feeling had been drained from him. "You say he left in a hurry three minutes after I'd gone. So he wasn't after me. Who else left?"

"No idea." Schaffer snapped the cigarette in half, dropped it to the floor. "The place is packed. And there's another door. I *can't* believe it. Why old Smithy? *Why* Torrance-Smythe. He was the cleverest of all."

"That's why he's dead," Smith said sombrely. "Now listen carefully. It's time you knew the score."

Schaffer looked at him steadily and said: "It's more than time."

Smith began to speak in a very low voice, in fluent completely idiomatic German, careful that his back was turned to the Gestapo officers at the far end of the bar. After a minute or two he saw Heidi returning to the room through the doorway behind the bar but ignored her as she ignored him. Almost immediately afterwards a gradual diminution in the babel of talk, followed by an almost complete silence, made him fall quiet himself and follow the direction of the gaze of hundreds of soldiers all of whom were looking towards the door.

There was reason for the silence, especially good reason, Smith thought, for soldiers almost totally cut off from womankind. Mary Ellison, clad in a belted raincoat, with a scarf over her head and a battered suitcase in her hand, was standing in the doorway. The silence seemed to deepen. Women are rare at any time in a high Alpine *Gasthaus*, unaccompanied young women even rarer, and beautiful young women on their own virtually unknown. For some moments Mary stood there uncertainly, as if uncertain of her welcome or not knowing what to do. Then she dropped her bag, and her face lit up as she caught sight of Heidi, a face transformed with joy. Marlene Dietrich in *The Blue Angel,* Smith thought inconsequentially. With a face and a figure and an acting talent like that, she could have had Hollywood tramping a path of beaten gold to her doorstep . . . Through the silent room she and Heidi ran towards each other and embraced.

"My dear Maria! My dear Maria!" There was a break in Heidi's voice that made Smith reflect that Hollywood might have been well advised to tramp out two paths of beaten gold. "So you came after all!"

"After all those years!" Mary hugged the other girl and kissed again. "It's wonderful to see you again, Cousin Heidi! Wonderful, wonderful, wonderful! Of *course* I came. Why ever not?"

"Well!" Heidi made no effort to lower her voice as she looked around significantly. "They're a pretty rough lot, hereabouts. You should carry a gun, always. Hunter battalion, they call themselves. They're well named!"

The soldiers broke out into a roar of laughter and the normal hubbub of sound resumed almost at once. Arm in arm, Heidi led Mary across to the small group of civilians standing at the far end of the bar. She stopped in front of the man in the centre of the group, a dark, wiry, intelligent-faced man who looked very very tough indeed, and performed the introductions.

"Maria, this is Captain von Brauchitsch. He—um—works in the Schloss Adler. Captain, my cousin, Maria Schenk."

Von Brauchitsch bowed slightly.

"You are fortunate in your cousins, Heidi. We were expecting you, Miss Schenk." He smiled. "But not someone as beautiful as this."

Mary smiled in turn, her face puzzled. "You were expecting—"

"He was expecting," Heidi said drily. "It is the captain's business to know what is going on."

"Don't make me sound so sinister, Heidi. You'll frighten Miss Schenk." He glanced at his watch. "The next cable car leaves in ten minutes. If I might escort the young lady—"

"The young lady is going to my room first," Heidi said firmly. "For a washup and a cafe schnapps. Can't you see that she's half-dead with cold?"

"I do believe her teeth are chattering," von Brauchitsch

67

said with a smile. "I thought it might have been me. Well, the cable car after the next one, then."

"And I'm going with her," Heidi announced.

"Both of you?" Von Brauchitsch shook his head and smiled again. Von Brauchitsch was always smiling. "My lucky night."

"Permits, travel documents, identity cards and letters you have," Heidi said. She fished up some papers from the recesses of her Tyrolean blouse and handed them to Mary who was sitting across from her on the bed in her room. "Plan of the castle and instructions. Do your homework well then give them back to me. I'll take them up. You might be searched —they're a suspicious bunch up there. And drink up that schnapps—first thing von Brauchitsch will do is to smell your breath. Just to check. He checks everything. He's the most suspicious of the lot."

"He seemed a very pleasant man to me," Mary said mildly.

"He's a very unpleasant Gestapo officer," Heidi said drily.

When Heidi returned to the bar, Smith and Schaffer had been rejoined by Carraciola, Thomas and Christiansen. All five appeared to be carefree in their drinking and chatting inconsequentially, but their low and urgent voices were evidence enough of the desperate worry in their minds. Or in the minds of some of them.

"You haven't seen old Smithy, then?" Smith asked quietly. "None of you saw him go? Then where in hell has he got to?"

There was no reply, but the shrugs and worried frowns were reply enough. Christiansen said: "Shall I go and have a look?"

"I don't think so," Smith said. "I'm afraid it's too late to go anywhere now."

Both doors of Zum Wilden Hirsch had suddenly burst open and half a dozen soldiers were coming quickly in through either door. All had slung machine carbines, Schmeissers, at the ready. They fanned out along the walls and waited, machine carbines horizontal, fingers on triggers, their eyes very calm, very watchful.

"Well, well," Christiansen murmured. "It was a nice war."

The sudden and total silence was emphasised rather than broken by the crisp footfalls on the wooden floor as a full colonel of the Wehrmacht came striding into the room and looked coldly around him. The gargantuan proprietor of the

Gasthaus came hurrying round from the back of the bar, tripping over chairs in the anxiety and fear limned so unmistakably clearly in his round pumpkin of a face.

"Colonel Weissner!" It required no acute ear to catch the shake in the proprietor's voice. "What in God's name—"

"No fault of yours, *Mein Herr*." The colonel's words were reassuring which was more than the tone of his voice was. "But you harbour enemies of the state."

"Enemies of the state." In a matter of seconds the proprietor's complexion had changed from a most unbecoming puce to an even more unbecoming washed-out grey while his voice now quavered like a high-C tuning fork. "What? I? I, Josef Wartmann—"

"Please." The colonel held up his hand for silence. "We are looking for four or five Alpenkorps deserters from the Stuttgart military prison. To escape, they killed two officers and a guardroom sergeant. They were known to be heading this way."

Smith nodded and said in Schaffer's ear: "Very clever. Very clever indeed."

"Now then," Weissner continued briskly. "If they're here, we'll soon have them. I want the senior officers present of drafts thirteen, fourteen and fifteen to come forward." He waited until two majors and a captain came forward and stood at attention before him. "You know all your officers and men by sight?"

The three officers nodded.

"Good. I wish you—"

"No need, Colonel." Heidi had come round from behind the bar and now stood before Weissner, hands clasped respectfully behind her back. "I know the man you're after. The ringleader."

"Ah!" Colonel Weissner smiled. "The charming—"

"Heidi, Herr Colonel. I have waited table on you up in the Schloss Adler."

Weissner bowed gallantly. "As if one could ever forget."

"That one." Her face full of a combination of righteous indignation and devotion to duty, Heidi pointed a dramatically accusing finger at Smith. "That's the one, Herr Colonel. He —he pinched me!"

"My dear Heidi!" Colonel Weissner smiled indulgently. "If we were to convict every man who ever harboured thoughts of—"

69

"Not that, Herr Colonel. He asked me what I knew or had heard about a man called General Cannabee—I think."

"General Carnaby!" Colonel Weissner was no longer smiling. He glanced at Smith, motioned guards to close in on him, then glanced back at Heidi. "What did you tell him?"

"Herr Colonel!" Heidi was stiff with outraged dignity. "I hope I am a good German. *And* I value my engagements at the Schloss Adler." She half-turned and pointed across the room. "Captain von Brauchitsch of the Gestapo will vouch for me."

"No need. We will not forget this, my dear child." He patted her affectionately on the cheek, then turned to Smith, the temperature of his voice dropping from warm to subzero. "Your accomplices, sir, and at once."

"At once, my dear Colonel?" The look he gave Heidi was as glacial as the colonel's voice. "Surely not. Let's get our priorities straight. First, her thirty pieces of silver. Then us."

"You talk like a fool," Colonel Weissner said contemptuously. "Heidi is a true patriot."

"I'm sure she is," Smith said bitterly.

Mary, her face still and shocked, stared down from the uncurtained crack in Heidi's dark room as Smith and the four others were led out of the front door of Zum Wilden Hirsch and marched off down the road under heavy escort to where several command cars were parked on the far side of the street. Brusquely, efficiently, the prisoners were bundled into two of the cars, engines started up and within a minute both cars were lost to sight round a bend in the road. For almost a minute afterwards Mary stood there, staring out unseeingly on the swirling snow, then pulled the curtains together and turned back towards the darkened room.

She said in a whisper: "How did it happen?"

A match scratched as Heidi lit and turned up the flame of the oil lamp.

"I can't guess." Heidi shrugged. "Someone, I don't know who, must have tipped Colonel Weissner off. But I put the finger on him."

Mary stared at her. "You—you—"

"He'd have been found out in another minute anyway. They were strangers. But it strengthens our hand. I—and you —are now above suspicion."

"Above suspicion!" Mary looked at her in disbelief then

went on, almost wildly: "But there's no point in going ahead now!"

"Is there not?" Heidi said thoughtfully. "Somehow, I feel sorrier for Colonel Weissner than I do for Major Smith. Is not our Major Smith a man of resource? Or do our employees in Whitehall lie to us. When they told me he was coming here, they told me not to worry, to trust him implicitly. A man of infinite resource—those were their exact words—who can extricate himself from positions of utmost difficulty. They have a funny way of talking in Whitehall. But already I trust him. Don't you?"

There was no reply. Mary stared at the floor, her eyes bright with unshed tears. Heidi touched her arm and said softly: "You love him as much as that?"

Mary nodded in silence.

"And does he love you?"

"I don't know. I just don't know. He's been too long in this business—even if he did know," she said bitterly, "he probably wouldn't tell himself."

Heidi looked at her for a long moment, shook her head and said: "They should never have sent you. How can you hope to—" She broke off, shook her head again, and went on: "It's too late now. Come on. We mustn't keep von Brauchitsch waiting."

"But—but if he doesn't come? If he can't escape—and how *can* he escape?" She gestured despairingly at the papers lying on the bed. "They're bound to check with Düsseldorf first thing in the morning about those forged references."

Heidi said without any particular expression in her voice: "I don't think he'd let *you* down, Mary."

"No," Mary said dolefully. "I don't suppose he would."

The big black Mercedes command car swept along the snow-packed road that paralleled the Blau See, the windscreen wipers just coping with the thickly swirling snow that rushed greyly back at the windscreen through powerful headlight beams. It was an expensive car and a very comfortable one, but neither Schaffer up front nor Smith in the rear seat experienced any degree of comfort whatsoever, either mental or physical. On the mental side there was the bitter prospect of the inevitable firing squad and the knowledge that their mission was over even before it had properly begun: on the physical side they were cramped in the middle of their seats, Schaffer flanked by driver and guard, Smith by Colonel

71

Weissner and guard, and both Smith and Schaffer suffering from pain in the lower ribs: the owners of the Schmeisser machine pistols the muzzles of which were grinding into the captives' sides had no compunction about letting their presence be known.

They were now, Smith estimated, halfway between village and barracks. Another thirty seconds and they would be through the barrack gates. Thirty seconds. No more.

"Stop this car!" Smith's voice was cold, authoritative, with an odd undertone of menace. "Immediately, do you hear? I must think."

Colonel Weissner, startled, turned and stared at him. Smith ignored him completely. His face reflected an intensely frowning concentration, a thin-lipped anger barely under control, the face of a man to whom the thought of disobedience of his curt instruction was unthinkable: most certainly not the face of a man going to captivity and death. Weissner hesitated, but only fractionally. He gave an order and the big car began to slow.

"You oaf! You utter idiot!" Smith's tone, shaking with anger, was low and vicious, so low that only Weissner could hear it. "You've almost certainly ruined everything and, by God, if you have, Weissner, you'll be without a regiment tomorrow!"

The car pulled into the roadside and stopped. Ahead, the red taillights of the command car in front vanished into the snow-filled darkness. Weissner said brusquely, but with a barely perceptible tremor of agitation in his voice: "What the devil are you talking about?"

"You knew about this American general, Carnaby?" Smith's face, eyes narrowed and teeth bared in anger, was within six inches of Weissner's. "How?" He almost spat the word out.

"I dined in the Schloss Adler last night. I—"

Smith looked at him in total incredulity.

"Colonel Paul Kramer told you? He actually talked to you about him?" Weissner nodded wordlessly. "Admiral Canaris' Chief of Staff! And now everybody knows. God in heaven, heads will roll for this." He screwed the heels of his palms into his eyes, lowered his hands wearily to his thighs, gazed ahead unseeingly and shook his head, very slowly. "This is too big, even for me." He fished out his pass and handed it to Weissner, who examined it in the beam of a none too steady flashlight. "Back to the barracks at once! I must get through to Berlin immediately. My uncle will know what to do."

"Your uncle?" By what seemed a great effort of will Weissner looked up from the pass he held in his hand: his voice was no steadier than the flashlight. "*Heinrich* Himmler?"

"Who do you think?" Smith snarled. "Mickey Mouse?" He dropped his voice to a low murmur. "I trust you never have the privilege of meeting him, Colonel Weissner." He gave Weissner the benefit of a long and speculative look singularly lacking in any encouragement, then turned away and prodded the driver none too lightly in the back. "The barracks—and make it quick!"

The car moved off. Anything that the nephew of the dreaded Heinrich Himmler, Chief of the Gestapo, said was good enough for the driver.

Smith turned to the guard by his side. "Take that damned thing out of my ribs!"

Angrily, he snatched the gun away. The guard, who had also heard of Himmler, meekly yielded up the machine pistol. One second later he was doubled up in helpless retching agony as the butt of the Schmeisser smashed into his stomach and another second later Colonel Weissner was pinned against the window of his Mercedes as the muzzle of the Schmeisser ground into his right ear.

Smith said: "If your men move, you die."

"Okay." Schaffer's calm voice from the front seat. "I have their guns."

"Stop the car," Smith ordered.

The car came to a halt. Through the windscreen Smith could see the lights of the barracks guardroom, now less than two hundred yards away. He gave Weissner a prod with the Schmeisser muzzle.

"Out!"

Weissner's face was a mask of chagrined rage but he was too experienced a soldier even to hesitate. He got out.

"Three paces from the car," Smith said. "Face down in the snow. Hands clasped behind your head. Schaffer, your gun on your guard. Out beside the colonel, you." This with his gun muzzle in the driver's neck.

Twenty seconds later, Schaffer at the wheel, they were on their way, leaving three men face downwards in the snow and the fourth, Smith's erstwhile guard, still doubled up in agony by the roadside.

"A creditable effort, young Himmler," Schaffer said approvingly.

"I'll never be that lucky again," Smith said soberly. "Take your time passing the barracks. We don't want any of the sentries getting the wrong idea."

At a steady twenty miles an hour they passed the main gates and then the secondary gates, apparently, as far as Smith could see, without exciting any comment. Just behind the three-pointed star on the car's radiator flew a small triangular pennant, the Camp Commandant's personal standard, and no one, it was safe to assume, would question the comings and goings of Colonel Weissner.

For half a mile or so beyond the secondary gates the road ran northwards in a straight line with, on the left, a sheer hundred-foot cliff dropping down into the waters of the Blau See, and, to the right, a line of pines, not more than fifty yards wide, backing up against another vertical cliff face which soared up until lost in the snow and the darkness.

At the end of the half-mile straight, the road ahead swept sharply to the right to follow a sharp indentation in the Blau See's shoreline, a dangerous corner marked by white fencing which would normally have been conspicuous enough by nighttime but which was at the moment all but invisible against the all-enveloping background of snow. Schaffer braked for the corner. A thoughtful expression crossed his face and he applied still heavier pressure to the brake pedal and glanced at Smith.

"An excellent idea." It was Smith's turn to be approving. "We'll make an agent out of you yet."

The Mercedes stopped. Smith gathered up the Schmeissers and pistols they had taken from Weissner and his men and got out. Schaffer wound down the driver's window, released the hand brake, engaged gear and jumped out as the car began to move. With his right arm through the window Schaffer walked and then, as the car began to gather speed, ran along beside the Mercedes, his hand on the steering wheel. Twenty feet from the cliff edge he gave a last steering correction, jerked the quadrant hand throttle wide open and leapt aside as the car accelerated. The wooden fence never had a chance. With a splintering crash barely audible above the roaring of the engine at maximum revs in first gear, the Mercedes went through the barrier as if it had been made of cardboard, shot out over the edge of the cliff and disappeared from sight.

Smith and Schaffer reached the safety of an unbroken stretch of fencing and peered down in time to see the car, upside down now and its headlamps still blazing, strike the surface of the lake with an oddly flat explosive sound, like distant gunfire. A column of water and weirdly phosphorescent spray reached halfway up the cliff side. When it subsided, they could at once locate from an underwater luminescence the position of the sinking car: the headlamps were still burning. Smith and Schaffer looked at each other then Smith thoughtfully removed his peaked cap and sent it sailing over the edge. The strong gusting wind blew the cap in against the cliff face, but it tumbled on down and landed, inside up, on still surfacing bubbles iridescently glittering from the light now far below. Then the light went out.

"So who cares?" Schaffer straightened up from the fencing and shrugged his shoulders. "Wasn't our car. Back to the village, hey?"

"Not on your life," Smith said emphatically. "And I mean that—literally. Come on. Other way."

Clutching their recently acquired weapons, they ran round the corner in the direction in which the car had been travelling. They had covered less than seventy yards when they heard the sound of car engines and saw wavering beams lighting up the splintered fence. Seconds later Smith and Schaffer were off the road, hidden in the pines and moving slowly back in the direction of a command car and two armoured cars that had now pulled up at the broken barrier.

"That's it, then, Herr Colonel." An Alpenkorps sergeant with shoulder-slung gun peered gingerly over the edge of the cliff. "Going too fast, saw it too late—or never saw it at all. The Blau See is over a hundred metres deep here, Herr Colonel. They're gone."

"Maybe they're gone and maybe they're not. I wouldn't trust that lot as far as my front door." Colonel Weissner's voice carried clearly and sounded bitter. "They may have faked it and doubled back. Send one party of men straight into the pines there as far as the cliff wall. Five metre spacing. Let them use their flashlights. Then another party of men five hundred metres in the car back towards the camp. You go with them, Sergeant. Again spread out to the cliff face. Let them come together. And be quick."

Schaffer, from his hiding place behind the bole of a pine, looked thoughtfully at Smith.

"I have to concede a point, boss, it's perhaps as well we

didn't go straight back to the village. Cunning old devil, isn't he?"

"And what does that make me?" Smith murmured.

"Okay, okay. I'll concede that point, too."

Five minutes passed. Comparatively little of the falling snow penetrated the thickly matted branches of the pines and the two men could clearly see the occasional flicker of flashlights as the line of men nearest them moved away to the south, their lights probing behind tree trunks and under windfalls as they searched for the two escaped prisoners. Colonel Weissner paced up and down, slowly, beside his command car, his head bowed as if immersed in thought. From time to time he consulted his watch. As Smith watched, he moved out to the unbroken fencing and remained there, peering down towards the surface of the Blau See.

By and by Smith and Schaffer could hear the distant sound of muffled voices and within a minute the sergeant moved into the beam of the command car headlamps, approached Colonel Weissner and saluted.

"Not even a footprint, Herr Colonel."

Weissner straightened and turned.

"There wouldn't be," he said sombrely. "I've just seen a hat floating in the water. A squalid end for such brave men, Sergeant. A squalid end."

FIVE

THE CABLE car moved slowly out of the lower station at the beginning of its long climb up to the castle. An impossible climb, Mary thought, a dangerous and impossible climb. Peering through the front windows she could just distinguish the outline of the first pylon through the thinly driving snow. The second and third pylons were invisible, but the intermittently shining cluster of lights suspended impossibly high in the sky showed clearly enough where they had to go. People have made it before, she thought dully, we'll probably make it, too. The way she felt then, with the botton gone from her world, she didn't particularly care whether she made it or not.

The cable car was a twelve-passenger vehicle, painted bright red outside, well-lit inside. There were no seats, only grabrails along the two sides. That the grabrails were very necessary became immediately and alarmingly obvious. The wind was now very strong and the car began to sway alarmingly only seconds after clearing the shelter of the lower station.

Apart from two soldiers and an apparent civilian, the only other passengers consisted of von Brauchitsch, Mary, and Heidi, the last now with a heavy woollen coat and cossack fur hat over her ordinary clothes. Von Brauchitsch, holding onto the grabrail with one hand, had his free arm round Mary's shoulders. He gave them a reassuring squeeze and smiled down at her.

"Scared?" he asked.

"No." And she wasn't, she hadn't enough emotion left to be scared, but even with no hope left she was supposed to be a professional. "No, I'm not scared. I'm terrified. I feel seasick already. Does—does this cable ever break?"

"Never." Von Brauchitsch was reassurance itself. "Just hang on to me and you'll be all right."

"That's what he used to say to me," Heidi said coldly.

"Fräulein," von Brauchitsch explained patiently, "I am gifted beyond the average, but I haven't yet managed to grow a third arm. Guests first."

With a cupped cigarette in his hand, Schaffer leaned against the base of an unmistakable telephone pole and gazed thoughtfully into the middle distance. There was reason both for the hooded cigarette and the thoughtful expression. Less than a hundred yards away from where he stood at the edge of the pines bordering the road running alongside the shore of the Blau See he could see guards, clearly illuminated by overhead lights, moving briskly to and fro in the vicinity of the barrack gates. Dimly seen behind them were the outline of the barracks themselves.

Schaffer shifted his stance and gazed upwards. The snow was almost gone now, the moon was threatening to break through, and he had no difficulty at all in distinguishing the form of Smith, his legs straddled across the lowest cross bar.

Smith was busily employed with a knife, a specially designed commando knife which, among other advanced features, had a built-in wire cutter. Carefully, methodically, he brought the wire cutter to bear. With eight consecutive snips eight consecutive telephone wires fell to the ground. Smith closed and pocketed his knife, distentangled his legs from the cross bar, wrapped his arms round the pole and slid down to the ground. He grinned at Schaffer.

"Every little helps," he said.

"Should hold them for a while," Schaffer agreed. Once more they gathered up their guns and moved off to the east, vanishing into the pine woods which bordered the rear of the barracks.

The cable car swayed more alarmingly than ever. It had now entered upon the last near-vertical lap of its journey. With von Brauchitsch's arm still around her shoulders, with her face still pressed against the front windows of the car, Mary stared up at the towering battlements, white as the driving snow, and thought that they reached up almost to the clouds themselves. As she watched, a break came in the wisping clouds and the whole fairy-tale castle was bathed in bright moonlight. Fear touched her eyes, she moistened her lips and gave an involuntary shiver. Nothing escaped von Brauchitsch's acute perception. He gave her shoulders another reassuring squeeze, perhaps the twentieth in that brief journey.

"Not to worry, Fräulein. It will be all right."

"I hope so." Her voice was the ghost of a whisper.

The same unexpected moonlight almost caught Smith and Schaffer. They had just crossed the station tracks and were moving stealthily along towards the left luggage office when the moon broke through. But they were still in the shadows of the overhanging station roof. They pressed back into those shadows and peered along the tracks, past the hydraulic bumpers which marked the end of the line. Clearly now, sharply limned as if in full daylight, red etched against the white, they could see one cable car approaching the lower station, the other climbing the last few vertical feet towards the header station and, above that, the dazzling outline of the Schloss Adler glittering under the bright moon.

"That helps," Schaffer said bitterly. "That helps a lot."

"Sky's still full of clouds," Smith said mildly. He bent to the keyhole of the left luggage office, used his skeleton keys and moved inside. Schaffer followed, closing the door.

Smith located their haversacks, cut a length of rope from the nylon, wrapped it round his waist and began stuffing some hand grenades and plastic explosives into a canvas bag. He raised his head as Schaffer diffidently cleared his throat.

"Boss?" This with an apprehensive glance through the window.

"Uh-huh?"

"Boss, has it occurred to you that Colonel Weissner probably knows all about this cache by this time? What I mean is, we may have company soon."

"We may indeed," Smith admitted. "Surprised if we don't have. That's why I've cut this itsy-bitsy piece of rope off the big coil and why I'm taking the explosives and grenades only from my rucksack and yours. It's a very big coil—and no one knows what's inside our rucksacks. So it's unlikely that anything will be missed."

"But the radio—"

"If we broadcast from here we might be caught in the act. If we take it away and they find it gone they'll know that that car at the bottom of the Blau See is empty. Is that it?"

"More or less."

"So we compromise. We remove it, but we return it here after we've broadcast from a safe place."

"What do you mean 'safe place'?" Schaffer demanded plaintively. The darkly saturnine face was unhappy. "There isn't a safe place in Bavaria."

"There's one not twenty yards away. Last place they'd look." He tossed Schaffer a bunch of skeleton keys. "Ever been inside a Bavarian ladies' cloakroom?"

Schaffer fielded the keys, stared at Smith, shook his head and left. Quickly he moved down the tracks, his light flashing briefly on and off. Finally his flashlight settled on a doorway with, above it, the legend DAMEN.

Schaffer looked at it, pursed his lips, shrugged his shoulders and got to work on the lock.

Slowly, with apparently infinite labour, the cable car completed the last few feet of its ascent and passed in under the roof of the Schloss Adler header station. It juddered to a halt, the front door opened and the passengers disembarked. They moved from the header station—built into the northwest base of the castle—up through a steeply climbing twenty-five-foot tunnel which had heavy iron doors and guards at either end. Passing the top gateway, they emerged into the courtyard, the entrance of which was sealed off by a massively barred iron gate guarded by heavily armed soldiers and Doberman pinschers. The courtyard itself was brightly illuminated by the light of dozens of uncurtained interior windows. In the very centre of the courtyard stood the helicopter which had that morning brought Reichsmarschal Rosemeyer to the Schloss Adler. Under the cover of a heavy tarpaulin—momentarily unnecessary because of the cessation of the snow—a dungareed figure, possibly the pilot, worked on the helicopter engine with the aid of a small but powerful arc lamp.

Mary turned to von Brauchitsch, still holding a proprietary grip on her arm, and smiled ruefully.

"So many soldiers. So many men—and, I'm sure, so few women. What happens if I want to escape from the licentious soldiery?"

"Easy." Von Brauchitsch really did have, Mary thought dully, a most charming smile. "Just jump from your bedroom window. One hundred metres straight down and there you are. Free!"

The ladies' cloakroom in the station was a superlatively nondescript place, bleakly furnished with hard-backed benches, chairs, deal tables, and a sagging wooden floor. The Spartans would have turned up their noses at it, in its sheer lack of decorative inspiration it could have been surpassed only by its counterpart in England. The expiring remains of a fire burnt dully in a black enamel stove.

Smith was seated by the central table, radio beside him, consulting a small book by the light of a hooded pencil flash and writing on a slip of paper. He checked what he had written, straightened and handed the book to Schaffer.

"Burn it. Page by page."

"Page by page? All?" Surprise in the saturnine face. "You won't be requiring this any more?"

Smith shook his head and began to crank the radio handle.

There was a very much better fire in the Operations Room in Whitehall, a pine-log fire with a healthy crackle and flames of a respectable size. But the two men sitting on either side of the fire were a great deal less alert than the two men sitting by the dying embers of the fire in the Bavarian Alps. Admiral Rolland and Colonel Wyatt-Turner were frankly dozing, eyes shut, more asleep than awake. But they came to full wakefulness, jerking upright, almost instantly, when the long-awaited call sign came through on the big transceiver manned by the civilian operator at the far end of the room. They glanced at each other, heaved themselves out of their deep armchairs.

"Broadsword calling Danny Boy." The voice on the radio was faint but clear. "Broadsword calling Danny Boy. You hear me? Over."

The civilian operator spoke into his microphone: "We hear you. Over."

"Code. Ready? Over."

"Ready. Over."

Rolland and Wyatt-Turner were by the operator's shoulder now, eyes fixed on his pencil as he began to make an instantaneous transcription of the meaningless jumble of letters beginning to come over the radio. Swiftly the message was spelt out: TORRANCE-SMYTHE MURDERED. THOMAS, CHRISTIANSEN AND CARRACIOLA CAPTURED.

As if triggered by an unheard signal, the eyes of Rolland and Wyatt-Turner lifted and met. Their faces were strained and grim. Their eyes returned to the flickering pencil.

ENEMY BELIEVE SCHAFFER AND SELF DEAD, the message continued. EFFECTING ENTRY INSIDE THE HOUR. PLEASE HAVE TRANSPORT STANDING BY NINETY MINUTES. OVER.

Admiral Rolland seized the microphone from the operator.

"Broadsword! Broadsword! Do you know who I am, Broadsword?"

"I know who you are, sir. Over."

"Pull out, Broadsword. Pull out now. Save yourselves. Over."

"You—must—be—joking." The words were spoken in slow-motion, a perceptible pause between each pair. "Over."

"You heard me." Rolland's voice was almost as slow and distinct. "You *heard* me. That was an order, Broadsword."

"Mary is already inside. Over and out."

The transceiver went dead.

"He's gone, sir," the operator said quietly.

"He's gone," Rolland repeated mechanically. "Dear God, he's gone."

Colonel Wyatt-Turner moved away and sat down heavily in his chair by the fire. For such a big, burly man he appeared curiously huddled and shrunken. He looked up dully as Admiral Rolland sank into the opposite chair.

"It's all my fault." The colonel's voice was barely distinguishable. "All my fault."

"We did what we had to do. All *our* fault, Colonel. It was my idea." He gazed into the fire. "Now this—this on top of everything else."

"Our worst day," Wyatt-Turner agreed heavily. "Our worst day ever. Maybe I'm too old."

"Maybe we're all too old." With his right forefinger Rolland began to tick off the fingers of his left hand. "HQ Commander-in-Chief, Portsmouth. Secret alarm triggered. Nothing missing."

"Nothing taken," Wyatt-Turner agreed wearily. "But the vigil emulsion plates show photostatic copies taken."

"Two. Southampton. Barge-movement duplicates missing. Three, Plymouth. Time lock in the naval HQ inoperative. We don't know what this means."

"We can guess."

"We can guess. Dover. Copy of a section of the Mulberry Harbour plans missing. An error? Carelessness? We'll never know. Five, Bradley's HQ guard sergeant missing. Could mean anything."

"Could mean everything. All the troop movements for Overlord's Omaha beach are there."

"Lastly, seven OS reports today. France, Belgium, Netherlands. Four demonstrably false. Other three unverifiable."

For long moments there was a heavy, a defeated silence, finally broken by Wyatt-Turner.

"If there was ever any doubt, there's none now." He spoke without looking up, his eyes gazing emptily into the fire. "The Germans have almost total penetration here—and we have almost none on the Continent. And now this—Smith and his men, I mean."

"Smith and his men," Rolland echoed. "Smith and his men. We can write them off."

Wyatt-Turner dropped his voice, speaking so softly that the radio operator couldn't overhear.

"And Operation Overlord, sir?"

"Operation Overlord," Rolland murmured. "Yes, we can write that off, too."

"Intelligence is the first arm of modern warfare," Wyatt-Turner said bitterly. "Or has someone said that before?"

"No intelligence, no war." Admiral Rolland pressed an intercom button. "Have my car brought round. Coming, Colonel? To the airfield?"

"And a lot farther than that. If I have your permission, sir."

"We've discussed it." Admiral Rolland shrugged. "I understand how you feel. Kill yourself if you must."

"I've no intention." Wyatt-Turner crossed to a cupboard and took out a sten gun, turned to Rolland and smiled: "We may encounter hostiles, sir."

"You may indeed." There was no answering smile on the admiral's face.

"You heard what the man said?" Smith switched off the transmitter, telescoped the aerial and glanced across at Schaffer. "We can pull out now."

"Pull out now? Pull out now?" Schaffer was outraged. "Don't you realise that if we do they'll get to Mary inside twelve hours." He paused significantly, making sure he had all Smith's attention. "And if they get to her they're bound to get to Heidi ten minutes later."

"Come off it, Lieutenant," Smith said protestingly. "You've only seen her once, for five minutes."

"So?" Schaffer was looking positively belligerent. "How often did Paris see Helen of Troy? How often did Antony see Cleopatra? How often did Romeo—" He broke off then went on defiantly: "And I don't care if she is a traitor spying on her own people."

"She was born and brought up in Birmingham," Smith said wearily.

"So who cares? I draw the line at nothing. Even if she is a Limey—" He paused. "English?"

"Come on," Smith said. "Let's return this radio. We may have callers soon."

"We mustn't be raising too many eyebrows," Schaffer agreed.

They returned the radio, locked the left luggage office and were just moving towards the station exit when they were halted by the sound of truck engines and a siren's ululation. They pressed back against a wall as headlights lit up the station entrance. The leading truck came to a skidding halt not ten yards away.

Schaffer looked at Smith. "Discretion, I think?"

"Discretion, indeed. Behind the ticket office."

The two men moved swiftly alongside the tracks and hid in the deep shadows behind the booking office. A sergeant, the one who had organised the search along the Blau See, came running through the entrance, followed by four soldiers, located the left luggage office, tried the door handle, reversed his machine pistol and hammered the lock without effect, reversed his gun again, shot away the lock and passed inside, flashlight in hand. He appeared at the doorway almost at once.

"Tell the captain. They didn't lie. The Englanders' gear is here!" One of the soldiers left and the sergeant said to the three remaining men: "Right. Get their stuff out and load it up."

"There goes my last pair of cotton socks," Schaffer murmured mournfully as their rucksacks were taken away. "Not to mention my toothbrush and—"

He broke off as Smith caught his arm. The sergeant had stopped the man carrying the radio, taken it from him, placed his hand on it and stood quite still. He was directly under one of the small swinging electric lights and the expression on his face could clearly be seen to change from puzzlement to disbelief to complete and shocked understanding.

"*Kapitan!*" the sergeant shouted. "*Kapitan.*"

An officer came hurrying through the station entrance.

"The radio, *Kapitan!* It's warm, very warm! It's been in use inside the last five minutes."

"In the last five minutes? Impossible!" He stared at the sergeant. "Unless—"

"Yes, *Herr Kapitan.* Unless."

"Surround the station," the officer shouted. "Search every room."

"Oh God!" Schaffer moaned. "Why can't they leave us alone?"

"Quickly," Smith said softly. He took Schaffer's arm and they moved through the dark shadows till they reached the ladies' cloakroom. Careful not to rattle his skeleton keys, Smith had the door open in seconds. They passed inside and locked the door behind them.

"This won't look so good in my obituary," Schaffer said dolefully. There was a perceptible edge of strain under the lightly spoken words.

"What won't?"

"Gave his life for his country in a ladies' lavatory in Upper Bavaria. How can a man rest in peace with that on his mind? . . . What's our friend outside saying?"

"If you shut up we might hear."

"And when I say everywhere, I mean everywhere." The German captain was barking out his commands in the best parade-ground fashion. "If a door is locked, break it open. If you can't break it open, shoot the lock away. And if you don't want to die in the next five minutes, never forget that those are violent and extremely dangerous men almost certainly armed with stolen Schmeisser machine pistols, apart from their own weapons. Make no attempt to capture them. Shoot on sight and shoot to kill."

"You heard?" Smith said.

"I'm afraid I did." There was a perceptible click as Schaffer cocked his machine pistol.

They stood side-by-side in the darkness listening to the sounds of the search, the calling of voices, the hammering of rifle butts on wood, the splintering of yielding doors, the occasional short burst of machine-gun fire where a door, presumably, had failed to yield to more conventional methods of persuasion. The sounds of the approaching search grew very close.

"They're getting warm," Schaffer murmured.

Schaffer had underestimated the temperature. Just as he finished speaking an unseen hand closed on the outer door handle and rattled the door furiously. Smith and Schaffer moved silently and took up position pressed close against the wall, one on either side of the door.

The rattling ceased. A heavy crashing impact from the outside shook the door on its hinges. A second such impact and the woodwork in the jamb by the lock began to splinter. Two more would do it, Smith thought, two more.

But there were no more.

"Gott in Himmel, Hans!" The voice beyond the door held —or appeared to hold—a mixture of consternation and outrage. "What are you thinking of? Can't you read?"

"Can't I—" The second voice broke off abruptly and when it came again it was in tones of defensive apology. *"Damen! Mein Gott! Damen!"* A pause. "If you had spent as many years on the Russian front as I have—" His voice faded as the two men moved away.

"God bless our common Anglo-Saxon heritage," Schaffer murmured fervently.

"What are you talking about?" Smith demanded. He had released his tense grip on the Schmeisser and realised that the palms of his hands were damp.

"This misplaced sense of decency," Schaffer explained.

"A far from misplaced and highly developed sense of self-preservation," Smith said drily. "Would *you* like to come searching for a couple of reputed killers like us, knowing that the first man to find us would probably be cut in half by a burst of machine-gun fire? Put yourself in their position. How do you think those men feel? How would you feel?"

"I'd feel very unhappy," Schaffer said candidly.

"And so do they. And so they seize on any reasonable excuse not to investigate. Our two friends who have just left have no idea whatsoever whether we're in here or not and, what's more, the last thing they want to do is to find out."

"Stop making with the old psychology. All that matters is that Schaffer is saved. Saved!"

"If you believe that," Smith said curtly, "you deserve to end up with a blindfold round your eyes."

"How's that again?" Schaffer asked apprehensively.

"You and I," Smith explained patiently, "are not the only people who can put ourselves in the places of the searchers. You can bet your life that the captain can and more than likely the sergeant, too—you saw how quickly he caught on to that damn radio. By and by one or other is going to come by, see this closed and undamaged door, blow his top and insist on a few of his men being offered the chance to earn a posthumous Iron Cross. What I mean is, Schaffer is not yet saved."

"What do we do, boss?" Schaffer said quietly. "I don't feel so funny any more."

"We create a diversion. Here are the keys—this one. Put it in the lock and hold it ready to turn. We'll be leaving in a hurry—troops of this calibre can't be fooled for long."

He dug into his knapsack, fished out a hand grenade, crossed the cloakroom into the washroom and, in almost total darkness, felt his way across it to where the window at the back should have been, finally located it from the source of a faint wash of light. He pressed his nose against the glass but could see nothing, cursed softly as he realised a washroom window would always certainly be frosted, located the latch and slowly swung the window wide. With infinite caution, a fraction of an inch at a time, he thrust his head slowly through the window.

Nobody blew his head off. There were soldiers immediately to be seen, it was true, soldiers armed and at the ready, but they weren't looking in his direction: there were five of them, spread out in an arc of a circle, perhaps fifteen yards from the station entrance, and every machine pistol was trained on that entrance. Waiting for the rabbits to bolt, Smith thought.

What was of much more interest was the empty truck parked only feet away from the window where he was: it was the reflected light from its sidelights that had enabled him to locate the window. Hoping that the truck was built along conventional lines, Smith armed the grenade, counted three, lobbed it under the back wheels of the truck and ducked behind the shelter of the washroom wall.

The two explosions—grenade and petrol tank—went off so almost simultaneously as to be indistinguishable in time. Shattered glass from the window above showered down on his head and his eardrums hurt fiercely both from the roar of sound and the proximity to the explosive shock wave. Smith made no attempt to inspect the damage he had done, less from the urgent need for haste to leave there than from the very obvious fact that the remains of the truck outside had burst into flames and to have lifted his head above that windowsill would have been a swift form of illuminated suicide: not that he could have done so in any event for the wind-driven flames from the truck were already beginning to lick through the shattered washroom window. On hands and knees Smith scuttled across the washroom floor, not rising till he had reached the cloakroom. Schaffer, who had his hand on the key and the door already open a fraction of an inch turned at Smith's approach.

"To the hills, boss?" he enquired.

"To the hills."

The trackside of the station was, predictably, deserted: those who had not automatically run to investigate the source of the explosion would have as automatically assumed that the explosion was in some way connected with an escape attempt or resistance on the part of the hunted men. However it was, the result was the satisfactory same.

They ran along the tracks till they came to the bumpers at the end of the line, skirted those and continued running until they were safely among the scatter of houses that rose steeply up the hillside on the eastern side of the village. They stopped to take breath and looked back the way they had come.

The station was on fire, not yet heavily on fire, but, with flames rising six to eight feet and black smoke billowing into the night sky, obviously already beyond any hope of extinction.

Schaffer said: "They're not going to be very pleased."

"I shouldn't think so."

"What I mean is, they're really going to go after us now. With everything they have. They've Doberman pinschers up at the castle and I've no doubt they have them at the camp too. They've only to bring them to the station, sniff our packs, have them circle the station, pick up our scent and that's it. Smith and Schaffer torn to shreds. I'll take on the Alpenkorps one-by-one but I draw the line at Doberman pinschers, boss."

"I thought it was horses you were scared of?" Smith said mildly.

"Horses, Doberman pinschers, you name it, I'm scared of it. All it's got to have is four feet." He looked gloomily at the burning station. "I'd make a rotten vet."

"No worry," Smith assured him. "We won't be here long enough for any of your four-footed pals to come bothering you."

"No?" Schaffer looked at him suspiciously.

"The castle," Smith said patiently. "That's what we're here for. Remember?"

88

"I hadn't forgotten." The flames from the blazing station were now licking thirty, forty feet up in the air. "You've gone and ruined a perfectly good station, you know that?"

"As you would say yourself," Smith reminded him, "it wasn't our station to start with. Come on. We've a call to make then we'll go see what kind of reception awaits us at the Schloss Adler."

Mary Ellison was just at that moment discovering what the reception in the Schloss Adler was like. In her case it was none too pleasant. Von Brauchitsch and Heidi beside her, she was gazing around the great hall of the castle, stone walls, stone flags, a dark oaken roof, when a door at the far end of the hall opened and a girl came towards them. There was an arrogance, a crisp authority about her: she marched, rather than walked.

But a very beautiful girl, Mary had to admit to herself, big, blonde, blue-eyed and beautiful. She could have been a pinup girl for the Third Reich. At the moment, the blue eyes were very cold.

"Good evening, Anne-Marie," von Brauchitsch said. There was a marked lack of cordiality in his voice. "This is the new girl, Fräulein Maria Schenk. Maria, this is the colonel's secretary, in charge of all female staff."

"Took your time about getting here, didn't you, Schenk?" If Anne-Marie had a soft, lilting, mellifluous voice she wasn't bothering to use it just then. She turned to Heidi and gave her an icy up-and-down. "And why you? Just because we let you wait table when the colonel has company—"

"Heidi is this girl's cousin," von Brauchitsch interrupted brusquely. "*And* she has my permission." The cold implication that she should confine herself to her duties was unmistakable.

Anne-Marie glared at him but made no attempt to press the point. Very few people would have done. Von Brauchitsch was just that sort of person.

"In here, Schenk." Anne-Marie nodded to a side door. "I have a few questions to ask."

Mary looked at Heidi, then at von Brauchitsch, who shrugged and said: "Routine investigation, Fräulein. I'm afraid you must."

Mary preceded Anne-Marie through the doorway. The door was firmly closed behind them. Heidi and von Brauchitsch looked at each other. Heidi compressed her lips and the expression that momentarily flitted over her face about matched the one Anne-Marie had been wearing: von Brauchitsch made the age-old helpless gesture of lifting his shoulders high, palms of the hands turned up.

Within half a minute the reason for von Brauchitsch's helpless gesture became obvious. Through the door there came first the sound of a raised voice, a brief scuffle then a sharp cry of pain. Von Brauchitsch exchanged another resigned glance with Heidi, then turned as he heard heavy footsteps behind him. The man approaching was burly, weather-beaten, middle-aged and in civilian clothes: but although not in uniform he could never have been mistaken for anything other then an army officer. The heavy blue-shaven jowls, bull neck, close-cropped hair and piercing blue eyes made him almost a caricature of the World War I Prussian Uhlan cavalry officer. That he was by no means as fossilised as he appeared was quite evident from the distinctly respectful manner in which von Brauchitsch addressed him.

"Good evening, Colonel Kramer."

"Evening, Captain. Evening, Fräulein." He had an unexpectedly gentle and courteous voice. "You wear an air of expectancy?"

Before either could answer, the door opened and Anne-Marie and Mary entered: Mary gave the impression of having been pushed into the room. Anne-Marie was slightly flushed and breathing rather heavily, but otherwise her beautiful Aryan self. Mary's clothes were disordered, her hair dishevelled and it was obvious that she had been crying. Her cheeks were still tear-stained.

"We'll have no more trouble with *her*," Anne-Marie announced with satisfaction. She caught sight of Kramer and the change in her tone was perceptible. "Interviewing new staff, Colonel."

"In your usual competent fashion, I see," Colonel Kramer said drily. He shook his head. "When will you learn that respectable young girls do not like being forcibly searched and having their underclothes examined to see if they were made in Piccadilly or Gorki Street?"

"Security regulations," Anne-Marie said defensively.

"Yes, yes." Kramer's voice was brusque. "But there are other ways." He turned away impatiently. The engaging of female staff was not the problem of the deputy chief of the German Secret Service. While Heidi was helping Mary to

90

straighten her clothes, he went on to von Brauchitsch: "A little excitement in the village tonight?"

"Nothing for us." Von Brauchitsch shrugged. "Deserters."
Kramer smiled.

"That's what I told Colonel Weissner to say. I think our friends are British agents."

"What?"

"After General Carnaby, I shouldn't wonder," Kramer said carelessly. "Relax, Captain. It's over. Three of them are coming up for interrogation within the hour. I'd like you to be present later on. I think you'll find it most entertaining and —ah—instructive."

"There were five of them, sir. I saw them myself when they were rounded up in Zum Wilden Hirsch."

"There *were* five," Colonel Kramer corrected. "Not now. Two of them—the leader and one other—are in the Blau See. They commandeered a car and went over a cliff."

Mary, her back to the men and Anne-Marie, smoothed down her dress and slowly straightened. Her face was stricken. Anne-Marie turned, saw Mary's curiously immobile position and was moving towards her when Heidi took Mary's arm and said quickly: "My cousin looks ill. May I take her to her room?"

"All right." Anne-Marie waved her hand in curt dismissal. "The one you use when you are here."

The room was bleak, monastic, linoleum-covered, with a made-up iron bed, chair, tiny dressing table, a hanging cupboard and nothing else. Heidi locked the door behind them.

"You heard?" Mary said emptily. Her face was as drained of life as her voice.

"I heard—and I don't believe it."

"Why should they lie?"

"*They* believe it." Heidi's tone was impatient, almost rough. "It's time you stopped loving and started thinking. The Major Smiths of this world don't drive over cliff edges."

"Talk is easy, Heidi."

"So is giving up. *I* believe he is alive. And if he is, and if he comes here and you're gone or not there to help him, you know what he'll be then?" Mary made no reply, just gazed emptily into Heidi's face. "He'll be dead. He'll be dead because you let him down. Would *he* let *you* down?"

Mary shook her head dumbly.

"Now then," Heidi went on briskly. She reached first under her skirt then down the front of her blouse and laid seven objects on the table. "Here we are. Lilliput .21 automatic, two spare magazines, ball of string, lead weight, plan of the castle and the instructions." She crossed to a corner of the room, raised a loose floorboard, placed the articles beneath and replaced the board. "They'll be safe enough there."

Mary looked at her for a long moment and showed her first spark of interest in an hour.

"You *knew* that board was loose," she said slowly.

"Of course. I loosened it myself a fortnight ago."

"You—you knew about this as far back as then?"

"Whatever else?" Heidi smiled. "Good luck, cousin."

Mary sank onto the bed and sat there motionless for ten minutes after Heidi had gone, then rose wearily to her feet and crossed to her window. Her window faced to the north and she could see the line of pylons, the lights of the village and, beyond that, the darkened waters of the Blau See. But what dominated the entire scene were the redly towering flames and billowing clouds of black smoke reaching up from some burning building at the far end of the village. For a hundred yards around it night had been turned into day and even if there had been a local fire brigade to hand it would have been clearly impossible for them to approach anywhere near the flames. When that fire went out all that would be left would be smoking ashes. Mary wondered vaguely what it might mean.

She opened her window and leaned out, but cautiously. Even for a person as depressed as she was, there was no temptation to lean too far: castle walls and volcanic plug stretched vertically downwards for almost three hundred feet. She felt slightly dizzy.

To the left and below a cable car left the castle header station and started to move down to the valley below. Heidi was in that car, leaning out a partially opened window and hopefully waving but Mary's eyes had again blurred with tears and she did not see her. She closed the window, turned away, lay down heavily on the bed and wondered again about John Smith, whether he were alive or dead. And she wondered again about the significance of that fire in the valley below.

Smith and Schaffer skirted the backs of the houses, shops and *Weinstuben* on the east side of the street, keeping to the dark shadows as far as it was possible. Their precautions, Smith realised, were largely superfluous: the undoubted centre of attraction that night was the blazing station and the street leading to it was jammed with hundreds of soldiers and villagers. It must, Smith thought, be a conflagration of quite some note, for although they could no longer see the fire itself, only the red glow in the sky above it, they could clearly hear the roaring crackle of the flames, flames three hundred yards away and with the wind blowing in the wrong direction. As a diversion, it was a roaring success.

They came to one of the few stone buildings in the village, a large barnlike affair with double doors at the back. The yard abutting the rear doors looked like an automobile scrapyard. There were half-a-dozen old cars lying around, most of them without tyres, some rusted engines, dozens of small useless engine and body parts and a small mountain of empty oil drums. They picked their way carefully through the debris and came to the doors.

Schaffer used skeleton keys to effect and they were inside, doors closed and both flashlights on, inside fifteen seconds.

One side of the garage was given over to lathes or machine tools of one kind or another, but the rest of the floor space was occupied by a variety of vehicles, mostly elderly. What caught and held Smith's immediate attention, however, was a big yellow bus parked just inside the double front doors. It was a typically Alpine post bus, with a very long overhang at the back to help negotiate mountain hairpin bends: the rear wheels were so far forward as to be almost in the middle of the bus. As was also common with Alpine post buses in winter, it had a huge angled snow-plough bolted on to the front of the chassis. Smith looked at Schaffer.

"Promising, you think?"

"If I was optimistic enough to think we'd ever get back to this place," Schaffer said sourly, "I'd say it was very promising. You knew about this?"

"What do you think I am? A bus diviner? Of course I knew about it."

Smith climbed into the driver's seat. The keys were in the ignition. Smith switched on and watched the fuel gauge climb up to the half-full mark. He located the headlamps switch and turned it on. They worked. He pressed the starter button and the engine caught at once. Smith killed it immediately. Schaffer watched the performance with interest.

"I suppose you know you need a PSV licence to drive one of those, boss?"

"I have one around somewhere. Leave half the explosives in

the back of the bus. And hurry. Heidi might be down with the next car."

Smith climbed down from the driver's seat, went to the front doors, unbolted both, top and bottom, and pushed gently. The doors gave an inch, then stopped.

"Padlocked," Smith said briefly.

Schaffer surveyed the massive steel plough on the front of the bus and shook his head sorrowfully.

"Poor old padlock," he said.

The snow had stopped now but the wind from the west was now very strong. The cold was intense. Masses of ragged dark cloud hurried across the sky and the entire valley was alternatively cast into the deepest shadow or bathed in contrastingly dazzling light as the moon was alternatively obscured by the clouds or shone through the shifting gaps between them. But there was no alternating light and shade at the far end of the village: the station still burnt furiously enough to render the moon's best efforts pretty ineffectual.

A cable car was coming slowly down the valley, less than a hundred yards now from the lower station. Impelled by the powerfully gusting wind, it swung wildly, terrifyingly across the night sky. But as it approached the end of its journey the motion quickly dampened down and disappeared altogether as it approached the station.

The cable car jerked to a stop. Heidi, the only passenger, climbed out: understandably enough, she was looking rather pale. She walked down the steps at the back of the station, reached ground level then stopped dead as she heard the softly whistled first few notes of "Lorelei." She whirled round, then slowly approached two shapes, clad all in white, huddled by the side of the station.

"The Major Smiths of this world *don't* drive off clifftops," she said calmly. She paused, then stepped forward suddenly and gave each man a quick hug and kiss on the cheek. "But you had me a little worried there."

"You just keep on worrying like that," Schaffer said. "No need to worry about him, though."

Heidi waved a hand in the direction of the other end of the village. From the cable-car station on the lower slopes they had an excellent if distant view of the fire. "Are you responsible for this?" she asked.

"It was a mistake," Smith explained.

"Yeah. His hand slipped," Schaffer added.

"You two should audition for a music hall act," Heidi said drily. Suddenly serious, she said: "Mary thinks you're both gone."

"Weissner doesn't," Smith said. "The car that went over the cliff went without us. They're on to us."

"Hardly surprising," she murmured. "Or hadn't you noticed the size of the fire." She paused, then went on bleakly: "They're not the only ones who are on to you. Kramer knows you're British agents after General Carnaby."

"Well, well, well," Smith said thoughtfully. "I wonder what little bird has been whispering in Kramer's shell-like ear. One with a very long-range voice, methinks."

"What *are* you talking about?"

"Nothing. It's not important."

"It's not important! But don't you *see?*" Her voice was imploring, almost despairing. "They *know*—or will any minute —that you're alive. They *know* who you are. They'll be expecting you up there."

"Ah, but you overlook the subtleties, my dear Heidi," Schaffer put in. "What they *don't* know is that *we* are expecting *them* to be expecting *us*. At least, that's what I think I mean."

"You're whistling in the dark, Lieutenant. And one last thing: your friends are being brought up to the castle any time now."

"For interrogation?" Smith asked.

"I don't expect they've been asked up for tea," she said acidly.

"Fair enough," Smith nodded. "We'll go up with them."

"In the same car?" The words didn't question Smith's sanity, but the tone and expression did.

"Not 'in.' With." Smith peered at his watch. "The post bus in Sulz's garage. Be there in eighty minutes. And oh!—bring a couple of crates of empty beer bottles."

"Bring a couple of—oh, all right." She shook her head in conviction. "You're both mad."

"Shines through in our every word and gesture," Schaffer agreed, then, suddenly serious, added: "Say a prayer for us, honey. And if you don't know any prayers, keep your fingers crossed till they ache."

"Please come back," she said. There was a catch in her voice. She hesitated, made to say more, turned and walked quickly away. Schaffer looked after her admiringly as she walked down the street.

"There goes the future Mrs. Schaffer," he announced. "Bit tetchy and snappy, perhaps." He pondered. "But funny, I thought she was close to crying at the end there."

"Maybe you'd be tetchy and snappy and tearful if you'd been through what she's been in the past two and a half years," Smith said sourly.

"Maybe she'd be less tetchy and tearful if she knew a bit more about what's going on."

"I haven't the time to explain everything to everybody."

"You can say that again. Devious, boss. That's the word for you."

"Like enough." Smith glanced at his watch. "I wish to God they'd hurry up."

"Speak for yourself." Schaffer paused. "When we—well, if we—get away, is she coming with us?"

"Is who coming with us?"

"Heidi, of course!"

"Heidi, of course. If we make it—and we can only do it through Mary, and Mary was introduced by—"

"Say no more." Schaffer stared after the retreating figure and shook his head. "She'll be a sensation in the Savoy Grill," he said dreamily.

SIX

THE SECONDS crawled by and became minutes, and the minutes in turn piled up with agonising slowness until almost quarter of an hour had passed. Brilliant moonshine and a contrastingly almost total darkness had alternated a score of times as the low, tattered, black clouds scudded across the valley, and the cold deepened until it reached down into the bones of the two watchers in the shadows. And still they waited. They waited because they had to: they couldn't reach the Schloss Adler without company and company was a long time in coming.

And they waited in silence, each man alone with his own thoughts. What was in Schaffer's mind Smith couldn't guess, probably he was blissfully envisaging himself as the instigator of a series of uncontrollable stampedes in a selection of the better known hostelries in the West End of London. Smith's own thoughts were much more pragmatic and concerned solely with the immediate future. He was becoming concerned, and seriously concerned, about the intense cold and how it would affect their chances of making the trip up to the castle intact. Stamp their feet and flail their arms as they might, that numbing cold tightened its grip on them with every minute that passed. What they were about to do needed both physical strength and quick reactions in full measure and that glacial cold was swiftly draining them of both. Briefly and bleakly he wondered what odds any reasonable bookmaker would have given against their chances of reaching the castle but dismissed the thought still-born. When no other option offered there was no percentage in figuring the percentages, and, besides, they were due to find out immediately: the long-awaited company was at hand.

Two Alpenkorps command cars, the leading one with wailing siren and flashing headlamps, swept up the village street just as the moon broke through the cloudwrack once again, flooding the valley with light. Smith and Schaffer looked up at the moon, then at each other and then, wordlessly, moved back and pressed more deeply into the shadows on the west side of the lower station. The two metallic clicks seemed unnaturally loud as they eased forward the safety catches of their Schmeisser machine pistols.

Engines stopped and headlamps faded and died almost on the same instant as the two cars pulled up beneath the steps. Men hurried out and lined up briefly before advancing single file up the station steps. A dozen altogether, Smith counted, an officer, eight guards and Carraciola, Thomas, and Christiansen. All eight guards had their guns at the ready, which seemed a rather superfluous precaution as the three prisoners had their hands manacled behind their backs. Ergo, the guns weren't there to guard the prisoners but against any rescue attempt by Smith and Schaffer. He and Schaffer, Smith thought wryly, must be acquiring quite a reputation for themselves. But, nonetheless, a reassuring spectacle: if the Germans had known the true reason for his, Smith's, presence in Bavaria, they would also have known that they could have taken the three prisoners up with only a pea shooter for protection and still have remained free from molestation.

The last of the twelve men passed inside the lower station. Smith touched Schaffer's arm. They slung their Schmeissers, scrambled quickly but quietly onto the ice-covered and steeply sloping roof of the station and silently and with no little difficulty crawled forwards and upwards to the front edge of the roof under which the cable car would appear as it moved out at the beginning of its long haul towards the castle. They were, Smith knew, terribly exposed: snow suits or not, a casual passer-by in the street below had only to glance upwards and their detection was certain. Fortunately, there appeared to be no casual passers-by: the free entertainment provided by the burning station was drawing a full house. And then, as the cable began to move, the moon disappeared behind clouds.

They waited, tensely, till the leading edge of the cable car appeared, swung their legs over the lip of the roof, waited till the suspension bracket passed beneath them, reached down for the cable, allowed themselves to be pulled off the roof, fell across the cable and lowered themselves gently until their feet touched the roof of the cable car.

Mary walked softly along the dimly lit, stone flagged passage, counting off doors as she went. Outside the fifth she stopped, put her ear to it, stopped, glanced through the keyhole, knocked quietly and waited for a response. There was none. She knocked again, more loudly, with the same result. She turned the handle and found the door locked. From her small handbag she produced a set of skeleton keys. When the door yielded, she slipped quickly inside, closed the door and switched on the light.

The room was a considerable improvement on the one she had been given, although furnished with the same regulation iron bedstead. It was close-carpeted, boasted a couple of armchairs, and had a small chair with an *Oberleutnant's* uniform on it, a large wardrobe and a chest of drawers with a holstered belt, gun and binoculars resting on its glass top.

Mary locked the door, withdrew the key, crossed the room, lifted the lower sash window and looked down. She was, she saw, directly above the roof of the cable-car header station, a very steeply downward sloping roof the upper edge of which was built into the castle wall itself. She withdrew her head, removed from her handbag a ball of string with a heavy bolt attached to one end, laid it on the bed, picked up the binoculars and took up station by the window. Shivering in the bitter night wind, she adjusted the focus on the field glasses, then traversed down the line of the aerial cables. And then she had it, dimly seen but unmistakable, the squat black outline of the cable car, now halfway between the bottom and middle pylons, swaying madly, frighteningly, across the sky in the high and gusting wind.

Smith and Schaffer lay stretched out on the roof, clutching desperately to the suspension bracket, the only anchorage available. The roof was solidly coated with white-sheeted ice, they could find no purchase anywhere for their feet, and their bodies slid uncontrollably in all directions with the violent buffeting of the car beneath them. The sheer physical strain on hands and arms and shoulders was even worse than Smith had feared: and the worst was yet to come.

Schaffer twisted his head and peered downwards. It was a dizzy, vertiginous and frankly terrifying spectacle. The entire valley below seemed to be swinging through a forty-five degree arc. One second he was looking at the line of pines that bordered the western slope of the valley, then the floor of the valley rushed by beneath them and seconds later he was staring at the line of pines that swept up the eastern side of the valley. He twisted his head upwards, but that was no improvement, the lights of the Schloss Adler careened wildly through the same dizzy arc: it was like being on a combination of roller coaster, big dipper and runaway Ferris wheel with the notable exception, Schaffer thought bleakly, that the coaster, dipper, and Ferris wheel were provided with safety belts and other securing devices designed to prevent the occupant from parting company with his machine. The wind howled its high and lonely threnody through the cables and the suspension bracket. Schaffer looked away, screwed his eyes shut, lowered his head between his outstretched arms and moaned.

"Still think the horse the world's worst form of transport?" Smith asked. His lips were close to Schaffer's ear.

"Give me my boots and saddle," Schaffer said, then, even more despairingly, "Oh, no! Not again!"

Once more, without any warning, the moon had broken through, flooding the two men in its pale cold light. Gauging their time when the strain on their arms was least, they pulled the snow hoods far over their heads and tried to flatten themselves even more closely on to the roof.

In the Schloss Adler two people were watching the wild upward progress of the cable car, now brilliantly illuminated by the moon. Through Mary's field glasses two clearly distinguishable shapes of men could be seen stretched out on the cable-car roof. For half a minute she kept the glasses trained on them, then slowly turned away, her eyes wide, almost staring, her face empty of expression. Fifty feet above her head a sentry with slung gun patrolling the battlements stopped and gazed down at the cable car crawling up the valley. But he didn't gaze for long. Although booted, gauntleted, and muffled to the ears, he shook with the cold. It was no night for idle spectating. He looked away indifferently and resumed his brisk sentry-go.

Indifference was a quality that was conspicuously lacking on top of the cable car. The cable car was on the last lap now, the section between the last pylon and the castle header station. Soon the moment of truth. A minute from then,

Smith thought, and they could both well be lying broken and lifeless on the rocks two hundred feet below.

He twisted his head upwards. The cold moon still sailed across a clear gap in the sky but was closing rapidly towards another bank of cloud. The castle battlements, with the header station at the base, seemed almost vertically above his head. So steeply was the car rising on this last section that the volcanic plug itself was now less than fourteen yards away. His gaze followed the volcanic plug downwards till it reached its base: down there, on the slopes below, patrolling guards and their Doberman pinschers were barely the size of beetles.

"Suits her, doesn't it?" Schaffer said suddenly. Harsh edges of strain burred in his voice and his face was tight and desperate. "A lovely name."

"What are you talking about?" Smith demanded.

"Heidi."

"Oh, my God!" Smith stared up at the rapidly closing header station. "Her name is Ethel."

"You didn't have to tell me." Schaffer tried to sound aggrieved but it didn't quite come off. He followed Smith's upward gaze and, after a long pause, said very slowly: "Jesus! Look at the slope of that goddamned roof!"

"I've been looking." Smith eased his knife from its sheath and made a quick grab at the suspension bracket as a particularly violent swing almost broke his grip with his other hand. "Get your knife ready. And for God's sake don't lose it."

The moon slid behind a black patch of cloud and the valley was flooded with darkness. Slowly, carefully, as the cable car approached the header station and the swaying motion dampened down, Smith and Schaffer eased their way to the after end of the car, rose gingerly but swiftly to their feet and grabbed the cable with their free hands while their feet tried to find what precarious hold they could on the treacherously ice-sheathed roof.

The front of the car passed under the lip of the header station roof. A moment later the suspension bracket followed and Smith lunged forward and upwards, flinging himself bodily on to the roof. His right arm struck downwards and the knife blade pierced the coating of ice and imbedded itself firmly in the wood beneath. Less than a second later Schaffer had landed beside him, the downward arcing knife making contact at exactly the same instant as himself.

The blade broke off at the hilt. Schaffer opened his hand,

dropped the haft and clawed desperately at the ice. The dragging nails ripped through the encrusting ice, quite failing to hold him. He reached his left hand to his mouth, tore off the gauntlet and dug both hands in with all the strength that was in him. He slowed, but not enough. His scrabbling toes failed to find any more purchase and he knew he was sliding out over the edge—and that when he went the first thing to halt his fall would be the rock-pile two hundred and fifty feet beneath at the base of the volcanic plug.

Smith had been badly winded by his fall. Several seconds elapsed before he realised that Schaffer wasn't where he should have been—lying on the roof beside him. He twisted round, saw the white blur of Schaffer's strained and desperate face, had a vague impression of Schaffer's eight fingernails scoring their way through the ice as his body, already up to mid-thigh, slid inexorably over the edge and brought his left hand flashing down with a speed and power that, even in those circumstances, made Schaffer grunt in pain as the vice-like grip clamped over his right wrist.

For some seconds they lay like that. Spread-eagled and motionless on the sloping roof, the lives of both dependent on the slim imbedded blade of Smith's knife, then Schaffer, urged by Smith's quivering left arm, began to inch his way slowly upwards. Thirty seconds later and he was level with Smith.

"This is a knife I have, not an ice axe," Smith said hoarsely. "Won't take much more of this. Have you another knife?"

Schaffer shook his head. Momentarily, speech was beyond him.

"Piton?"

The same shake of the head.

"Your flash?"

Schaffer nodded, reached under the cumbersome snow smock with his left hand and eventually managed to wriggle his flashlight free.

"Unscrew the bottom," Smith said. "Throw it away—and the battery." Schaffer brought his left hand across to where his right was pinioned by Smith, removed base and battery, flattened the now empty cylinder base a little, reversed his grip and gouged the flashlight into the ice, downwards and towards himself. He moved his right hand and Smith released his grip. Schaffer remained where he was. Smith smiled and said: "Try holding me."

Schaffer caught Smith's left wrist. Tentatively, his hand still hooked in readiness, Smith removed his hand from the haft of the knife. Schaffer's imbedded flashlight held firm. Cautiously at first, then with increasing confidence as the sharp blade cut through the protective sheathing of ice, Smith carved out a secure handhold in the wooden roof of the station, passed his knife to Schaffer, wriggled out of his snow smock, undid a few turns of the knotted rope round his waist and secured the free end to Schaffer's belt. He said: "With the knife and flash, think you can make it?"

"Can I make it?" Schaffer tested both knife and flashlight and smiled, a pretty strained effort, but his first for some time. "After what I've been through—well, ever seen a monkey go up a coconut palm tree?"

Fifty feet above their heads, Mary withdrew from the window and laid the binoculars on the dressing table. Her hands shook and the metal of the binoculars rattled like castanets against the glass top. She returned to the window and began to pay out the weighted string.

Smith came up the last few feet of the sloping roof at the end of the rope, caught Schaffer's hand, stood upright on the flat inner section of the roof and at once began to unwind the rest of the knotted rope from his waist. Schaffer, although the temperature was far below freezing, wiped his brow like a man in a heat wave.

"Brother!" He mopped his brow some more. "If I can ever do you a favour, like lending you car fare—"

Smith grinned, clapped his shoulder, reached up into the gloom, caught the weighted end of the suspended string and quickly bent the nylon on to it. He gave two gentle tugs and the rope began to move upwards as Mary hauled it in through the window. Smith waited until two more gentle return tugs indicated that the rope was securely fastened and began to climb.

He was halfway up to the window when the moon broke through. In his Alpenkorps uniform he was perfectly silhouetted against the gleaming white of the castle walls. He hung there motionless, not daring to move, not so much as even daring to glance upwards or downwards lest the movement attract some hostile attention.

Twenty-five feet below him Schaffer peered cautiously over the edge of the header station roof. The guards and dogs were still patrolling the area round the foot of the volcanic plug, they had only to give one casual upwards glance and Smith's discovery was inevitable. Then some hair-prickling sixth sense made Schaffer look sharply upwards and he became very still indeed. The sentry, another circuit of the battlements completed, was standing with hands splayed out on the parapet, gazing out over the valley, perhaps watching the now dying flames from the burnt-out station: he had to lower his eyes only a fraction and that was that. Slowly, with his right hand, Schaffer brought up the Luger with the long perforated silencer screwed to its muzzle and laid it, in the best police fashion, across his left wrist. He had no doubt he could kill his man with one shot, the only question was when best to do it, how to weigh the balance of possibilities. If he waited until the man sighted them, he might give a warning shout or thrust himself back into cover before Schaffer could kill him. If he shot the sentry before he sighted them, then there would be no question of either escape or warning. But there was the possibility that the man might pitch forward over the battlements, crash off the roof of the header station and fall into the valley below, close by the patrolling men and dogs. A possibility only, Schaffer decided, not a probability: the slamming effect of the Luger shell would almost certainly knock him backwards off his feet. Schaffer had never before gunned down an unsuspecting man, but he coldly prepared to do so now. He lined up the luminous sight on the man's breastbone and began to squeeze the trigger.

The moon went behind a cloud.

Slowly, stiffly, Schaffer lowered his gun. Schaffer, once again, wiped sweat from his forehead. He had the feeling that he wasn't through with brow-mopping for the night.

Smith reached the window, clambered over the sill, gave the rope two tugs as a signal for Schaffer to start climbing and passed into the room. It was almost totally dark inside, he'd just time to make out the iron bedstead which had been dragged to the window as anchorage for the rope when a pair of arms wound tightly round his neck and someone started murmuring incoherently in his ear.

"Easy on, easy on," Smith protested. He was still breathing heavily and needed all the air he could get, but summoned enough energy to bend and kiss her. "Unprofessional conduct, what's more. But I won't report it this time."

She was still clinging to him, silent now, when Lieutenant Schaffer made his appearance, dragging himself wearily over the sill and collapsing on the iron bedstead. He was breathing very heavily indeed and had about him the air of one who has suffered much.

"Have they no elevators in this dump?" he demanded. It took him two breaths to get the words out.

"Out of training," Smith said unsympathetically. He crossed to the door and switched on the light, hurriedly switched it off again. "Damn. Get the rope in then pull the curtains."

"This is the way they treated them in the Roman galleys," Schaffer said bitterly. But he had the rope inside and the curtains closed in ten seconds. As Smith was maneuvering the bed back into its original position, Schaffer was stuffing the nylon into their canvas bag, a bag which, in addition to snow suits and Schmeissers, contained some hand grenades and a stock of plastic explosives. He had just finished tying the neck of the bag when a key scraped in the lock.

Smith motioned Mary to stay where she was as he moved quickly to take up position behind the door: Schaffer, for all his alleged exhaustion, had dropped flat to the floor behind the bed with all the speed and silence of a cat. The door opened and a young *Oberleutnant* strode into the room, stopping short as he saw Mary, her hand to her mouth. His face registered astonishment, an astonishment almost immediately replaced by an anticipatory half-smile as he stepped forward beyond the opened door. Smith's arm came down and the young officer's eyes turned up in his head.

Smith studied the plans of the castle given him by Mary while Schaffer trussed up the *Oberleutnant* with the nylon, gagged him with tape and shoved him, jackknifed, into the bottom of the cupboard. For good measure he pulled the top of the bed against the door.

"Ready when you are, boss."

"That's now. I have my bearings. First left, down the stairs, third left. The gold drawing room. Where Colonel Kramer holds court. Complete with minstrels' gallery."

"What's a minstrels' gallery?" Schaffer enquired.

"A gallery for minstrels. Then the next right-hander takes us to the east wing. Down again, second left. Telephone exchange."

"Why there?" Schaffer asked. "We've already cut the lines."

"Not the ones between here and the barracks, we haven't.

Want them to whistle up a regiment of Alpenkorps?" He turned to Mary. "Helicopter still here?"

"It was when I arrived."

"The helicopter?" Schaffer showed his puzzlement. "What gives with the whirlybird, then?"

"This gives with the whirlybird. They could use it either to whip Carnaby out of here—they *might* just be nervous if they think we're on the loose—or they might use it to block our getaway."

"*If* we get away."

"There's that. How are you on immobilising helicopters, Lieutenant Schaffer? Your report states that you were an up-and-coming racing driver and a very competent mechanic before they scraped the bottom of the barrel and dragged you in."

"I volunteered," Schaffer said with dignity. "About the competence, I dunno. But give me a four-pound hammer and I'll sure as little fishes immobilise anything from a bulldozer to a bicycle."

"And without the four-pounder? This is not a boilermakers' convention."

"I have been known to use finesse."

Smith said to Mary: "How can we get a sight of this machine?"

"Just five paces that way." She pointed to the door. "Every passage window in the Schloss Adler opens onto the courtyard."

Smith opened the door, glanced up and down the passage and crossed to an opposite window. Schaffer was by his side.

The comings and goings of the moon made no difference to the state of illumination in the Schloss Adler courtyard. Two big overhead arc lamps burned by the heavily barred entrance gates. A third burned at the opposite end of the courtyard, over the main doorway leading into the castle itself. At a height of about ten feet four waterproof storm lamps were fastened to the east and west walls of the courtyard. Lights burned from a dozen windows on the east and northern sides. And the brightest light of all came from an arc lamp that had been rigged above the helicopter and under the temporary protection of a stretched tarpaulin. A figure in green overalls and a high-peaked cap was working on the helicopter's engine. Smith touched Schaffer's arm and they moved back into the room where Mary was waiting, closing the door behind them.

"Seems a straightforward operation," Schaffer said. "Fixing it so that the chopper doesn't fly again, I mean. I cross to the main gates, overpower the four men on guard, strangle the four Doberman pinschers, knock off two or three other characters—armed characters—who appear to be patrolling the place all the time, overpower about twenty soldiers who appear to be drinking beer in some sort of canteen across the way, dispose of the guy who's working on the engine and *then* immobilise the chopper. I mean, just immobilising the chopper itself wouldn't be anything, really, would it?"

"We'll think of something," Smith said soothingly.

"I'll bet you think of something," Schaffer said moodily. "That's what I'm afraid of."

"Time's a-wasting. We won't be needing those any more." Smith folded the plan, handed it to Mary, then frowned as she put it in her bag. "You know better than that. The Lilliput: it should be on your person, not in the bag. Here." He handed her the Mauser he'd taken from Colonel Weissner. "This in your bag. Hide the Lilliput on you."

"When I get to my room I will," she said primly.

"All those leering Yankee lieutenants around," Schaffer said sadly. "Thank heavens I'm a changed man."

"His mind is set on higher things," Smith explained. He glanced at his watch. "Give us thirty minutes."

They slipped cautiously through the doorway then strode briskly and confidently along the passage, making no attempt to conceal their presence. The bag with the Schmeissers, rope, grenades and explosives Smith swung carelessly from one hand. They passed a bespectacled soldier carrying a sheaf of papers and a girl carrying a laden tray, neither of whom paid any attention to them. They turned right at the end of the passage, reached a circular flight of stairs and went down three floors until they came to the level of the courtyard. A short broad passage, with two doors on either side, took them to the main door leading out to the courtyard.

Smith opened the door and looked out. The scene was very much as Schaffer had feelingly described it, with far too many armed guards and police dogs around for anyone's peace of mind. The overalled mechanic was still at work on the helicopter's engine. Smith quietly closed the door and turned his attention to the nearest right-hand door in the passage. It was locked. He said to Schaffer: "Keep an eye open at the end of the passage there."

Schaffer went. As soon as he was in position, Smith

107

brought out skeleton keys. The third key fitted and the door gave under his hand. He signalled Schaffer to return.

With the door closed and locked behind them, they looked around the room, a room faintly but for their purposes adequately lit by the backwash of light shining through the unshuttered window from the courtyard. It was, quite apparently, the fire-fighting HQ of the castle. The walls were hung with drums of rolled hoses, asbestos suits, helmets and fire axes: wheeled hand pumps, CO_2 cylinders, and a variety of smaller cylinders for fighting oil and electrical fires took up much of the floor space.

"Ideal," Smith murmured.

"Couldn't be better," Schaffer agreed. "What are you talking about?"

"If we leave anyone in here," Smith explained, "he's unlikely to be discovered unless there's an actual outbreak of fire. Agreed? So." He took Schaffer by the arm and led him to the window. "The lad working on the chopper there. About your size, wouldn't you say?"

"I wouldn't know," Schaffer said. "And if you've got in mind what I think you have in mind, then I don't want to know, either."

Smith drew the shutters, crossed to the door and switched on the overhead light.

"You got any better ideas?"

"Give me time," he complained.

"I can't give you what we haven't got. Take your jacket off and keep your Luger lined up on that door. I'll be back in a minute."

Smith left, closing but not locking the door behind him. He passed through the outer doorway, walked a few paces across the courtyard, halted at the base of a set of steps leading up to the helicopter and looked up at the man working above him, a tall rangy man with a thin intelligent face and lugubrious expression on it. If he'd been working barehanded with metal tools in that freezing temperature, Smith thought, he'd have had a lugubrious expression on his face, too.

"You the pilot?" Smith asked.

"You wouldn't think so, would you?" the overalled man said bitterly. He laid down a spanner and blew on his hands. "Back in Tempelhof I have two mechanics for this machine, one a farmhand from Schwabia, the other a blacksmith's assistant from the Harz. If I want to keep alive I do my own mechanics. What do you want?"

"Not me. Reichsmarschal Rosemeyer. The phone."

"The Reichsmarschal?" The pilot was puzzled. "I was speaking to him less than fifteen minutes ago."

"A call just came through from the Chancellory in Berlin. It seems urgent." Smith let a slight note of impatience creep into his voice. "You better hurry. Through the main door there, then the first on the right."

Smith stood aside as the guard clambered down, looked casually around him. A guard with a leashed Doberman was no more than twenty feet away, but paying no attention to them: with his pinched bluish face sunk deep in his upturned collar, his hands thrust down into his greatcoat pockets and his frozen breath hanging heavily in the air, he was too busy concentrating on his own miseries to have time to spare for ridiculous suspicions. Smith turned to follow the pilot through the main door, unobtrusively unholstering his Luger and gripping it by the barrel.

Smith hadn't intended chopping down the pilot with his gun butt but was left with no option. As soon as the pilot had passed through the side door and seen Schaffer's Luger pointing at his chest from a distance of four feet his shoulders lifted—the preliminary, Smith knew, not to violence or resistance but to a shout for help. Schaffer caught him as he pitched forward and lowered him to the floor.

Quickly they unzipped the overall from the unconscious man, bound and gagged him and left him lying in a corner. The overall was hardly a perfect fit for Schaffer, but, then, overalls are rarely a perfect fit for anybody. Schaffer switched the pilot's hat for his own, pulled the peak low over his eyes and left.

Smith switched off the light, unshuttered the window, raised the lower sash and stood, Luger in hand, just far enough back from the window so as not to be seen from outside. Schaffer was already climbing the steps up to the helicopter. The guard was now only feet from the base of the ladder. He'd his hands out of his pockets now and was flailing his arms across his shoulders in an attempt to keep warm.

Thirty seconds later Schaffer climbed down the ladder again, carrying some piece of equipment in his left hand. He reached the ground, lifted the piece of equipment for a closer inspection, shook his head in disgust, lifted his right hand in a vague half-greeting to the uncaring German guard and headed for the main door again. By the time he reached the fire-fighting room, Smith had the window shuttered again and the light on.

"That was quick," Smith said approvingly.

"Fear lent him wings, as the saying goes," Schaffer said sourly. "I'm always quick when I'm nervous. Did you see the size of the teeth in that great slavering monster out there?" He held up the piece of equipment for inspection, dropped it to the floor and brought his heel down on it. "Distributor cap. I'll bet they haven't another in Bavaria. Not for that engine. And now, I suppose you want me to go and impersonate the telephone operator."

"No. We don't want to exhaust all your Thespian stamina."

"My what?" Schaffer asked suspiciously. "That sounds kinda like a nasty crack to me."

"Your acting resources. The only other impersonation you'll be called on to make tonight is that of Lieutenant Schaffer, OSS, the innocent American abroad."

"That shouldn't be too difficult," Schaffer said bitterly. He draped the overalls he'd just removed over the unconscious pilot. "A cold night. Anyway, the telephone exchange."

"Soon. But I'd like to check first how far they've got with old Carnaby-Jones. Let's take a look."

Two floors higher up and midway along the central passage Smith stopped outside a doorway. At a nod from him, Schaffer reached for a light switch. Except for a faint glow of light at either end, the passage was now completely dark. Smith laid a gentle hand on the doorknob and quietly eased the door open. Fifteen inches, no more. Both men swiftly slid through the narrow gap, Smith quickly and softly closing the door to again.

The room, if so enormous a chamber could be called a room, must have been at least seventy feet long by thirty wide. The farther end of the room was brightly and warmly lit by three large chandeliers: comparatively, the end of the room where Smith and Schaffer stood was shrouded in near darkness.

They stood, not on the floor, but on a platform some dozen feet above the floor. It was a massive and grotesquely carved oaken minstrels' gallery which completely spanned the thirty-foot width of that end and ran perhaps a quarter of the way down both the longer sides of the room. There were rows of wooden benches, an organ on one side of the door through which they had just passed, a battery of pipes on the other. Whoever had built that place had obviously liked the organ and choir singing: or maybe he just thought he did. From the centre of the front of the gallery, opposite the rear door, a flight of steps with intricately scrolled wooden banisters led down to what was very obviously the gold drawing room.

It was aptly named, Smith thought. Everything in it was gold or golden or gilt. The enormous wall-to-wall carpet was deep gold in colour, the thickness of the pile would have turned a polar bear green with envy. The heavy baroque furniture, all twisted snakes' and gargoyles' heads, was gilt, the huge couches and chairs covered in a dusty gold lamé. The chandeliers were gilded and, above the enormous white and gilt-plated fireplace, in which a crackling pine log fire burned, hung an almost equally enormous white and gilt-plated mirror. The great heavy curtains could have been made from beaten gold. The ceiling-high oak panelling was a mistake, it continued to look obstinately like oak panelling, maybe the original covering gold paint had worn off. All in all, Smith reflected, it was a room only a mad Bavarian monarch could have conceived of, far less lived in.

Three men were seated comfortably round the great fire, to all appearances having an amicable discussion over afterdinner coffee and brandy, which was being served to them from —almost inevitably—a golden trolley by Anne-Marie. Anne-Marie, like the panelling, was a disappointment: instead of a gold lamé dress she wore a long white silk sheath gown which, admittedly, went very well with her blond colouring and snow tan. She looked as if she were about to leave for the opera.

The man with his back to him Smith had never seen before but, because he immediately recognised who the other men were, knew who this man must be: Colonel Paul Kramer, Deputy Chief of the German Secret Service, regarded by M.I.6 as having the most brilliant and formidable brain in German Intelligence. The man to watch, Smith knew, the man to fear. It was said of Kramer that he never made the same mistake twice—and that no one could remember where he'd last made a mistake for the first time.

As Smith watched, Colonel Kramer stirred, poured some more brandy from a Napoleon bottle by his side and looked first at the man on his left, a tall, ageing, but still good-looking man in the uniform of a Reichsmarschal of the Wehrmacht—at that moment, wearing a very glum expression on

111

his face—then at the man seated opposite, an iron-grey-haired and very distinguished-looking character in the uniform of a lieutenant general of the U. S. Army. Without a comptometer to hand, it was difficult to say which of the two generals was wearing the more decorations.

Kramer sipped his brandy and said wearily: "You make things very difficult for me, General Carnaby. Very very difficult indeed."

"The difficulties are of your own making, my dear Kramer," Cartwright Jones said easily. "Yours and General Rosemeyer's here . . . There *is* no difficulty." He turned to Anne-Marie and smiled. "If I might have some more of that excellent brandy, my dear. My word, we've nothing like this in SHAEF. Marooned in your Alpine redoubt or not, you people know how to look after yourselves."

In the gloom at the back of the minstrels' gallery, Schaffer nudged Smith with his elbow.

"What gives with old Carnaby-Jones knocking back the Napoleon, then?" he asked in a low indignant murmur. "Why isn't he being turned on a spit or having the French fits coming out of scopolamine?"

"Ssssh!" Smith's nudge carried a great deal more weight and authority than Schaffer's had done.

Jones smiled his thanks as Anne-Marie poured him some more brandy, sipped from the glass, sighed in satisfaction and continued: "Or have you forgotten, General Rosemeyer, that Germany is also a signatory to the Hague conventions?"

"I haven't forgotten," Rosemeyer said uncomfortably. "And if I had my way . . . General, my hands are tied. I have my orders from Berlin."

"And you can tell Berlin all they're entitled to know," Jones said easily. "I am General—Lieutenant General—George Carnaby, United States Army."

"And Chief Coordinator of Planning for the Second Front," Rosemeyer added morosely.

"The second front?" Jones asked with interest. "What's that?"

Rosemeyer said heavily and with earnest gravity: "General, I've done all I can. You must believe me. For thirty-six hours now, I've held off Berlin. I've persuaded—I've *tried* to persuade the High Command that the mere *fact* of your capture will compel the Allies to alter all their invasion plans. But this, it seems, is not enough. For the last time, may I request—"

"General George Carnaby," Jones said calmly. "United States Army."

"I expected nothing else," Rosemeyer admitted tiredly. "How could I expect anything else from a senior army officer? I'm afraid the matter is now in Colonel Kramer's hands."

Jones sipped some more brandy and eyed Kramer thoughtfully. "The colonel doesn't seem very happy about it either."

"I'm not," Kramer said. "But the matter is out of my hands, too. I also have my orders. Anne-Marie will attend to the rest of it."

"*This* charming young lady?" Jones was politely incredulous. "A maestro of the thumbscrew?"

"Of the hypodermic syringe," Kramer said shortly. "She used to be a trained nurse." A bell rang and Kramer picked up a phone by his side. "Yes? Ah! They have, of course, been searched? Very good. Now." He looked across at Jones. "Well, well, well. Some interesting company coming up, General. Very interesting indeed. Parachutists. A rescue team—for you. I'm sure you'll be delighted to meet one another."

"I really can't imagine what you're talking about," Jones said idly.

"The rescue team we've seen before," Smith murmured to Schaffer. "And no doubt we'll be renewing old acquaintance before long. Come on."

"What? Now?" Schaffer jerked an urgent thumb in the direction of Jones. "Just when they're going to get to work on him?"

"Out of your social depth, Lieutenant," Smith whispered. "They're civilised. First, they finish the brandy. *Then* the works."

"It's like I said," Schaffer said mournfully. "I'm from Montana."

The two men left as quietly as they had come and as quietly closed the door behind them. Against the loom of light at either end of the corridor, they could see that the passageway was clear. Smith switched on the light. They walked briskly along the passage, dropped down a flight of stairs, turned left and halted outside a doorway which bore above it the legend TELEFON ZENTRALE.

"Telephone exchange," Schaffer said.

Smith shook his head in admiration, put his ear to the door, dropped to one knee, peered through the keyhole and, while still in that position, softly tried the handle. Whatever

113

slight sound he made was masked by the muffled sound of a voice speaking over a telephone. The door was locked. Smith slowly released the handle, straightened and shook his head.

"Suspicious bunch of devils," Schaffer said sourly. "The skeletons?"

"The operator would hear us. Next door."

Next door wasn't locked. The door gave before Smith's pressure on the handle. The room beyond was in total darkness and appeared to be empty.

"Moment, bitte!" a cold voice said behind them.

Quickly, but not too quickly, Smith and Schaffer turned round. A few feet away stood a soldier, levelled carbine in his hand, his eyes moving in active suspicion from the two men to the kit bag in Smith's hands. Smith glared at the man, raised an imperative forefinger to his lips.

"Dummkopf!" Smith's voice was a low furious whisper through clenched teeth. *"Silenz! Englander!"*

He turned away impatiently and peered tensely through the partly opened doorway. Again he held up an imperious hand that commanded silence. After a few more seconds he straightened, lips compressed, looked significantly at Schaffer and moved slightly to one side. Schaffer took his position and started peering in turn. Curiosity, Smith could see, was replacing suspicion in the soldier's face. Schaffer straightened and said softly: "What in God's name do we do?"

"I don't know," Smith said in a worried whisper. "Colonel Kramer told me he wanted them alive. But—"

"What is it?" the soldier demanded in a voice as low as their own. With the mention of Colonel Kramer the last of his suspicions had gone. "Who is it?"

"You still here," Smith said irritably. "All right, go on. Have a look. But be quick!"

The soldier, his face and eyes now alight with intense curiosity and what might have been dreams of rapid promotion, moved forward on tiptoe as Schaffer courteously stepped to one side to let him see. A pair of Lugers grinding simultaneously into both temples effectively put an end to any ideas of rapid military advancement that he might briefly have entertained. He was propelled, stumbling, into the room and, by the time he'd picked himself up and turned round, the door was closed, the light on and both pistols lined at his head.

"Those are silencers you see on our guns," Smith said quietly. "No heroics, no shooting. Dying for the Fatherland is one thing, dying uselessly for no reason at all is another and very stupid thing. Don't you agree?"

The soldier looked at them, calculated his chances, accepted the fact that he had none and nodded. Schaffer produced a length of rope and said: "You may be overeager, son, but you're no fool. Lie down with your hands behind your back."

The room, Smith saw, was small and lined with metal shelves and filing cabinets. Some sort of storage room for office records. The chances of anyone coming along weren't high and it was, anyway, a chance they had to take. He waited till Schaffer had bound and gagged the prisoner, put his Luger away, helped Schaffer to bind the man to two of the metal legs supporting the shelves, turned to the window, slid up the lower sash and peered out.

The valley to the north stretched out before him, the lights of the village and the smouldering embers of the railway station visible through very gently falling snow. Smith looked to his right. The lighted window of the telephone exchange was only a few feet away. Down from the window a heavy lead-sheathed cable attached to a wire almost equally as heavy stretched down the castle wall into the darkness.

"That the one?" Schaffer was by his side now.

"That's the one. Let's have the rope."

Smith eased his legs into a double bowline, wriggled over the windowsill and cautiously lowered himself to the full extent of his arms while Schaffer, standing by the window with the rope belayed round one of the stanchions of the shelving, took the strain. Smith released his grip on the sill and was lowered jerkily by Schaffer till he was about ten or twelve feet down. Then, using a free hand and both feet to fend himself off from the wall he began to swing himself in a pendulum arc across the face of the castle, an assist from Schaffer up above adding momentum to his swing. On the fifth swing the fingers of his left hand hooked round the lead cable and wire. As Schaffer eased off tension on the rope Smith got both hands round the cable and quickly climbed up the few feet to the window above. He was almost certain that the lead cable he had in his hands *was* the telephone outlet, but only almost: he had no desire to slice the blade of his knife through high-powered electricity supply lines.

He hitched a wary eye over the windowsill, saw that the telephone operator, his back almost directly to him, was talking animatedly on the phone, lifted himself another six inches, observed a cable of what appeared to be exactly similar dimensions to the one he was holding running along the skirting board to some point behind the exchange and then not reappearing again. He lowered himself a couple of feet, grasped cable and wire firmly with his left hand, inserted the point of his knife between cable and wire a few inches below that and started sawing. A dozen powerful saw cuts and he was through.

He replaced the knife in its sheath, hoisted himself up again and had another look through the window. The operator was still animated, but this time not with his voice but with a hand which he was using furiously to crank a handle at the side of the exchange. After a few seconds of this profitless exercise he gave up and just sat there staring at the switchboard and shaking his head in bafflement. Smith made a signal to Schaffer, released his grip on the cable and swung back across the castle wall.

Mary glanced at her watch for the tenth time in less than as many minutes, stubbed out the half-cigarette she'd been nervously smoking, rose from her chair, opened her handbag, checked that the safety catch of the Mauser inside was in the off position, closed the bag and crossed the room. She had just turned the handle and begun to open the door when knuckles rapped on the outside. She hesitated, glanced at the bag in her hand and looked round almost wildly to see where she could dispose of it. But it was too late to dispose of anything. The door opened and a cheerfully smiling von Brauchitsch stood framed in the doorway.

"Ah, Fräulein!" He glanced at the bag and smiled again. "Lucky me! Just in time to escort you wherever you're going."

"To escort me——" She broke off and smiled. "My business is of no consequence. It can wait. You wanted to see me, Captain?"

"Naturally."

"What about?"

"What about, she says! About nothing, that's what. Unless you call yourself nothing. Just to see you. Is that a crime? The prettiest girl we've seen——" He smiled again, this man who was always smiling, and took her arm. "Come, a little Bavarian hospitality. Coffee. We have an armoury that's been converted into the finest *cafe-stube*——"

"But—but my duties?" Mary said uncertainly. "I must see the colonel's secretary—"

"That one! Let her wait!" There was a marked lack of cordiality in von Brauchitsch's voice. "You and I have a lot to talk about."

"We have?" It was impossible to resist the infectious smile, not to reply in kind. "Such as?"

"Düsseldorf."

"Düsseldorf?"

"Of course! That's my home town, too."

"Your home town, too!" She smiled again and gave him the briefest of squeezes. "How small a world. That *will* be nice."

She wondered vaguely, as she walked along, how one could smile and smile and, inside, feel as chilled as the tomb.

SEVEN

FOR THE second time in fifteen minutes Smith and Schaffer stopped at the doorway outside the gold room's minstrels' gallery, switched out the passage light, paused, listened, then passed silently inside. This time, however, Smith reached through the crack of the almost closed door and switched the light back on again. He did not expect to be using that door again, that night or any other night, and he had no wish to raise any eyebrows, however millimetric the raising: survival was a matter of the infinitely careful consideration of all possible dangers, no matter how remote that possibility might at times appear.

This time, Smith and Schaffer did not remain at the back of the minstrels' gallery. They moved slowly to the front, till they had come to the head of the broad flight of stairs leading down to the floor of the gold room and then sat down on the front oaken benches, one on each side of the gallery's passageway. They were still shrouded in deep gloom, completely invisible from below.

Colonel Kramer's stock of V.S.O.P. Napoleon brandy was certainly taking a beating that night, Smith reflected. The colonel, Reichsmarschal Rosemeyer, Jones and Anne-Marie had been joined by three others—Carraciola, Thomas and Christiansen. Those last three were no longer manacled and under heavy guard. On the contrary there was no sign of any guard, and the three men were sitting deeply relaxed and side by side on one of the massive gold lamé covered couches, glasses of brandy, and no small ones at that, in their hands. Even Anne-Marie now held a glass in her hand. It appeared to be an occasion for a celebration of some note.

118

Kramer lifted his glass towards the three men seated on the couch.

"Your health, gentlemen. Your very good health." He turned to the Reichsmarschal. "Three of the best in Europe, sir."

"I suppose they are necessary," Rosemeyer said in resigned distaste. "At least, their courage is beyond dispute. Your health, gentlemen."

"Your health, gentlemen," Jones said bitterly. He sat forward in his chair and hurled his glass into the fire. The glass shattered and there was a momentary tongue of flame as the brandy ignited. *"That's* how I drink the health of double agents."

Schaffer leaned across the passageway and whispered: "I thought you said he couldn't act?"

"Nobody's ever paid him 25,000 bucks a night before," Smith said sardonically.

"Tut, tut, General. Best Venetian glass." Kramer shook his head deprecatingly then smiled. "But an understandable fit of pique. When your heroic rescuers turn out to be, well, birds of a different feather—"

"Double agents!" In his contempt, Jones almost spat out the words.

Kramer smiled again, tolerantly, and turned to the three men on the couch.

"And the return trip, gentlemen? As well organised as your outward journey?"

"That's about the one thing the close-mouthed so-and-so told us," Carraciola said with some bitterness. "A Mosquito bomber is to come to pick us up. Salen, a little village north of Frauenfeld in Switzerland. There's a little civilian airfield just to the north of Salen."

Schaffer bent across the passage again and said in an admiring whisper: "You really are a fearful liar."

"So Salen it is," Kramer was saying. "We know all about it. The Swiss are very good at looking the wrong way when it suits them: but for reasons of our own we find it convenient not to protest too much. Odd things happen at Salen . . . However. A little message to London. Arrange pick-up times and so forth. Then a helicopter to the border—so much easier than walking, gentlemen—a rubber dinghy for the Rhine and then a short walk. You'll be back in Whitehall, reporting General Carnaby's transfer to Berlin, before you know it."

"Back in London?" Thomas shook his head in slow emphasis. "Not on your nelly, Colonel. With Smith and that Yank still at large? What happens if they find out what's really happening? What happens if they remain at large? What happens if they get a message through to London—"

"What do you take us for?" Kramer said tiredly. "You will also, of course, be reporting the unfortunate demise of your leader. As soon as we located that still-warm radio set in the left luggage office we put on bloodhounds from the barracks. Your precious Major Smith was the last man to handle that set and he left a pretty clear trail. The hounds traced him along the east side of the village as far as a garage and then up to the lower station of the *Luftseilbahn*."

"The cable car?" Thomas was frankly disbelieving.

"The cable car. Our Major Smith is either a very foolhardy or a very dangerous man—I must confess I know nothing of him. And there, at the lower station, the hounds completely lost the scent. The handlers circled the station with the hounds and then brought them into the cable car itself. But the trail was cold. Our quarry appeared to have vanished into thin air.

"It was then that one of the searchers had the original idea of examining the thin air, so to speak. He climbed up and examined the roof of the lower station. Surprise, surprise, unmistakable signs in the snow and ice that two men had been up there before him. From that it was only a logical step to examine the roof of the cable car itself, and sure enough—"

"They're inside!" Christiansen exclaimed.

"And won't get out again." Colonel Kramer leaned back comfortably in his chair. "Have no fear, gentlemen. Every exit is blocked—including the header station. We've doubled the guards outside and the rest have begun to carry out a floor to floor search."

In the gloom of the minstrels' gallery Smith and Schaffer exchanged thoughtful glances.

"I don't know," Thomas said uneasily. "He's a resourceful devil—"

Kramer held up a hand.

"Fifteen minutes. I guarantee it." He shifted his glance to Jones. "I don't pretend to look forward to this, General, but shall we get on with your—ah—medication?"

Jones glared at Carraciola, Christiansen, and Thomas and said, very slowly and distinctly: "You—bloody—swine!"

"Against all my principles, General Carnaby," Rosemeyer

said uncomfortably. "But if we could only dispense with force—"

"Principles? You make me sick!" Jones stood up and made a strangled noise in his throat. "The hell with you all! The Hague Conventions! Principles! Officers and gentlemen of the Third bloody Reich!" He stripped off his uniform jacket, rolled up a sleeve and sat down again.

There was a brief and uncomfortable silence, then Kramer nodded to Anne-Marie who put down her glass and moved off to a side door leading off the gold drawing room. In was obvious to everyone that Anne-Marie wasn't feeling in the least uncomfortable: the half-smile on her face was as near to that of pleasurable anticipation as she could permit herself in the presence of Rosemeyer and Kramer.

Again Smith and Schaffer exchanged glances, no longer thoughtful glances, but the glances of men who know what they have to do and are committed to doing it. Carefully, silently, they eased themselves up from the choir stalls, adjusted the straps of their shoulder-slung Schmeissers until the machine pistols were in the horizontal position then started slowly down the stairs, well apart and as close as possible to their respective banisters, to minimise the danger of creaking treads.

They were halfway down, just beginning to emerge from the dark gloom of the gallery, when Anne-Marie re-entered the room. She was carrying a small stainless-steel tray; on the tray were a glass beaker, a phial containing some colourless liquid and a hypodermic syringe. She set the glass tray down on an occasional table close to Jones and broke the phial into the narrow beaker.

Smith and Schaffer had reached the foot of the stairs and were now advancing towards the group round the fireplace. They had now completely emerged from the shadows and were in full view of anyone who cared to turn his head. But no one cared to turn his head, every seated person in the drawing room was engrossed in the scene before him, watching in varying degrees of willing or unwilling fascination as Anne-Marie carefully filled the hypodermic syringe and held it up to the light to examine it. Smith and Schaffer continued to advance, their footfalls soundless on the luxuriously deep pile of the gold carpet.

Carefully, professionally, but with the trace of the smile still on her lips, Anne-Marie swabbed an area of Jones' forearm with cotton wool soaked in alcohol and then, as watchers unconsciously bent forward in their seats, picked up Jones' wrist in one hand and the hypodermic in the other. The hypodermic hovered over the swabbed area as she located the vein she wanted.

"Just a waste of good scopolamine, my dear," Smith said. "You won't get anything out of him."

There was a moment's frozen and incredulous stillness, the hypodermic syringe fell soundlessly to the floor, then everyone whirled round to stare at the two advancing figures, carbines moving gently from side to side. Predictably, Colonel Kramer was the first to recover and react. Almost imperceptibly, his hand began to drift to a button on a panel beside his chair.

"That button, Colonel," Smith said conversationally.

Slowly, reluctantly, Kramer's hand retreated from the button.

"On the other hand," Smith went on cordially, "why not? By all means, if you wish."

Kramer glanced at him in narrow-eyed and puzzled suspicion.

"You will notice, Colonel," Smith continued by way of explanation, "that my gun is not pointing at you. It is pointed at him"—he swung his gun to cover Carraciola—"at him" —the gun moved to Thomas—"at him"—it covered Christiansen—"and at him!" Smith swung round abruptly and ground the muzzle of the Schmeisser into Schaffer's ribs. "Drop that gun! Now!"

"Drop the gun?" Schaffer stared at him in shock and baffled consternation. "What in the name of God—"

Smith stepped swiftly forward and, without altering his grip on his gun, lifted the barrel sharply upwards and drove the butt of the Schmeisser into Schaffer's stomach. Schaffer grunted in agony, doubled forwards with both hands clutched over his midriff, then, seconds later, obviously in great pain, began to straighten slowly. Glaring at Smith, the dark eyes mad in his face, he slipped the shoulder strap and the Schmeisser fell to the carpet.

"Sit there." With the muzzle of his gun Smith gestured to a chair halfway between Rosemeyer's and the couch where the three men were sitting.

Schaffer said slowly, painfully: "You goddamned lousy, dirty, double-crossing—"

"That's what they all say. You're not even original." The

contempt in Smith's voice gave way to menace. "That chair, Schaffer."

Schaffer lowered himself with difficulty into his chair, rubbed his solar plexus and said, "You – – –. If I live to be a hundred—"

"If you live to be a hundred you'll do nothing," Smith said contemptuously. "In your own idiom, Schaffer, you're a punk and a pretty second-rate one at that." He settled himself comfortably in a chair beside Colonel Kramer. "A simple-minded American," he explained carelessly. "Had him along for local colour."

"I see," Kramer said. It was obvious that he did not see. He went on uncertainly: "If we might have an explanation—"

Smith waved him negligently to silence.

"All in good time, my dear Kramer, all in good time. As I was saying, my dear Anne-Marie—"

"How did you know her name was Anne-Marie?" Kramer asked sharply.

Smith smiled enigmatically, ignored him completely, and continued: "As I was saying, scopolamine is a waste of time. All scopolamine will do, as you're all aware, is to reveal the truth about our friend here, which is that he is not Lieutenant General George Carnaby, Chief Coordinator of Planning for the Second Front, but a certain Cartwright Jones, an American actor being paid precisely 25,000 dollars to impersonate General Carnaby." He looked over to Jones and bowed. "My congratulations, Mr. Jones. A very creditable performance. Pity you'll have to spend the rest of the war in a concentration camp."

Kramer and Rosemeyer were on their feet, the others leaning far forward on the couch, an almost exactly identical expression of disbelief showing in every face. If Cartwright Jones had been earth's first visitor from outer space he couldn't possibly have been the object of more incredulous consternation.

"Well, well, well," Smith said with interest. "Surprise, surprise, surprise." He tapped Kramer on the arm and gestured in the direction of Carraciola, Thomas and Christiansen. "Odd, wouldn't you say, Kramer? They seem just as astonished as you are?"

"Is this true?" Rosemeyer demanded hoarsely of Jones. "What he says? Do you deny—"

In a voice that was no more than a whisper, Jones said: "How—how in God's name—who *are* you, sir?"

123

"A stranger in the night." Smith waved a hand. "Dropped in in the passing, you might say. Maybe the Allies will let you have that twenty-five thousand after the war. I wouldn't bank on it though, if international law allows you to shoot a captured enemy soldier dressed as a civilian, maybe the opposite holds good too." Smith stretched and politely patted a yawn to extinction. "And now, Anne-Marie, if I could—with your permission, my dear Kramer—have a glass of that excellent Napoleon. Clinging to the roofs of cable cars works the devil with my circulation."

The girl hesitated, looked at Kramer and Rosemeyer, found neither encouragement nor discouragement, shrugged, poured a glass and handed it to Smith, who sniffed the bouquet approvingly, drank a little and bowed again to Jones.

"My congratulations, sir. You are a connoisseur." He sipped again, turned to Kramer and said sadly: "To think you have been wasting such excellent liquor on enemies of the Third Reich."

"Don't listen to him, Colonel Kramer, don't listen to him!" Carraciola shouted wildly. "It's a bluff! He's just trying—"

Smith lined up his gun on Carraciola's chest and said softly: "Keep quiet or I'll make you quiet, you damned traitor. You'll have your chance—*and* we'll see who's bluffing." He lowered his gun to his knees and went on tiredly: "Colonel Kramer, I don't fancy talking and having to keep a gun on this unlovely trio all the time. Have you a guard you can trust? A man who won't talk afterwards, I mean?"

He sat back in his chair, sipped his brandy and ignored the malevolent stares from his four erstwhile colleagues. Kramer looked at him for a very long moment, then nodded thoughtfully and reached for a phone.

The armoury—now converted into a *cafe-stube*—of the Schloss Adler was very much in keeping with the remainder of the castle, something out of a medieval dream or nightmare, according to how individual tastes and inclinations lay. It was a large, darkly panelled, stoneflagged room with enormous adze-cut smoke-blackened beams and walls behung with ancient and rusty suits of armour, ancient and rusty weapons of all kinds and scores of armorial bearings, some of which could have been genuine. Three-sided half-booths lined the walls and half-a-dozen slab-topped monastery refectory tables, flanked by massive oak benches, paralleled the shorter axis of the room. The oil lamps, suspended by iron chains from the ceiling, were turned low, lending the atmosphere in the armoury an air of intimacy or brooding menace, according to one's original mood on entering. There was no doubt in Mary's mind as to its effect upon her. Her gaze followed half-a-dozen heavily armed and jackbooted men who were just leaving the armoury, then came back reluctantly to the man sitting close beside her in the corner booth.

"Well, what did I tell you?" von Brauchitsch said expansively. "Coffee to match the surroundings!"

Coffee to match the surroundings, Mary thought, would have tasted of hemlock. She said: "What did those men want? They seemed to be looking for someone."

"Forget them. Concentrate on von Brauchitsch."

"But you spoke to them. What did they *want?*"

"They say there are spies in the castle!" Von Brauchitsch threw his head back, laughed, and spread his hands, palms up. "Imagine! Spies in the Schloss Adler! The Gestapo HQ! They must have flown in on their broomsticks. The military commandant is an old woman. He has spies in about once a week. Now what was I saying about Düsseldorf?" He broke off, glancing at her empty coffee cup. "My apologies, my dear Fräulein. Come, more coffee."

"No, really. I must go."

Von Brauchitsch laughed again and put his hand on hers.

"Go where? There *is* nowhere to go inside the Schloss Adler. Nonsense, nonsense." He turned in his seat and called: "Fräulein! Two more coffees. And with schnapps, this time."

While he was ordering, Mary glanced quickly at her watch and a momentary expression of desperation crossed her face, but by the time von Brauchitsch turned back she was smiling sweetly at him. She said: "You were saying about Düsseldorf—"

The company in the gold drawing room had now been increased by one, a tall, cold-faced and hard-eyed sergeant who held a carbine cradled in a pair of strong and very capable-looking hands. He was standing behind the couch on which Carraciola, Thomas and Christiansen were seated, and he was giving them his entire attention, apart from a frequent sideways glance at Schaffer. He had about him a reassuring air of competence.

"A very much more civilised arrangement," Smith said approvingly. He rose, leaving his Schmeisser lying on the floor, crossed to the brandy decanter on the sideboard, poured himself another drink and made his way back to the fireplace where he placed his glass on the mantelpiece.

"This will take but minutes, only," Smith said in a soft and ominous voice. "Anne-Marie, bring in three more capsules of scopolamine." He smiled at her. "And I needn't remind *you* to bring the hypodermics."

"Colonel Kramer!" Carraciola said desperately. "This is madness! Are you going to allow—"

"Guard!" Smith's voice was harsh. "If that man talks again, silence him!"

The guard jabbed his carbine muzzle none too lightly into Carraciola's back. Carraciola subsided, fuming, his fists clenched till the ivory showed.

"What do you take Reichsmarschal Rosemeyer and Colonel Kramer for?" Smith demanded cuttingly. "Credulous fools? Little children? Imbeciles of your own calibre, who imagine you can get away with a cretinous masquerade of this nature? The scopolamine will be used *after* I have established my own bona-fides and *after* I have disproved yours. Anne-Marie?"

Anne-Marie smiled and marched away. It was not every night that she got the chance to administer three injections of scopolamine. Then she stopped and turned, eyebrows raised in interrogation, as Smith called her name again.

"One moment, Fräulein." Smith, brandy glass in hand, was staring unseeingly into the middle distance and the watchers could see a slow smile coming to his face, a smile obviously heralding the birth of a new idea and one that pleased him very much. "Of course, of course," Smith said softly. "And bring three notebooks, will you, my dear?"

"*Three* notebooks?" Colonel Kramer's tone was neutral, his eyes watchful. "*Three* capsules? You give the impression that we have *four* enemies of the Reich here."

"Only three enemies that matter," Smith said in weary patience. "The American?" The fact that he neither bothered to glance at Schaffer nor even permit a trace of contempt to creep into his voice showed unmistakably his opinion of the American. "He doesn't even know what day of the week it is. Now then." He picked up a cigar from an inlaid marquetry box, lit it and sipped some more brandy. "Let's be fair and establish my bona-fides first. Pointers first, then proof. In the best judicial fashion.

"First, why did I invite another guard in and lay down my

126

own gun?" He paused and went on sarcastically: "Of course! Because I wanted to increase the odds against myself. Secondly, why didn't I kill Colonel Weissner and his men when I had them at my mercy—if, that is, I'm an enemy of the Third Reich—earlier this evening? I had some difficulty, I might tell you, in restraining our fire-eating young American here from turning himself into a one-man firing squad. Very aggressive, he was."

"I'll damned well tell you why," Carraciola said viciously. "Because you knew the shots would be heard!"

Smith sighed, lifted the flap of his jacket, produced an automatic and fired. The sound of the impact of the bullet thudding into the couch inches from Carraciola's shoulder completely blanketed the soft plop made by the automatic itself. Smith carelessly threw the silenced Luger into a nearby empty chair and smiled quizzically at Carraciola.

"Didn't know I had that, did you? I didn't kill Colonel Weissner because German does not kill German."

"You are German?" Kramer's eyes were still watchful but the tone perhaps a shade less neutral.

"Johann Schmidt, at your service." This with a little bow and a click of the heels. "Captain John Smith of the Black Watch."

"From the Rhineland, by your accent?"

"Heidelberg."

"But that is *my* home town."

"Indeed?" Smith smiled his interest. "Then I think we have a mutual friend."

Momentarily, a faraway look came to Kramer's eyes and he said softly, apparently apropos of nothing: "The columns of Charlemagne."

"Ah, and the fountain in the courtyard of the dear old Friedrichsbau," Smith said nostalgically. He glanced at Kramer, and the nostalgia gave way to a pseudomournful reproof. "How could you, my dear Colonel? To proceed. Why —third point, I think—why did I stage this elaborate car accident—because I *knew* those three impostors wouldn't dare come into the open until they thought I was dead. Anyway, if I *were* the impostor, would I have come back when I knew the game was up? Anyway, to come back for what?" He smiled wearily and nodded at Jones. "To rescue *another* impostor?"

Kramer said thoughtfully: "I must say I'm rather begin-

127

ning to look forward to hearing what our three friends here have to say."

"I'll tell you *now* what I've bloody well got to say." Christiansen was on his feet, ignoring the guard's gun, his voice shaking with fury. "He's fooling you, he's fooling all of us. He's a damned liar and you're too damned stupid to see the wool over your eyes. A tissue of – – – lies, beginning to end—"

"That will do!" Kramer's hand was up, his eyes bleak, his tone icy. "You condemn yourselves from your own mouths. Every statement made so far by this officer is demonstrably true. Sergeant Hartmann"—this to the guard with the carbine —"if any of those men speak again, do you think you could silence him without silencing him permanently?"

Hartmann produced a small woven-leather truncheon from his tunic and slipped the looped thong over his wrist.

"You know I can, Herr Colonel."

"Good. Pray continue, Captain Schmidt."

"Thank you. I hadn't finished." Smith felt like pouring himself another brandy, a celebration brandy or, alternatively, pinning a medal on Christiansen for having so unerringly if unwittingly exposed the chink in Kramer's armour, a wounded intellectual vanity, the lacerated professional pride of a brilliant man being reminded of his capacity for being duped by one of those who had already duped him. "For the same excellent reason I came here by the roof of the cable car—they'd *never* have come into the open if they'd known I was here—and alive. Incidentally, Kramer, hasn't it occurred to you that it's impossible to enter the Schloss Adler from the roof of the header station without the assistance of a rope and someone inside?"

"Damnation!" Coming so soon after Christiansen's reminder of his fallibility, Smith's question left Kramer's self-confidence badly shaken. "I never thought—"

"Von Brauchitsch," Smith said carelessly. "He had his orders direct from Berlin." He placed his glass on the mantelpiece, walked across and stood before the three spies. "Tell me, how did *I* know Jones was an impostor? Why did you *not* know he was one? And if I'm not what I claim to be then what in God's name am I doing here at all. Perhaps you would like to explain that?"

The three men glared up at him in baleful silence.

"Perhaps they would indeed," Kramer said heavily. He came and stood by Smith, staring down at the three men with an oddly expressionless gaze that was more disturbing than any show of anger could ever have been. After another and longer silence he said: "Captain Schmidt, this has gone far enough."

"Not yet."

"I require no more," Kramer persisted.

"I promised you proof—those were but the pointers. A proof to satisfy the Deputy Chief of the German Secret Service—and that proof is in three parts. A yes or no, Colonel Kramer, if you please. Do you or do you not know the name of our top man in Britain?" Kramer nodded. "Then suppose we ask them?"

The three men on the couch looked at each other, then at Smith. They looked in silence. Thomas licked dry lips, a movement that did not go unnoticed by Kramer. Smith produced a small red notebook from his tunic pocket, removed a rubber band, tore out the central page, then carefully replaced the band on the book and the book in his pocket. He wrote something on the page and handed it to Kramer, who glanced at it and nodded. Smith took the paper from him, walked across to the fire and burned it.

"Now then," Smith said. "You have here, in the Schloss Adler, the most powerful radio transmitter in Central Europe—"

"You are singularly well-informed, Captain Schmidt," Kramer said wryly.

"Smith. I live Smith. I breathe Smith. I *am* Smith. Put a radio-telephone call through to Field Marshal Kesselring's HQ in northern Italy. Ask for his Chief of Military Intelligence."

Kramer said softly: "The mutual friend you mentioned?"

"An old alumnus of Heidelberg University," Smith nodded. "Colonel Wilhelm Wilner." He smiled. "Willi-Willi."

"You know that? Then it will not be necessary to call him."

"Admiral Canaris would like you to."

"And you know my chief, too?" Kramer's voice was even softer.

"My self-esteem urges me to say that I do—but modesty and the truth compel me to admit I don't," Smith said disarmingly. "I just work for him."

"I'm convinced already, convinced beyond all doubt," Rosemeyer said. "But do as he says, Colonel."

Kramer did as he was told. He put a call through to the radio room, hung up and waited patiently. Smith lay back in his armchair, brandy in one hand, cigar in the other, the picture of relaxed confidence. If Schaffer and the three men on the couch beside him were either relaxed or confident they entirely failed to show it. Behind them Hartmann, their guard, watched his four charges hopefully, as if eager to show his expertise with a blackjack. If either Rosemeyer or Jones were thinking any thoughts at all, those thoughts didn't break through to the surface. Anne-Marie, not quite knowing what was going on, hovered around indecisively, a tentative smile of anticipation still on her face. She was the only person who moved during the period of waiting and that only because Smith crooked a finger at her and indicated his empty brandy glass: so complete was the ascendancy he had achieved that she obeyed the unspoken command without hesitation and brought back a very generous measure of brandy which she sat down by his side table to the accompaniment of a winning smile. Smith gave her a winning smile in return. But no one spoke, not once, during that seemingly interminable wait.

The phone bell rang.

Kramer lifted it and, after a few preliminary exchanges, presumably with operators, said: "Colonel Wilhelm Wilner. My dear friend, Willi-Willi. How are you?" After the introductory courtesies were over, Kramer said: "We have an agent here who claims to know you. A Captain John Smith. Have you ever—ah, so you know him? Good, good!" A pause, then he continued: "Could you describe him?"

He listened intently, looking at Smith as a voice crackled over the receiver. Suddenly he beckoned to Smith, who rose and crossed over to where Kramer was sitting.

"Your left hand," Kramer said to Smith, took it in his own, then spoke into the phone. "Yes, the tip of the little finger is missing . . . and the right forearm has what?" Smith bared his right forearm wthout being told. "Yes, yes, two parallel scars, three centimetres apart . . . What's that? . . . Tell him he's a traitor?"

"And tell him he's a renegade," Smith smiled.

"And you're a renegade," Kramer said on the phone. "Chambertin, you say. Ah! Thank you, thank you. Good-bye, my old friend." He replaced the receiver.

"We both prefer French wine," Smith said apologetically and by way of explanation.

"Our top double agent in the Mediterranean," Kramer said wonderingly. "And I'd never even heard of you."

"Maybe that's why he is what he is," Rosemeyer said drily.

"I've been lucky." Smith shrugged, then said briskly: "Well, then. My credentials?"

"Impeccable," Kramer said. "My God, they're impeccable."

"So," Smith said grimly. "Now for our friends' credentials. As you know, Christiansen, Thomas and Carraciola—the real Christiansen, Thomas and Carraciola—while working for—"

"What in God's name are you talking about?" Christiansen shouted. He was on his feet, his face suffused with uncontrollable anger. "The real Christiansen—" His eyes turned up as Hartmann's blackjack caught him behind the ear and he sagged to the floor.

"He was warned," Kramer said grimly. "You didn't hit him too hard, Sergeant?"

"A two-minute tap," Hartmann said reassuringly.

"Good. I think you may now proceed without interruption, my dear Schmidt."

"Smith," Smith corrected him. "As I was saying, our real agents while working for the British counter-espionage have not only been responsible for the deep infiltration of the German Secret Service into the British espionage network in France and the Low Countries but have also set up an excellent chain of spies in England—a most successful ring, as Admiral Canaris well knows."

"It's not my territory," Kramer said. "But that, of course, I know."

Smith said coldly: "To your feet, you impostors, and sit at the table there. Sergeant, lend a hand to that man on the floor there. He appears to be coming round."

Their faces baffled and uncomprehending, Carraciola and Thomas made their way towards the table and sat down, where they were shortly joined by a very shaky and sick-looking Christiansen. The sergeant remained by him just long enough to ensure that he didn't fall off his chair, then took three paces back and covered them all with his carbine again.

From the other side of the table Smith flung down in front of the three men the little notebooks that Anne-Marie had brought. Then he produced his own elastic-banded notebook from his pocket and laid it on the small table beside Kramer.

"If they are who they claim to be," Smith said quietly, "it would be reasonable, would it not, my dear Kramer, to expect them to be able to write the names and the addresses or contacts of our agents in England and of the British agents who have been supplanted on the Continent by our men." He

131

paused significantly. "And then compare their lists to the genuine one in my book there."

"It would indeed," Kramer said slowly. "Proof at one stroke. Masterly, my dear Captain Schmidt—Smith, I mean." He smiled, almost wanly. "I'm afraid I'm not myself tonight. But tell me, Captain." He touched the banded notebook by his side. "This list of agents—I mean, carrying it around on your person. Does this not contravene every rule we have?"

"Of course it does. Rules can only be broken by the man who made them. You think that even I would dare without his authority? Admiral Walter Canaris will be in his Berlin office now." Smith nodded towards the telephone.

"What do you take me for?" Kramer smiled and turned to the three men at the table. "Well, you heard."

"There's something terribly far wrong—" Carraciola began despairingly.

"There is indeed," Kramer interrupted bleakly.

"I don't *doubt* Smith's bona-fides." Carraciola was almost in anguish now. "Not any more. But there's been some ghastly mistake—"

"You are the ones who have made it," Smith said curtly.

"Write," Kramer commanded. "Sergeant Hartmann."

Sergeant Hartmann stepped forward, his leather-thonged blackjack at the ready. The three men bent their heads and wrote.

EIGHT

THE ARMOURY was almost deserted now. Some time previously, a couple of sergeants had entered, moved around among the coffee tables and taken at least a score of grumbling men away for unspecified duties. Mary did not have to guess at what those unspecified duties might be. She glanced secretly at her watch for what must have been the twentieth time, rubbed her forehead wearily, rose to her feet and smiled palely at von Brauchitsch.

"I'm so sorry, Captain. I must go. I really must go. A most dreadful headache."

"I *am* sorry, my dear Maria." A troubled contrition had replaced his habitual smile. "You should have told me earlier. You don't look at all well. A long journey from the Rhineland, then all this schnapps—"

"I'm afraid I'm not used to it," Mary said ruefully. "I'll be all right when I've lain down."

"Of course, of course. Come, my dear, let me escort you to your room."

"No, no!" Then, realising she had spoken with uncalled-for vehemence, she smiled again and touched his hand. "I'll be all right. Really I will."

"Captain von Brauchitsch knows what's best." The face was serious but friendly, the voice authoritative but with an underlying tone of humour, and Mary knew there was no answer to it. "I positively insist. Come along."

He tucked her arm protectively under his and led her from the armoury.

Arm in arm they walked along the passageway leading from the armoury-cum-*cafe-stube* towards the central block of the castle. The passageway, in contrast to the last time they had walked along there, was completely deserted and Mary commented on the fact.

"It's the witches on their broomsticks," von Brauchitsch laughed. "The commandant hasn't caught them yet, but give him another few years and you never know. All those poor souls you saw being hauled out of the armoury are now probably poking about the eaves or climbing up the flagpoles. You never know where spies get to nowadays."

"You seem to treat the possibility lightly enough," Mary said.

"I'm a Gestapo officer. I'm paid and trained to use my head, not an overheated imagination," he said curtly, then squeezed her arm and apologised. "Sorry, that tone of voice was aimed at someone else, not you." He halted abruptly, peered out a window into the courtyard and said: "Now that is strange."

"What's strange?"

"The helicopter there," von Brauchitsch said thoughtfully. "Army regulations state that High Command helicopters must be kept in instant readiness at all times. But that one has part of its engine cover dismantled and a tarpaulin stretched in position over it. Wouldn't call that instant readiness, would you?"

"I suppose helicopters need repairing from time to time the same as any other machine." Her throat was suddenly dry and she wished von Brauchitsch wouldn't hold her so closely, he was bound to notice her accelerating heartbeat. "What's so unusual about that?"

"What's so unusual is that there was no one working on that machine almost half an hour ago when we first passed by here," von Brauchitsch said. "Unheard of for a Reichsmarschal's personal pilot to walk away and leave a job half done."

"Would it be unheard of for him to take a piece of mechanism inside and repair it under cover?" Mary asked sweetly. "Or perhaps you haven't seen a thermometer tonight?"

"I'm getting as bad as the old commandant and his witch hunts," von Brauchitsch said sadly. He moved on, shaking his head. "You see before you a horrible example of the dangers of being too long in my business: the obvious answer is far too obvious for shrewd and cunning intellects like ours. I must remember that later on tonight."

"You're going to exercise this great mind again tonight?" Mary asked lightly.

"In there, as a matter of fact," von Brauchitsch nodded as they passed by an ornate door. "The gold drawing room." He glanced at his watch. "In twenty minutes! So soon! Your charming company, Fräulein."

"Thank you, kind sir. You—you have an appointment?" Her heart was back at its old tricks again.

"An evening of musical appreciation. Even the Gestapo has its finer side. We are going to listen to a nightingale sing." He quickened his pace. "Sorry. Fräulein, but I've just remembered I've one or two reports to prepare."

"I'm sorry if I've kept you from your work, Captain," she said demurely. How much does he know? she thought wildly. How much does he suspect? What action has he suddenly decided to take? The von Brauchitschs of this world didn't just suddenly remember anything for the excellent reason that they never forgot it in the first place. "It's been most kind of you."

"The pleasure was one-sided," von Brauchitsch protested gallantly. "Mine and mine alone." He stopped outside her bedroom door, took her hand in his and smiled. "Good night my dear Maria. You really are the most charming girl."

"Good night." She returned smile for smile. "And thank you."

"We really must get to know each other better," von Brauchitsch said in farewell. He opened her door, bowed, kissed her hand, gently closed the door behind her and rubbed his chin thoughtfully. "Very much better, my dear Maria," he said softly to himself. "Very much better indeed."

Carraciola, Thomas and Christiansen bent over their notebooks and scribbled furiously. At least the first two did: Christiansen had not yet recovered from the blow on the head and was making heavy weather of his writing. Kramer, who was standing apart with Smith and talking to him in low tones, looked at them in curiosity and with just a trace of uneasiness.

"They seem to be finding plenty of inspiration from somewhere," he said carefully.

"The spectacle of an open grave is often thought provoking," Smith said cynically.

"I am afraid I don't quite follow?"

135

"Do you know what those men will be fifteen minutes from now?"

"I'm tired," Kramer said. He sounded it. "Please don't play with words, Captain Schmidt."

"Smith. In fifteen minutes they'll be dead. And they know it. They're fighting desperately for extra minutes to live: when you have as little time left as they have, even a minute is a prize snatched from eternity. Or the last despairing fling of the ruined gambler. Call it what you like."

"You wax lyrical, Captain," Kramer grumbled. He paced up and down for almost a minute, no longer troubling to watch the men at the table then stopped and planted himself squarely in front of Smith. "All right," he said wearily. "I've been on the spit long enough. I confess I'm baffled. Out with it. What in God's name is behind all this?"

"The simplicity of true genius, my dear Kramer. Admiral Rolland, the head of M.I.6. And he *is* a genius, make no mistake."

"So he's a genius," Kramer said impatiently. "Well?"

"Carraciola, Thomas and Christiansen were caught three weeks ago. Now, as you are aware, they were concerned only with northwest Europe and were not known here."

"By reputation, they were."

"Yes, yes. But only that. Admiral Rolland reckoned that if three fully briefed men impersonated our three captured men and were despatched here for a perfectly plausible reason, they would be persona grata of some note, honoured guests and completely accepted by you. And, of course, once they were accepted by you, they could operate inside the Schloss Adler with complete security and safety."

"And?"

"Well, don't you see?" It was Smith's turn to be impatient. "Rolland knew that if General Carnaby"—he broke off and scowled across the room at Carnaby-Jones—"or that impostor masquerading as General Carnaby were taken here, his opposite number in the German Army would be sent to interrogate him." Smith smiled. "Even in Britain they are aware that the prophet must go to the mountain, not the mountain to the prophet: the Army calls upon the Gestapo, not vice versa."

"Go on, go on!"

"The Wehrmacht Chief of Staff, Reichsmarschal Julius Rosemeyer, would have been just as priceless to the Allies as General Carnaby to us."

"The Reichsmarschal!" Kramer spoke in a shocked whisper, his eyes straying across the room to Rosemeyer. "Kidnap!"

"Your precious trusted agents there," Smith said savagely. "And they would have got away with it."

"My God! God in heaven! It's—it's diabolical!"

"Isn't it?" Smith said. "Isn't it just?"

Kramer left him abruptly, crossed the room to Rosemeyer and sat down in the chair beside him. For perhaps two minutes they talked together in low tones, occasionally glancing in Smith's direction. Kramer it was, Smith could see, who did most of the talking, Rosemeyer who did all of the reacting. Kramer, Smith reflected, must be putting it across rather well; a printed diagram could have been no clearer than the successive expressions of curiosity, puzzlement, astonishment and, finally, shocked realisation that reflected on Rosemeyer's face. After some seconds' silence, both men rose to their feet and walked across to where Smith stood. The Reichsmarschal, Smith saw, was a little paler than normal, and when he spoke it required neither a sensitive ear nor imagination to detect a slight tremor in his voice.

He said: "This is an incredible story, Captain Smith, incredible. But inevitable. It must be. The only explanation that can cover all the facts, put all the pieces of the jigsaw together." He attempted a smile. "To change the metaphor, I must say that it comes as a considerable shock to find that one is the missing key in a baffling code. I am eternally in your debt, Captain Smith."

"Germany is eternally in your debt," Kramer said. "You have done her a great service. We shall not forget this. I am sure the Führer himself will personally wish to honour you with some mark of his esteem."

"You are too kind, gentlemen," Smith murmured. "To do my duty is reward enough." He smiled faintly. "Perhaps our Führer will give me two or three weeks' leave—the way I feel tonight my nerves aren't what they were. But if you gentlemen will excuse me—my present task is not yet completed."

He moved away and walked slowly up and down, brandy glass in hand, behind the three men bent over the table. From time to time he glanced at one of the notebooks and smiled in weary cynicism, neither the smile nor the significance of the smile going unremarked by anyone in the room except the three writing men. He stopped behind Thomas, shook his head in disbelief and said: "My God!"

"Let's finish it now!" Rosemeyer demanded impatiently.

"If you please, Reichsmarschal, let us play this charade out to the bitter end."

"You have your reasons?"

"I most certainly have."

Briskly, but not hurriedly, von Brauchitsch walked away from Mary's room, his footfalls echoing crisply on the stone-flagged corridor. Once round the corner of the corridor he broke into a run.

He reached the courtyard and ran across to the helicopter. There was no one there. Quickly he ran up a few steps and peered through the Perspex cupola of the cockpit. He reached ground again and hailed the nearest guard, who came stumbling across, a leashed Doberman trailing behind him.

"Quickly," von Brauchitsch snapped. "Have you seen the pilot?"

"No, *Herr Kapitan*," the guard answered nervously. He was an elderly man, long past front-line service and held the Gestapo in great fear. "Not for a long time."

"What do you mean by a long time?" von Brauchitsch demanded.

"I don't know. That's to say," the guard added hastily, "half an hour. More. Three-quarters, I would say, *Herr Kapitan*."

"Damnation," von Brauchitsch swore. "So long. Tell me, when the pilot is carrying out repairs is there a place near here he uses as a workshop?"

"Yes, sir." The guard was eager to oblige with some positive information. "That door there, sir. The old grain store."

"Is he in there now?"

"I don't know, *Herr Kapitan*."

"You should know," von Brauchitsch said coldly. "It's your job to keep your eyes open. Well, just don't stand there, oaf! Go and find out."

The elderly guard trotted away while von Brauchitsch, shaking his head angrily over his impatience with the old soldier, crossed the courtyard and questioned the guards at the gate, three tough, competent, young storm troopers who, unlike the patrol guard, could be guaranteed not to miss anything. He received the same negative answer there.

He strode back towards the helicopter and intercepted the elderly guard running from the old grain store.

"There's nobody there, *Herr Kapitan.*" He was slightly out of breath and highly apprehensive at being the bearer of what might be ill news. "It's empty."

"It would be," von Brauchitsch nodded. He patted the old shoulder and smiled. "No fault of yours, my friend. You keep a good watch."

Unhurriedly, almost, now, he made for the main entrance door, pulling out a set of master keys as he went. He struck oil with the first door he opened. The pilot lay there, still unconscious, the smashed distributor cap beside him, the pair of overalls on top of him a mute but entirely sufficient explanation of the way in which the distributor cap had been removed without detection. Von Brauchitsch took a flashlight from a long rack on the wall, cut the pilot's bonds, freed his gag and left him lying there with the door wide open. The passage outside was a heavily travelled one, and someone was bound to be along soon.

Von Brauchitsch ran up the stairs to the passage leading to the bedrooms, slowed down, walked easily, casually past Mary's bedroom and stopped at the fifth door beyond that. He used his master keys and passed inside, switching on the light as he went in. He crossed the room, lifted the lower sash window and nodded when he saw that nearly all the snow on the sill had been brushed or rubbed away. He leaned farther out, switched on his flashlight and flashed the beam downwards. The roof of the header station was fifty feet directly below and the markings and footprints in the snow told their own unmistakable story.

Von Brauchitsch straightened, looked at the odd position of the iron bedstead against the wardrobe door and tugged the bed away. He watched the wardrobe door burst open and the bound and gagged figure inside roll to the floor without as much as hoisting an eyebrow. This had been entirely predictable. From the depth of the bound man's groans it was obvious that he was coming round. Von Brauchitsch cut him free, removed his gag and left. There were more urgent matters demanding his attention than holding the hands of young *Oberleutnants* as they held their heads and groaned their way back to consciousness.

He stopped outside Mary's room, put his ear to the door and listened. No sound. He put his eye to the keyhole and

139

peered. No light. He knocked. No reply. He used his master keys and passed inside. No Mary.

"Well, well, well," von Brauchitsch murmured. "Very interesting indeed."

"Finished?" Smith asked.

Thomas nodded. Christiansen and Carraciola glowered. But all three were sitting back and it was obvious that all three were, in fact, finished. Smith walked along behind them, reaching over their shoulders for the notebooks. He took them across the room and laid them on the little table by Kramer's chair.

"The moment of truth," Smith said quietly. "One book should be enough."

Kramer, reluctantly almost picked up the top book and began to read. Slowly he began to leaf his way through the pages. Smith drained his glass and sauntered unconcernedly across the room to the decanter on the sideboard. He poured some brandy, carefully recapped the bottle, walked a few aimless steps and halted. He was within two feet of the guard with the carbine.

He sipped his brandy and said to Kramer: "Enough?"

Kramer nodded.

"Then compare it with my original."

Kramer nodded. "As you say, the moment of truth."

He picked up the notebook, slid off the rubber band and opened the cover. The first page was blank. So was the next. And the next . . . Frowning, baffled, Kramer lifted his eyes to look across the room to Smith.

Smith's brandy glass was falling to the ground as Smith himself, with a whiplash violent movement of his body brought the side of his right hand chopping down on the guard's neck. The guard toppled as if a bridge had fallen on him. Glasses on the sideboard tinkled in the vibration of his fall.

Kramer's moment of utter incomprehension vanished. The bitter chagrin of total understanding flooded his face. His hand stretched out towards the alarm button.

"Uh-uh! Not the buzzer, Mac!" The blow that had struck down the guard had held no more whiplash than the biting urgency in Schaffer's voice. He was stretched his length on the floor where he'd dived to retrieve the Schmeisser now trained, rock steady, on Kramer's heart. For the second time that night, Kramer's hand withdrew from the alarm button.

Smith picked up the guard's carbine, walked across the room and changed it for his silenced Luger. Schaffer, his gun still trained on Kramer, picked himself up from the floor and glared at Smith.

"A second-rate punk," he said indignantly. "A simple-minded American. That's what you said. Don't know what goddamned day of week it is, do I?"

"All I could think of on the spur of the moment," Smith said apologetically.

"That makes it even worse," Schaffer complained. "And did you have to clobber me so goddamned realistically?"

"Local colour. What are you complaining about? It worked." He walked across to Kramer's table, picked up the three notebooks and buttoned them securely inside his tunic. He said to Schaffer: "Between them, they shouldn't have missed anything . . . Well, time to be gone. Ready, Mr. Jones?"

"And hurry about it," Schaffer added. "We have a streetcar to catch. Well, anyhow, a cable car."

"It's a chicken farm in the boondocks for me." Jones looked completely dazed and he sounded exactly the same way. "Acting? My God, I don't know anything about it."

"This is all you want?" Kramer was completely under control again, calm, quiet, the total professional. "Those books? Just those books?"

"Well, just about. Lots of nice names and addresses. A bedtime story for M.I.6."

"I see." Kramer nodded his understanding. "Then those men are, of course, what they claim to be?"

"They've been under suspicion for weeks. Classified information of an invaluable nature was going out and false—and totally valueless—information was coming in. It took two months' work to pinpoint the leakages and channels of false information to one or more of the departments controlled by those men. But we knew we could never prove it on them—we weren't even sure if there was more than one traitor and had no idea who that one might be—and, in any event, proving it without finding out their contacts at home and abroad would have been useless. So we—um—thought this one up."

"You mean, *you* thought it up, Captain Smith," Rosemeyer said.

"What does it matter?" Smith said indifferently.

"True. It doesn't. But something else does." Rosemeyer smiled faintly. "When Colonel Kramer asked you if the books were all you wanted, you said 'just about.' Indicating that there was possibly something else. It is your hope to kill two birds with one stone, to invite me to accompany you?"

"If you can believe that, Reichsmarschal Rosemeyer," Smith said unkindly, "it's time you handed your baton over to someone else. I have no intention of binding you hand and foot and carrying you over the Alps on my shoulder. The only way I could take you is at the point of a gun and I very much fear that you are a man of honour, a man to whom the safety of his skin comes a very long way behind his loyalty to his country. If I pointed this gun at you and said to get up and come with us or be gunned down, nobody in this room doubts that you'd just keep on sitting. So we must part."

"You are as complimentary as you are logical." Rosemeyer smiled, a little, bitter, smile. "I wish the logic had struck me as forcibly when we were discussing this very subject a few minutes ago."

"It is perhaps as well it didn't," Smith admitted.

"But—but Colonel Wilner?" Kramer said. "Field Marshal Kesselring's Chief of Intelligence. Surely he's not—"

"Rest easy. Willi-Willi is not on our payroll. What he said he believed to be perfectly true. He believes me to be the top double agent in Italy. I've been feeding him useless, false and out-of-date information for almost two years. Tell him so, will you?"

"Kind of treble agent, see?" Schaffer said in a patient explaining tone. "That's one better than double."

"Heidelberg?" Kramer asked.

"Two years at the university. Courtesy of the—um—Foreign Office."

Kramer shook his head. "I still don't understand—"

"Sorry. We're going."

"In fact, we're off," Schaffer said. "Read all about it in the postwar memoirs of Pimpernel Schaffer—"

He broke off as the door opened wide. Mary stood framed in the doorway and the Mauser was very steady in her hand. She let it fall to her side with a sigh of relief.

"Took your time about getting here, didn't you?" Smith said severely. "We were beginning to get a little worried about you."

"I'm sorry. I just couldn't get away. Von Brauchitsch—"

"No odds, young lady." Schaffer made a grandiose gesture with his right arm. "Schaffer was here."

"The new girl who arrived tonight!" Kramer whispered.

He looked slightly dazed. "The cousin of that girl from the—"

"None else," Smith said. "She's the one who has been helping me to keep Willi-Willi happy for a long time past. *And* she's the one who opened the door for us tonight."

"Boss," Schaffer said unhappily. "Far be it from me to rush you—"

"Coming now." Smith smiled at Rosemeyer. "You were right, the books weren't all I wanted. You were right, I did want company. But unlike you, Reichsmarschal, those I want have a high regard for their own skins and are entirely without honour. And so they will come." His gun waved in the direction of Carraciola, Thomas and Christiansen. "On your feet, you three. You're coming with us."

"Coming with us?" Schaffer said incredulously. "To England?"

"To stand trial for treason. It's no part of my duties to act as public executioner . . . God alone knows how many hundreds and thousands of lives they've cost already. Not to mention Torrance-Smythe and Sergeant Harrod." He looked at Carraciola, and his eyes were very cold. "I'll never know, but I think you were the brains. It was you who killed Harrod back up there on the mountain. If you could have got that radio codebook you could have cracked our network in south Germany. That would have been something, our network here has never been penetrated. The radio codebook was a trap that didn't spring . . . And you got old Smithy. You left the pub a couple of minutes after I did tonight and he followed you. But he couldn't cope with a man—"

"Drop those guns." Von Brauchitsch's voice was quiet and cold and compelling. No one had heard or seen the stealthy opening of the door. He stood just inside, about four feet from Mary and he had a small-calibre automatic in his right hand. Smith whirled round, his Luger lining up on the doorway, hesitated a fatal fraction of a second because Mary was almost directly in line with von Brauchitsch. Von Brauchitsch, his earlier gallantry of the evening abruptly yielding to a coldly professional assessment of the situation, had no such inhibitions. There was a sharp flat crack, the bullet passed through Mary's sleeve just above the elbow and Smith exclaimed in pain as he clutched his bleeding hand and heard his flying Luger strike against some unidentified furniture. Mary tried to turn around but von Brauchitsch was too quick and too strong. He jumped forward, hooked his arm round her and caught the wrist with the gun and thrust his own over

143

her shoulder. She tried to struggle free. Von Brauchitsch squeezed his wrist, she cried out in pain, her hand opened and her gun fell to the floor. Von Brauchitsch seemed to notice none of this, his unwinking right eye, the only vulnerable part of him that could be seen behind Mary's gun was levelled along the barrel of his automatic.

Schaffer dropped his gun.

"You shouldn't have tried it," von Brauchitsch said to Smith. "An extremely silly thing to do . . . In your circumstances, I'd have done exactly the same silly thing." He looked at Kramer. "Sorry for the delay, Herr Colonel. But I *thought* the young lady was very anxious and restive. *And* she knows precious little about her native Düsseldorf. *And* she doesn't know enough not to let people hold her hand when she's telling lies—as she does most of the time." He released the girl and half-turned her round, smiling down at her. "A delightful hand, my dear—but what a fascinating variation of pulse rates."

"I don't know what you're talking about and I don't care." Kramer gave vent to a long luxurious sigh and drooped with relief. "Well *done*, my boy, well done. My God! Another minute—" He heaved himself to his feet, crossed over to Schaffer, prudently keeping clear of von Brauchitsch's line of fire, searched him for hidden weapons, found none, did the same to Smith with the same results, handed him a white handkerchief to stem the flow of blood, looked at Mary and hesitated. "Well, I don't see how she very well can be, but . . . I wonder. Anne-Marie?"

"Certainly, Herr Colonel. It will be a pleasure. We've met before and she knows my methods. Don't you, my dear?" With a smile as nearly wolflike as any beautiful Aryan could give, Anne-Marie walked across to Mary and struck her viciously across the face. Mary cried in pain, staggered back against the wall and crouched there, eyes too wide in a pale face, palms pressed behind her for support from the wall, a trickle of blood coming from the corner of her mouth. "Well?" Anne-Marie demanded. "Have you a gun?"

"Anne-Marie!" There was protest and aversion in Kramer's face. "Must you—"

"I know how to deal with cheap little spies like her!" She turned to Mary and said: "I'm afraid they don't like watching how I get results. In there!"

She caught Mary by the hair, pulled her to the side door, opened it and pushed her violently inside. The sound of her

body crashing to the floor and another gasp of pain came together. Anne-Marie closed the door behind them.

For the next ten seconds or so there could be clearly heard
the sound of blows and muffled cries of pain. Von Brauchitsch waved Smith and Schaffer back with his gun, advanced,
hitched a seat on the edge of one of the big armchairs,
winced as he listened to the sound of the struggle and said to
Kramer drily: "I somehow think the young lady would have
preferred me to search her. There's a limit to the value of
false modesty."

"I'm afraid Anne-Marie sometimes lets her enthusiasm
carry her away," Kramer conceded. His mouth was wrinkled
in distaste.

"Sometimes?" Von Brauchitsch winced again as more
sounds filtered through the door, the crash of a body against
a wall, a shriek of pain, low sobbing moans, then silence.
"Always. When the other girl is as young and beautiful as
herself."

"It's over now." Kramer sighed. "It's all over now." He
looked at Smith and Schaffer. "We'll fix that hand first, then
—well, one thing about the Schloss Adler, there is no shortage of dungeons." He broke off, the fractional widening of
his eyes matching a similar slumping of his shoulders, and he
said carefully to von Brauchitsch: "You are far too good a
man to lose, Captain. It would seem that we were wasting
our sympathy on the wrong person. There's a gun four feet
from you pointing at the middle of your back."

Von Brauchitsch, his gun hand resting helplessly on his
thigh, turned slowly round and looked over his shoulder.
There was indeed a gun pointing at the middle of his back, a
Lilliput .21 automatic, and the hand that held it was discon-
certingly steady, the dark eyes cool and very watchful. Apart
from the small trickle of blood from her cut lip and rather
dishevelled hair, Mary looked singularly little the worse for
wear.

"It's every parent's duty," Schaffer said pontifically, "to
encourage his daughter to take up judo." He took the gun
from Von Brauchitsch's unresisting hand, retrieved his own
Schmeisser, walked across to the main door and locked it.
"Far too many folk coming in here without knocking." On
his way back he looked through the opened door of the side
room, whistled, grinned and said to Mary: "It's a good thing
I have my thoughts set on someone else. I wouldn't like to be
married to you if you lost your temper. That's regular sick-

bay dispensary in there. Fix the major's hand as best you can. I'll watch them." He hoisted his Schmeisser and smiled almost blissfully: "Oh, brother, how I'll watch them."

And he watched them. While Mary attended to Smith's injured hand in the small room where Anne-Marie had so lately met her Waterloo, Schaffer herded his six charges into one of the massive couches, took up position by the mantelpiece, poured himself some brandy, sipped it delicately and gave the prisoners an encouraging smile from time to time. There were no answering smiles, for all Schaffer's nonchalance and lighthearted banter there was about him not only a coldly discouraging competence with the weapon in his hand but also the unmistakable air of one who would when the need arose and without a second's hesitation, squeeze the trigger and keep on squeezing it. Being at the wrong end of a Schmeisser machine pistol does not make for an easy cordiality in relationships.

Smith and Mary emerged from the side room, the latter carrying a cloth-covered tray. Smith was pale and had his right hand heavily bandaged. Schaffer looked at the hand then lifted an enquiring eyebrow to Mary.

"Not so good." She looked a little pale herself. "Forefinger and thumb are both smashed. I've patched it as best I can but I'm afraid it's a job for a surgeon."

"If I can survive Mary's first aid," Smith said philosophically, "I can survive anything. We have a more immediate little problem here." He tapped his tunic. "Those names and addresses here. Might be an hour or two before we get them through to England and then another hour or two before those men can be rounded up." He looked at the men seated on the couch. "*You* could get through to them in a lot less than that and warn them. So we have to ensure your silence for a few hours."

"We could ensure it forever, boss," Schaffer said carelessly.

"That won't be necessary. As you said yourself, it's a regular little dispensary in there." He removed the tray cloth to show bottles and hypodermic syringes. He held up a bottle in his left hand. "Nembutal. You'll hardly feel the prick."

Kramer stared at him. "Nembutal? I'll be damned if I do."

Smith said in a tone of utter conviction: "You'll be dead if you don't."

NINE

SMITH HALTED outside the door marked RADIO RAUM, held up his hand for silence, looked at the three scowling captives and said: "Don't even *think* of tipping anyone off or raising the alarm. I'm not all that keen on taking you back to England. Lieutenant Schaffer, I think we might immobilise those men a bit more."

"We might at that," Schaffer agreed. He went behind each of the three men in turn, ripped open the top buttons on their tunics and pulled the tunics down their backs until their sleeves reached their elbows and said in the same soft voice: "That'll keep their hands out of trouble for a little."

"But not their feet. Don't let them come anywhere near you," Smith said to Mary. "They've nothing to lose. Right, Lieutenant, when you're ready."

"Ready now." Carefully, silently, Schaffer eased open the door of the radio room. It was a large, well-lit, but very bleak room, the two main items of furniture being a massive table by the window on the far wall and, on the table, an almost equally massive transceiver in gleaming metal: apart from two chairs and a filing cabinet the room held nothing else, not even as much as a carpet to cover the floorboards.

Perhaps it was the lack of a carpet that betrayed them. For the first half of Schaffer's stealthy advance across the room the operator, his back to them, sat smoking a cigarette in idle unconcern, listening to soft Austrian *Schrammel* music coming in over his big machine: suddenly, alerted either by the faintest whisper of sound from a creaking floorboard or just by some sixth sense, he whirled round and jumped to his feet. And he thought as quickly as he moved. Even as he raised

147

his arms high in apparently eager surrender, he appeared to move slightly to his right, shifting the position of his right foot. There came the sudden strident clamour of an alarm bell ringing in the passage outside. Schaffer leapt forward, his Schmeisser swinging, and the operator staggered back against his transceiver, then slid unconscious to the floor. But Schaffer was too late. The bell rang and kept on ringing.

"That's all I need!" Smith swore bitterly. "That's all I bloody well need." He ran through the radio-room door out into the passage, located the glass-cased alarm bell some feet away and struck it viciously with the butt of his Schmeisser. The shattered glass tinkled to the floor and the clangour abruptly ceased.

"Inside!" Smith gestured to the open doorway of the radio room. "All of you. Quickly." He ushered them all inside, looked around, saw a side door leading off to the right and said to Mary: "Quickly. What's in there? Schaffer?"

"Horatio hold the bridge," Schaffer murmured. He moved across and took up position at the radio-room door. "We could have done without this, boss."

"We could without a lot of things in this world," Smith said wearily. He glanced at Mary. "Well?"

"Storage rooms for radio spares, looks like."

"You and Jones take those three in there. If they breathe, kill them."

Jones looked down at the gun held gingerly in his hand and said: "I am not a serviceman, sir."

"I have news for you," Smith said. "Neither am I."

He crossed hurriedly to the transceiver, sat down and studied the confusing array of dials, knobs and switches. For fully twenty seconds he sat there, just looking.

Schaffer said from the doorway: "Know how to work it, boss?"

"A fine time to ask me," Smith said. "We'll soon find out, won't we?" He switched the machine to "Send," selected the ultra short-wave band and lined up his transmitting frequency. He opened another switch and picked up a microphone.

"Broadsword calling Danny Boy," he said. "Broadsword calling Danny Boy. Can you hear me? Can you hear me?"

Nobody heard him or gave indication of hearing him. Smith altered the transmitting frequency fractionally and tried again. And again. And again. After the sixth or seventh repetition, Smith started as a crash of machine-pistol fire came from the doorway. He twisted round. Schaffer was stretched full length on the floor, smoke wisping from the barrel of his Schmeisser.

"We got callers, boss," Schaffer said apologetically. "Don't think I got any but I sure as hell started their adrenalin moving around."

"Broadsword calling Danny Boy," Smith said urgently, insistently. "Broadsword calling Danny Boy. For God's sake, why don't they answer?"

"They can't come round the corner of the passage without being sawn in half." Schaffer spoke comfortably from his uncomfortable horizontal position on the floor. "I can hold them off to Christmas. So what's the hurry?"

"Broadsword calling Danny Boy. Broadsword calling Danny Boy. How long do you think it's going to be before someone cuts the electricity?"

"For God's sake, Danny Boy," Schaffer implored. "Why don't you answer? Why don't you answer?"

"Danny Boy calling Broadsword." The voice on the radio was calm and loud and clear, so free from interference that it might have come from next door. "Danny Boy—"

"One hour, Danny Boy," Smith interrupted. "One hour. Understood? Over."

"Understood. You have it, Broadsword?" The voice was unmistakably that of Admiral Rolland. "Over."

"I have it," Smith said. "I have it all."

"All sins are forgiven. Mother Machree coming to meet you. Leaving now."

There came another staccato crash of sound as Schaffer loosed off another burst from his Schmeisser. Admiral Rolland's voice on the radio said: "What was that?"

"Static," Smith said. He didn't bother to switch off. He rose, took three paces back and fired a two-second burst from his machine pistol, his face twisting in pain as the recoil slammed into his shattered hand. No one would ever use that particular radio again. He glanced briefly at Schaffer, but only briefly: the American's face, though thoughtful, was calm and unworried: there were those who might require helpful words, encouragement and reassurance, but Schaffer was not one of them. Smith moved swiftly across to the window and lifted the lower sash with his left hand.

The moon was almost obscured behind some darkly drifting cloud. A thin weak light filtered down into the half-seen obscurity of the valley below. Once again the snow was beginning to fall, gently. The air was taut, brittle, in the intensity of its coldness, an Arctic chill that bit to the bone. The icy wind that gusted through the room could have come off the polar icecap.

They were on the east side of the castle, Smith realised, the side remote from the cable-car header station. The base of the volcanic plug was shrouded in a gloom so deep that it was impossible to be sure whether or not the guards and Dobermans were patrolling down there: and, for the purposes of present survival, it didn't really matter. Smith withdrew from the window, pulled the nylon from the kit bag, tied one end securely to the metal leg of the radio table, threw the remainder of the rope out into the night then, with his left hand, thoroughly scuffed and rubbed away the frozen encrusted snow on both the windowsill and for two or three feet beneath it: it would, he thought, have to be a hypercritical eye that didn't immediately register the impression that there had been fairly heavy and recent traffic over the sill. He wondered, vaguely, whether the rope reached as far as the ground and dismissed the thought as soon as it had occurred to him: again, it didn't really matter.

He crossed the room to where Schaffer lay spread-eagled in the doorway. The key was in the lock on the inside of the door and the lock, he observed with satisfaction, was on the same massive scale as everything else in the Schloss Adler. He said to Schaffer: "Time to close the door."

"Let's wait till they show face again then discourage them some more," Schaffer suggested. "It's been a couple of minutes since the last guy peeked his head round the corner there. Another peek, another salvo from Schaffer and it might give us another couple of minutes' grace—enough time to make it feasible for us to have shinnied down that little old rope there and made our getaway."

"I should have thought of that." An icy snow-laden gust of wind blew across the room, from open window through open door, and Smith shivered. "My God, it's bitter!"

"Loss of blood," Schaffer said briefly, then added, unsympathetically: "And all that brandy you guzzled back there. When it comes to opening pores—"

He broke off and lay very still, lowering his head a fraction to sight along the barrel of his Schmeisser. He said softly: "Give me your flashlight, boss."

"What is it?" Smith whispered. He handed Schaffer the flash.

"Discretion," Schaffer murmured. He switched on the flash and placed it on the floor, pushing it as far away from himself as he could. "I reckon if I were in their place I'd be discreet, too. There's a stick poking round the corner of the passage and the stick has a mirror tied to it. Only, they haven't got it angled right."

Smith peered cautiously round the doorjamb, just in time to see stick and suspended mirror being withdrawn from sight, presumably to make adjustments. A few seconds later and the stick appeared again, this time with the mirror angled at more or less forty-five degrees. Mirror and stick disintegrated under the flatly staccato hammering of Schaffer's machine pistol. Schaffer stood up, took careful aim at the single overhead light illuminating the passage and fired one shot. Now the sole light in the passage came from the flashlight on the floor, the light from which would not only effectively conceal from the Germans at the far end of the passage what was going on at the radio-room door but, indeed, make it very difficult to decide whether or not the door itself was open or shut.

Smith and Schaffer moved back into the radio room, soundlessly closed the door behind them and as soundlessly turned the key in the lock. Schaffer used the leverage of his Schmeisser to bend the key so that it remained firmly jammed in the wards of the lock.

They waited. At least two minutes passed, then they heard the sound of excited voices at the far end of the passage followed almost at once by the sound of heavy boots pounding down the passage. They moved away from the door, passed inside the radio spares room, leaving just a sufficient crack in the doorway to allow a faint backwash of light to filter through. Smith said softly: "Mary, you and Mr. Jones for Thomas there. A gun in each temple." He took Christiansen for himself, forced him to kneel and ground his gun into the back of his neck. Schaffer backed Carraciola against a wall, the muzzle of his Schmeisser pressed hard against his teeth. At the other end of the machine pistol Schaffer smiled pleasantly, his teeth a pale gleam in the near darkness. The stillness inside the little room was complete.

The half-dozen Germans outside the radio-room door bore no resemblance to the elderly guard von Brauchitsch had interrogated in the courtyard. They were elite soldiers of the Alpenkorps, ruthless men who had been ruthlessly trained.

No one made any move to approach the door handle or lock: the machinelike efficiency with which they broached that door without risk to themselves was clearly the result of a well-drilled procedure for handling situations of precisely this nature.

At a gesture from the *Oberleutnant* in charge, a soldier stepped forward and with two diagonal sweeps emptied the magazine of his machine pistol through the door. A second used his machine pistol to stitch a neat circle in the wood, reversed his gun and knocked in the wooden circle with the butt. A third armed two grenades and lobbed them accurately through the hole provided while a fourth shot away the lock. The soldiers pressed back on each side of the door. The two flat cracks of the exploding grenades came almost simultaneously and smoke came pouring through the circular hole in the door.

The door was kicked open and the men rushed inside. There was no longer any need to take precautions—any men who had been in the same confined space as those two exploding grenades would be dead men now. For a moment there was confusion and hesitation until the blue acrid smoke was partially cleared away by the powerful cross-draught; then the *Oberleutnant*, locating the source of this draught with the aid of a small hand flashlight, ran across to the open window, checked at the sight of the rope disappearing over the sill, leaned out the window, rubbed his now-streaming eyes and peered downwards along the beam of his light. The beam reached perhaps halfway down the side of the volcanic plug. There was nothing to be seen. He caught the rope in his free hand and jerked it savagely: it was as nearly weightless as made no difference. For a moment he focussed his light on the disturbed snow on the window ledge then swung back into the room.

"Gott in Himmel!" he shouted. "They've got away. They're down already! Quickly, the nearest phone!"

"Well, now." Schaffer listened to the fading sound of running footsteps, removed the muzzle of his Schmeisser from Carraciola's teeth and smiled approvingly. "That was a good boy." Gun in Carraciola's back, he followed Smith out into the wrecked radio room and said thoughtfully: "It isn't going to take them too long to find out there are no footprints in the snow down there."

"It's going to take them even less time to discover that this rope is gone." Swiftly, ignoring the stabbing pain in his right hand, Smith hauled the nylon in through the window. "We're going to need it. *And* we're going to need some distractions."

"I'm distracted enough as it is," Schaffer said.

"Take four or five plastic explosives, each with different fuse length settings. Chuck them into rooms along the corridor there."

"Distractions coming up." Schaffer extracted some plastic explosives from the kit bag, cut the slow-burning RDX fuses off to varying lengths, crimped on the chemical igniters, said, "Consider it already done," and left.

The first three rooms he came to were locked and he wasted neither time nor the precious ammunition of his silenced Luger in trying to open them. But each of the next five rooms was unlocked. In the first three, all bedrooms, he placed charges in a Dresden fruit bowl, under an officer's cap and under a pillow: in the fourth room, a bathroom, he placed it behind a W.C. and in the fifth, a store room, high up on a shelf beside some highly inflammable cardboard cartons.

Smith, meanwhile, had ushered the others from the still smoke-filled, eye-watering, throat-irritating atmosphere of the radio room into the comparatively purer air of the passageway beyond, and was waiting the return of Schaffer when his face became suddenly thoughtful at the sight of some fire-fighting gear—a big CO_2 extinguisher, buckets of sand and a fireman's axe—on a low platform by the passage wall.

"You *are* slipping, Major Smith." Mary's eyes were red-rimmed and her tear-streaked face white as paper, but she could smile at him. "Distractions, you said. I've had the same thought myself, and I'm only me."

Smith gave her a half-smile, the way his hand hurt he felt he couldn't afford the other half, and tried the handle of a door beside the low platform, a door lettered AKTEN RAUM —Records Office. Such a door, inevitably, was locked. He took the Luger in his left hand, placed it against the lock, squeezed the trigger and went inside.

It certainly looked like a Records Office. The room was heavily shelved and piled ceiling-high with files and papers. Smith crossed to the window, opened it wide to increase the draught, then scattered large piles of paper on the floor and put a match to them. The paper flared up at once, the flames feet-high within seconds.

"Kinda forgot this, didn't you?" Schaffer had returned and was bearing with him the large CO_2 cylinder. He crossed to

153

the window. "Gardyloo or mind your heads or whatever the saying is."

The cylinder disappeared through the open window. The room was aleady so furiously ablaze that Schaffer had difficulty in finding his way back to the door again. As he stumbled out, his clothes and hair singed and face smoke-blackened, a deep-toned bell far down in the depths of the Schloss Adler began to ring with a strident urgency. "For God's sake, what next?" Schaffer said in despair. "The fire brigade?"

"Just about," Smith said bitterly. "Damn it, damn it, why couldn't I have checked first? Now they know where we are."

"A heat-sensing device linked to an indicator?"

"What else. Come on."

They ran along the central passageway, driving the prisoners in front of them, dropped down a central flight of stairs and were making for the next when they heard the shouting of voices and the clattering of feet on treads as soldiers came running up from the castle courtyard.

"Quickly! In behind there!" Smith pointed to a curtained alcove. "Hurry up! Oh, God—I've forgotten something!" He turned and ran back the way he had come.

"Where the hell has he—" Schaffer broke off as he realised the approaching men were almost upon them, whirled and jabbed the nearest prisoner painfully with the muzzle of his Schmeisser. "In that alcove. Fast." In the dim light behind the curtains he changed his machine pistol for the silenced Luger. "Don't even think of touching those curtains. With the racket that bell's making, they won't even hear you die."

Nobody touched the curtains. Jackbooted men, gasping heavily for breath, passed by within feet of them. They clattered furiously up the next flight of stairs, the one Smith and the others had just descended, and then the footsteps stopped abruptly. From the next shouted words it was obvious that they had just caught sight of the fire and had abruptly and for the first time realised the magnitude of the task they had to cope with.

"Emergency! Sergeant, get on that phone!" It was the voice of the *Oberleutnant* who had led the break-in to the radio room. "Fire detail at the double! Hoses, more CO_2 cylinders. Where in God's name is Colonel Kramer? Corporal! Find Colonel Kramer at once."

The corporal didn't answer, the sound of jutting heels striking on the treads as he raced down the stairs was answer enough. He ran by the alcove and ran down the next flight of stairs until the sound of his footfalls was lost in the metallic clamour of the alarm bell. Schaffer risked a peep through a crack in the curtains just as Smith came running up on tiptoe.

"Where the hell have you been?" Schaffer's voice was low and fierce.

"Come on, come on! Out of it!" Smith said urgently. "No, Jones, *not* down that flight of stairs, you want to meet a whole regiment of Alpenkorps coming up it? Along the passage to the west wing. We'll use the side stairs. For God's sake, hurry. This place will be like Piccadilly Circus in a matter of seconds."

Schaffer pounded along the passage beside Smith and when he spoke again the anxiety-born fierceness of tone had a certain plaintive quality to it. "Well, where the hell have you been?"

"The man we left tied up in the room beside the telephone exchange. The Records Office is directly above. I just remembered. I cut him free and dragged him out to the passage. He'd have burnt to death."

"You did that, did you?" Schaffer said wonderingly. "You do think of the most goddamned unimportant things, don't you?"

"It's a point of view. Our friend lying in the passage back there wouldn't share your sentiments. Right, down those stairs and straight ahead. Mary, you know the door."

Mary knew the door. Fifteen paces from the foot of the stairs she stopped. Smith spared a glance through the passage window on his left. Already smoke and flame were showing through the windows and embrasures in the northeast tower of the castle. In the courtyard below, dozens of soldiers were running around, most of them without what appeared to be any great sense of purpose or direction. One man there wasn't running. He was the overalled helicopter pilot and he was standing very still indeed, bent low over the engine. As Smith watched he slowly straightened, lifted his right arm and shook his fist in the direction of the burning tower.

Smith turned away and said to Mary: "Sure this is the room? Two stories below the window we came in?"

Mary nodded. "No question. This is it."

Smith tried the door handle: the room was locked. The time for skeleton keys and such-like finesse was gone: he placed the barrel of his Luger against the lock.

The corporal dispatched by his *Oberleutnant* to locate Colonel Kramer was faced by the same problem when he turned the handle of the gold drawing room, for, when Smith and the others had left there for the last time Schaffer had locked the door and thoughtfully thrown the key out a convenient passage window. The corporal first of all knocked respectfully. No reply. He knocked loudly, with the same lack of result. He depressed the handle and used his shoulder and all he did was to hurt his shoulder. He battered at the lock area with the butt of his Schmeisser but the carpenters who had built the Schloss Adler doors had known what they were about. He hesitated, then brought his machine pistol right way round and fired a burst through the lock, praying to heaven that Colonel Kramer wasn't sleeping in a chair in direct line with the keyhole.

Colonel Kramer was sleeping, all right, but nowhere near the direct line of the keyhole, he was stretched out on the gold carpet with a considerately placed pillow under his head. The corporal advanced slowly into the drawing room, his eyebrows reaching for his hair and his face almost falling apart in shocked disbelief. Reichsmarschal Rosemeyer was stretched out beside the colonel. Von Brauchitsch and a sergeant were sprawled in armchairs, heads lolling on their shoulders, while Anne-Marie—a very dishevelled and somewhat bruised-looking Anne-Marie—was stretched out on one of the big golden lamé couches.

Like a man in a daze, still totally uncomprehending, the corporal approached Kramer, knelt by his side and then shook him by the shoulder, with gentle respect at first and then with increasing vigour. After some time it was borne in upon him that he could shake the colonel's shoulder all night and that would be all he would have for it.

And then, illogically and for the first time, he noticed that all the men were without jackets, and that everyone, including Anne-Marie, had their left sleeves rolled up to the elbow. He looked slowly around the drawing room and went very still as his gaze rested on a tray with bottles, beakers and hypodermic syringes. Slowly, on the corporal's face, shocked incomprehension was replaced by an equally shocked understanding. He took off through the doorway like the favourite in the Olympics 100 metres final.

Schaffer tied the nylon rope round the head of the iron bedstead, tested the security of the knot, lifted the lower sash window, pushed the rope through and peered unhappily down the valley. At the far end of the village a pulsating red glow marked the smouldering embers of what had once been the railway station. The lights of the village itself twinkled clearly. Immediately below and to the right of where he stood could be seen four patrolling guards with as many dogs —Kramer hadn't spoken idly when he'd said the outside guards had been doubled—and the ease with which he could spot them Schaffer found all too readily understandable when he twisted his head and stared skywards through the thinly driving snow. The moon had just emerged from behind a black bar of cloud and was sailing across a discouragingly large stretch of empty sky. Even the stars could be seen.

"I'm going to feel a mite conspicuous out there, boss," Schaffer said complainingly. "And there's a wolf-pack loose down below there."

"Wouldn't matter if they had a battery of searchlights trained on this window," Smith said curtly. "Not now. We've no option. Quickly!"

Schaffer nodded dolefully, eased himself through the window, grasped the rope and halted momentarily as a muffled explosion came from the eastern wing of the castle.

"Number one," Schaffer said with satisfaction. "Bang goes a bowl of Dresden fruit—or a Dresden bowl of fruit. I do hope," he added anxiously, "that there's nobody using the toilet next door to where that bang just went off."

Smith opened his mouth to make impatient comment but Schaffer was already gone. Fifteen feet only and he was standing on the roof of the header station. Smith eased himself awkwardly over the sill, wrapped the rope round his right forearm, took the strain with his left hand and looked at Mary. She gave him an encouraging smile, but there was nothing encouraging about her expression when she transferred her gaze back to the three men who were lined up facing a wall, their hands clasped behind their necks. Carnaby-Jones was also covering them but, in his case, he held the gun as if it might turn and bite him at any moment.

Smith joined Schaffer on the roof of the header station. Both men crouched low to minimise the chances of being spotted from below. For the first ten feet out from the wall the roof was quite flat then dropped away sharply at an angle of thirty degrees. Smith thoughtfully regarded this steep slope and said: "We don't want a repeat performance of what happened to us last time we were out there. We could do with a good piton to hammer into the castle wall here. Or the roof. Some sort of belay for our rope."

"Pitons we don't need. Look at this." With his bare hands Schaffer scraped the snow-encrusted roof of the header station to reveal a fine wire netting and, below that, iron bars covering a pane of plate glass perhaps two feet by one. "Skylights, I believe they're called. Those bars look pretty firm to me."

He laid both hands on one of the bars and tugged firmly. It remained secure. Smith laid his left hand on the same bar and they pulled together. It still remained secure. Schaffer grinned in satisfaction, passed the rope round the bar and made no mistake about the knot he tied. Smith sat down on the roof and put his hand to the rope. Schaffer caught his wrist and firmly broke Smith's grip.

"No, you don't." Schaffer lifted Smith's right hand: the thick wrapping of bandages were already sodden, saturated with blood. "You can win your V.C. next time out. This time, you'd never make it. This one is on me." He paused and shook his head in wonder. "My God, Schaffer, you don't know what you're saying."

He removed the kit bag he'd been carrying round his neck, crawled to the break in the roof, gripped the rope and slid smoothly down the sloping surface. As he approached the roof edge he turned round with infinite care until he was pointing head downwards. Slowly, inch by almost imperceptible inch, the rope above him caught securely between his feet, he lowered himself still farther until his head was projecting over the edge of the roof. He peered downwards.

He was, he discovered, directly above one of the cables. Two hundred feet below, but to his left, this time, guards and Dobermans were floundering uphill through the deep snow at the best speed they could make, heading for the main entrance to the castle courtyard. The word had gone out, Schaffer realised, and every available man was being pulled in either to fight the fire or to help in the search for the men who had started the fire. Which meant, Schaffer concluded, that some of the garrison must have checked the state of the ground beneath the radio-room window and found there nothing but virgin and undisturbed snow . . .

He twisted his head and looked upwards. There was no sign of any guard patrolling the battlements, which was what he would have expected: there was no point in keeping a posted lookout for an enemy without when every indication pointed to the fact that the enemy were still within.

Schaffer eased himself downwards another perilous six inches till head and shoulders were over the edge of the roof. Only two things mattered now: was there a winch attendant or guard inside the header station and, if there were, could he, Schaffer, hold onto the rope with one hand while with the other he wriggled his Luger free and shot the guard? Schaffer doubted it. His OSS training had been wide-ranging and intensive but no one had ever thought it necessary that they should master the techniques of a high-wire circus performer. His mouth very dry and his heart pounding so heavily as to threaten to dislodge his precarious hand and toe holds, Schaffer craned his head and looked inside.

There was neither guard nor winch attendant inside: or, if there were any such, he was so well concealed that Schaffer couldn't see him. But logic said that no one would be hiding there for there was no conceivable reason why anyone should be hiding: logic also said that any person who might have been there would, like the patrolling guards below and the sentry on the battlements, have been called inside the castle to help fight fire and enemy. All Schaffer could see was a cable car, heavy winching machinery and heavy banks of lead-acid batteries: he was soon convinced that that was all that there was to see. No cause for concern.

But what he did see, something that did dismay him considerably, was that there was only one way for him to get into the station. There was no possibility of his sliding down the rope onto the floor of the station for the excellent reason that the roof of the station, in typically alpine eaves fashion, overhung the floor by at least six feet. The only way in was by dropping down onto the *Luftseilbahn's* heavy steel cable then overhanding himself up inside the station. Schaffer wasted no time in considering whether this was physically possible. It *had* to be possible. There was no other way in.

Carefully and with no little difficulty Schaffer inched himself back up the rope and the slope of the roof until he was about three feet clear of the edge. He eased his foot grip on the rope and swung round through 180° until he was once more facing up the slope with his legs now dangling over the edge. He looked up. The crouched figure of Smith showed tension in every line although the face was as expressionless as ever. Schaffer lifted one hand, made a circle with thumb

159

and forefinger, then eased himself over the edge until his searching feet found the cable.

He eased himself farther until he was sitting astride the cable, transferred his grip to the cable and swung down until he was suspended by hands and feet and looking up towards the moon. As a view, Schaffer reflected, it was vastly preferable to contemplating that two-hundred-foot drop down into the valley below. He started to climb.

He almost failed to make it. For every six inches he made up the cable, he slid back five. The cable was covered by a diabolically slippery coating of oil and sheath ice and only by clenching his fists till his forearms ached could he make any kind of progress at all and the fact that the cable stretched up at forty-five degrees made the difficult the well-nigh impossible. Such a means of locomotion would have been suicidal for the virtually one-handed Smith and quite impossible for either Mary or Carnaby-Jones. Once, after he had made about twelve feet, Schaffer looked down to gauge his chances if he let go and dropped down to the floor beneath and rapidly concluded that the chances were either that he would break both legs or, if he landed at all awkwardly, would pitch out two hundred feet down to the valley below. As Schaffer later recounted it, this last possibility, combined with the vertiginous view of the long long way to the floor of the valley, did him more good than an extra pair of arms. Ten seconds later, sweating and gasping like a long distance runner and very close to the last stages of exhaustion, he hauled himself onto the roof of the cable car.

He lay there for a full minute until the trembling in his arms eased and pulse and breathing rates returned to not more than a man in a high fever might expect to have, lowered himself quietly and wearily to the floor, took out his Luger, slid the safety catch and began to make a quick check that the header station really was empty of the enemy, a superfluous precaution, reason told him, any concealed person would have been bound both to see and hear his entry, but instinct and training went deeper than reason. There was no one there. He looked behind winches, electric motors and batteries. He had the place to himself.

The next thing was to ensure that he continued to have the place to himself. At the lower end of the sloping archway leading up to the castle courtyard, the heavy iron door stood wide. He passed through this doorway and padded softly up the cobbled pathway until he came to the courtyard exit.

Here, too, was another iron gate, as wide open as the other. Schaffer moved as far forward as the shadowing safety of the tunnel's overhang permitted and looked cautiously around the scene before him.

There was certainly, he had to admit, plenty to be seen and under more auspicious circumstances it would have done his heart good. The courtyard scene was as frenzied as the earlier glimpse they had had from the passage, but this time the action was much more purposive and controlled. Shouting, gesticulating figures were supervising the unrolling of hoses, the coupling up to hydrants, the relays of men carrying extinguishers and buckets of sand. The main gates stood open and unguarded, even the sentries must have been pressed into action: not that the unguarded doors offered any warmly beckoning escape route, only a suicide would have tried making his escape through a courtyard crowded with sixty or seventy scurrying Alpenkorps troops.

Over to his left the helicopter still stood forlorn and useless. There was no sign of the pilot. Suddenly a loud flat explosion echoed inside the confining walls of the square. Schaffer lifted his head to locate its source, saw fresh clouds of smoke billowing from an upper window in the east wing and briefly wondered which of his diversionary explosives that might be. But only for a brief moment. Some instinct made him glance to his right and his face went very still. The men he'd seen floundering up the slope outside, guards with the Doberman pinschers, were coming through the main gate, the clouds of frozen breaths trailing in the air behind them evidence enough of their exhausting run uphill through that knee-high snow. Schaffer backed away slowly and silently: German soldiers he could cope with or avoid but Dobermans were out of his class. He swung the heavy iron door to, careful not to make the least whisper of sound, slid home two heavy bolts, ran quickly down the arched passageway, closed and padlocked the lower door and put the key in his pocket.

He looked up, startled, at a loud crashing of glass and the subsequent tinkle as the shattered fragments fell to the floor. Automatically, the barrel of his Luger followed his glance.

"Put that cannon away," Smith said irritably. Schaffer could clearly see his face now, pressed close to the iron bars. "Who do you think is up here—Kramer and company?"

"It's my nerves," Schaffer explained coldly. "You haven't

161

been through what Lieutenant Schaffer's just been through. How are things up there?"

"Carraciola and friends are face down on the roof, freezing to death in the snow and Mary has the Schmeisser on them. Jones is still up there. Won't even put his head outside. Says he's no head for heights. I've given up arguing with him. How are things your end?"

"Quiet. If anyone is having any passing thoughts about the cable car, there are no signs of it. Both doors to the courtyard are locked. They're iron and even if someone does start having suspicious thoughts, they should hold them for a while. And, boss, the way I came in is strictly for the birds. And I mean strictly. What you need is wings. Your hand the way it is you could never make it. Mary and the old boy couldn't try it. Carraciola and the rest—well, who cares about Carraciola and the rest."

"What winch controls are there?" Smith asked.

"Well, now." Schaffer approached the winch. "A small lever marked 'Normal' and 'Notfall'—"

"Are there batteries down there?" Smith interrupted.

"Yeah. Any amount."

"Put the lever to 'Notfall'—Emergency. They could cut off the main power from inside the castle."

"O.K., it's done. Then there are 'Start' and 'Stop' buttons, a big mechanical handbrake and a gear lever affair marked 'Forwards' and 'Backwards.' With a neutral position."

"Start the motor," Smith ordered. Schaffer pressed the "Start" button and a generator whined into life, building up to its maximum revolutions after perhaps ten seconds. "Now release the brake and select forward gear. If it works, stop the car and try the other gear."

Schaffer released the brake and engaged gear, sliding the gear handle progressively over successive stops. The car moved forward, gently at first, but gathering speed until it was clear of the header station roof. After a few more feet Schaffer stopped the car, engaged reverse gear and brought the car back up into its original position. He looked up at Smith. "Smooth, huh?"

"Lower it down till it's halfway past the edge of the roof. We'll slide down the rope onto the top of the cable car, then you can bring us up inside."

"Must be all the fish you eat," Schaffer said admiringly. He set the car in motion.

"I'm sending Carraciola, Thomas and Christiansen down

first," Smith said. "I wouldn't care for any of us to be on the top of the same cable car as that lot. Think you can hold them till we get down?"

"You don't improve morale by being insulting to subordinate officers," Schaffer said coldly.

"I didn't know you'd any left. While you're doing that I'll have another go at persuading Juliet up there to come and join us." He prodded Carraciola with a far from gentle toe. "You first. Down that rope and onto the top of the cable car."

Carraciola straightened until he was kneeling, glanced down the slope of the roof to the depths of the valley beyond.

"You're not getting me on that lot. Not ever." He shook his head in finality, then stared up at Smith, his black eyes implacable in their hate. "Go on, shoot me. Kill me now."

"I'll kill you if you ever try to escape," Smith said. "Don't you know that, Carraciola?"

"Sure I know it. But you won't kill me in cold blood, just standing here. You're a man of principle, aren't you Major? Ethics, that's the word. The kind of noble sucker who risks his life to free an enemy soldier who might burn to death. Why don't you shoot, Major?"

"Because I don't have to." With his left hand Smith grabbed Carraciola's hair and jerked his head back till Carraciola, gasping with the pain of it, was staring skywards, while he reversed the grip on his Luger and raised it high. Nausea and pain flooded through him as the ends of the broken finger bone grated together, but none of this showed in his face. "I just knock you out, tie a rope round your waist and lower you down over the edge, maybe eight or ten feet. Schaffer eases out the car till it touches you, then he climbs in the back door, goes to the front door and hauls you inside. You can see my right hand's not too good, maybe I won't be able to tie a secure enough knot round you, maybe I won't be able to hold you, maybe Schaffer might let you go when he's hauling you inside. I don't much care, Carraciola."

"You double-dealing bastard!" Tears of pain filled Carraciola's eyes and his voice was low and venomous. "I swear to God I'll live to make you wish you'd never met me."

"Too late." Smith thrust him away contemptuously and Carraciola had to grab wildly at the rope to prevent himself from sliding over the break of the roof. "I've been wishing that ever since I found out who and what you really are. Vermin soil my hands. Move now or I damn well will shoot you.

Why the hell should I bother taking you back to England?"

Carraciola believed him. He slid down the rope until first his feet then his hands found the security of the supporting bracket of the cable car. Smith gestured with his gun towards Thomas. Thomas went without a word. Ten seconds later Christiansen followed him. Smith watched the cable car begin to move up inside the station, then looked upwards to the window from which the rope dangled.

"Mr. Jones?"

"I'm still here." Carnaby-Jones' voice had a quaver to it and he didn't as much as venture to risk a glance over the windowsill.

"Not for much longer, I hope," Smith said seriously. "They'll be coming for you, Mr. Jones. They'll be coming any moment now. I hate to say this, but I must. It is my duty to warn you what will happen to you, an enemy spy. You'll be tortured, Mr. Jones—not simple everyday tortures like pulling out your teeth and toenails, but unspeakable tortures I can't mention with Miss Ellison here—and then you'll finish in the gas chambers. *If* you're still alive."

Mary clutched his arm. "Would they—would they really do that?"

"Good God, no!" Smith stared at her in genuine surprise. "What on earth would they want to do that for?" He raised his voice again: "You'll die in a screaming agony, Mr. Jones, an agony beyond your wildest nightmares. And you'll take a long time dying. Hours. Maybe days. And screaming. Screaming all the time."

"What in God's name am I to do?" The desperate voice from above was no longer quavering, it vibrated like a broken bedspring. "What *can* I do?"

"You can slide down that rope," Smith said brutally. "Fifteen feet. Fifteen little feet, Mr. Jones. My God, you could do that in a pole vault."

"I can't." The voice was a wail. "I simply can't."

"Yes, you can," Smith urged. "Grab the rope now, close your eyes, out over the sill and down. Keep your eyes closed. We can catch you."

"I can't! I can't!"

"Oh God!" Smith said despairingly. "Oh, my God! It's too late now."

"It's too—what in heaven's name do you mean?"

"The lights are going on along the passage," Smith said, his voice low and tense. "And that window. And the next.

They're coming for you, Mr. Jones, they're coming now. Oh God, when they strip you off and strap you down on the torture table—"

Two seconds later Carnaby-Jones was over the sill and sliding down the nylon rope. His eyes were screwed tightly shut. Mary said admiringly: "You really are the most fearful liar ever."

"Schaffer keeps telling me the same thing," Smith admitted. "You can't all be wrong."

The cable car, with the three men clinging grimly to the suspension bracket, climbed slowly up into the header station and jerked to a halt. One by one the three men, under the persuasion of Schaffer's gently waving Luger, lowered themselves the full length of their arms and dropped the last two or three feet to the floor. The last of them, Thomas, seemed to land awkwardly, exclaimed in muffled pain and fell heavily sideways. As he fell, his hands shot out and grabbed Schaffer by the ankles. Schaffer, immediately off balance, flung up his arms in an attempt to maintain equilibrium and, before he could even begin to bring his arms down again, was winded by a diving rugby tackle by Christiansen. He toppled backwards, his back smashing into a generator with an impact that drove from his lungs what little breath had been left in them. A second later and Christiansen had his gun, driving the muzzle cruelly into a throat gasping for air.

Carraciola was already at the lower iron door, shaking it fiercely. His eye caught sight of the big padlock in its hasp. He swung round, ran back towards Schaffer, knocked aside the gun in Christiansen's hand and grabbed Schaffer by the throat.

"That padlock. Where's the key to that bloody padlock?" The human voice can't exactly emulate the hiss of a snake, but Carraciola's came pretty close to it then. "That door has been locked from the inside. You're the only person who could have done it. *Where is that key?*"

Schaffer struggled to a sitting position, feebly pushing aside Carraciola's hand. "I can't breathe!" The moaning, gasping breathing lent credence to the words. "I can't breathe. I—I'm going to be sick."

"Where *is* that damned key?" Carraciola demanded.

"Oh God, I feel ill!" Schaffer hoisted himself slowly to a kneeling position, his head bent, retching sounds coming from his throat. He shook his head from side to side, as if to clear away the muzziness, then slowly raised it, his eyes unfocussed. He mumbled: "What do you want? What did you say?"

"The key!" If the need for silence hadn't been paramount, Carraciola's voice would have been a frustrated scream of rage. Half a dozen times, in brutal and rapid succession, he struck Schaffer across the face with the palm and back of his hand. "Where is that key?"

"Easy on, easy on!" Thomas caught Carraciola's hand. "Don't be such a damned fool. You want him to talk, don't you?"

"The key. Yes, the key." Schaffer hoisted himself wearily to his feet and stood there swaying, eyes half-closed, face ashen, blood trickling from both corners of his mouth. "The batteries there, I think I hid them behind the batteries. I don't know, I can't think. No, wait." The words came in short, anguished gasps. "I didn't. I meant to, but I didn't." He fumbled in his pockets, eventually located the key and brought it out, offering it vaguely in Carraciola's direction. Carraciola, the beginnings of a smile on his face, reached out for the key but, before he could reach it, Schaffer abruptly straightened and with a convulsive jerk of his arm sent the key spinning through the open end of the station to land in the valley hundreds of feet below. Carraciola stared after the vanished key in total incredulity then, his suffused and enraged face mute evidence of his complete loss of self-control, stooped, picked up Schaffer's fallen Schmeisser and swung it viciously across the American's head and face. Schaffer fell like a tree.

"Well," Thomas said acidly. "Now that we've got that out of our systems. We can shoot the lock away."

"You can commit suicide with ricochets—that door's iron, man." Carraciola had indeed got it out of his system for he was back on balance again. He paused, then smiled slowly. "What the hell are we all thinking of? Let's play it clever. If we did get through that door the first thing we'd probably collect would be a chestful of machine-gun bullets. Remember, the only people who know who we really are have bloody great doses of Nembutal inside them and are liable to remain unconscious for a long time. To the rest of the garrison we're unknowns—and to the few who saw us arrive, we're prisoners. In both cases we're automatically enemies."

"So?" Thomas was impatient.

"So, as I say, we play it clever. We go down in this cable car and play it clever again. We phone old Weissner. We ask him to phone the Schloss Adler, tell him where Smith is and, in case Smith does manage to get down to the village on the other cable car after us, we ask him to have a reception committee waiting for him at the lower station. Then we go to the barracks—they're bound to have a radio there—and get in touch with you know who. Flaws?"

"Nary a flaw." Christiansen grinned. "And then we all live happily ever afterwards. Come on, what are we waiting for?"

"Into the cable car, you two." Carraciola waited until they had boarded, walked across the floor until he was directly under the smashed skylight and called: "Smith!" Schaffer's silenced Luger was in his hand.

On the roof above Smith stiffened, handed the trembling Carnaby-Jones—his eyes were still screwed shut—over to the care of Mary, took two steps towards the skylight and stopped. It was Wyatt-Turner who had said of Smith that he had a built-in radar set against danger and Carraciola's voice had just started it up into instantaneous operation and had it working with a clarity and precision that would have turned Decca green with envy.

"Schaffer?" Smith called softly. "Lieutenant Schaffer? Are you there?"

"Right here, boss." Midwest accent, Schaffer to the life. Smith's radar-scope went into high and had it been geared to warning bells he'd have been deafened for life. He dropped to hands and knees and crawled soundlessly forward. He could see the floor of the station now. The first thing that came into his vision was a bank of batteries, then an outflung hand, then, gradually, the rest of the spread-eagled form of Schaffer. Another few inches forward and he sensed as much as saw a long finger pointing in his direction and flung himself to one side. The wind from the Luger's shell riffled his hair. Down below someone cursed in anger and frustration.

"That's the last chance you'll ever have, Carraciola," Smith said. From where he lay he could just see Schaffer's face—or the bloody mask that covered his face. It was impossible to tell whether he was alive or dead. He looked dead.

"Wrong again. Merely the postponement of a pleasure. We're leaving now, Smith. I'm going to start the motor. Want Schaffer to get his—Christiansen has the Schmeisser on him. Don't try anything."

"You make for that control panel," Smith said, "and your first step into my line of vision will be your last. I'll cut you down, Carraciola. Schaffer's dead. I can see he's dead."

"He's damn all of the kind dead. He's just been clobbered by a gun butt."

"I'll cut you down," Smith said monotonously.

"Goddam it, I tell you he's not dead!" Carraciola was exasperated now.

"I'm going to kill you," Smith said quietly. "If I don't, the first guards through that door surely will. You can see what we've done to their precious Schloss Adler—it's well alight. Can't you guess the orders that have gone out—shoot on sight. Any stranger, shoot on sight—and shoot to kill. You're a stranger, Carraciola."

"For God's sake, will you listen to me?" There was desperation in the voice now. "I can prove it. He *is* alive. What can you see from up there?"

The signal strengths of Smith's danger radar set began to fade. He said: "I can see Schaffer's head."

"Watch it, then." There was a thud and a silenced Luger bounced to a stop a few inches from Schaffer's head. A moment later Carraciola himself came into Smith's field of vision. He looked up at Smith and at the Schmeisser muzzle staring down at him and said: "You won't be needing that." He stooped over Schaffer, pinched his nose with one hand and clamped his other hand over the mouth. Within seconds the unconscious man, fighting for the air that would not come, began to move his head and to raise feeble hands in the direction of his face. Carraciola took his hands away, looked up at Smith and said: "Don't forget, Christiansen still has that Schmeisser on him."

Carraciola walked confidently across to the control panel, made the generator switch, released the mechanical handbrake and engaged gear, pushing the lever all the way across. The cable car leapt forward with a violent jerk. Carraciola ran for it, jumped inside, turned and slammed shut the door of the cable car.

On the roof above, Smith laid down his useless Schmeisser and pushed himself wearily to his feet. His face was bleak and bitter.

"Well, that's it, then," Mary said. Her voice was unnaturally calm. "Finish. All finish. Operation Overlord—and us. If that matters."

"It matters to me." Smith took out his silenced automatic and held it in his good left hand. "Keep an eye on Junior here."

TEN

"NO!" FOR perhaps two dazed, incredulous seconds that were the longest seconds she had ever known, Mary had quite failed to gather Smith's intention: when shocked understanding did come, her voice rose to a scream. "No! No! For God's sake, no!"

Smith ignored the heartbroken voice, the desperate clutching hand and walked to the end of the flat section of the roof. At the lower edge of the steeply sloping roof section the leading edge of the cable car had just come into view: a cable car with, inside it, three men who were exchanging delighted grins and thumping one another joyously on the back.

Smith ran down the ice-coated pitch of the roof, reached the edge and jumped. The cable car was already seven or eight feet beyond him and almost as far below. Had the cable car not been going away from him he must surely have broken both legs. As it was, he landed with a jarring teeth-rattling crash, a crash that caused the cable car to shudder and sway and his legs to buckle and slide from beneath him on the ice-coated roof. His injured right hand failed to find a purchase on the suspension bracket and in his blindly despairing grab with his left hand he was forced to drop his Luger. It slid to the edge of the roof and fell away into the darkness of the valley below. Smith wrapped both arms round the suspension bracket and fought to draw some whooping gasps of air into his starving lungs: he had been completely winded by the fall.

In their own way, the three men inside the cable car were as nearly stunned as Smith himself. The smiles had frozen on their faces and Christiansen's arm was still poised in mid-air where it had been arrested by the sound and the shock of

Smith's landing on the cable-car roof, Carraciola, predictably, was the first to recover and react. He snatched the Schmeisser from Christiansen and pointed it upwards.

The cable car was now forty to fifty feet clear of the castle and the high wind was beginning to swing it, pendulum-like, across the sky. Smith, weakened by the impact of the fall, the pain in his hand and the loss of blood, hung on grimly and dizzily to the suspension bracket, his body athwart the roof of the car. He felt sick and exhausted and there seemed to be a mist in front of his eyes.

From shoulder to knee and only inches from his body a venomous burst of machine-pistol fire stitched a pattern of holes in the cable-car roof: the mists cleared away from Smith's eyes more quickly than he would have believed possible. A Schmeisser magazine held far more shells than that. They would wait a second or two to see if a falling body passed any of the side windows—with that violently swinging transverse movement it was virtually impossible for anyone to fall off over the leading or trailing ends of the car—and if none came, then they would fire again. But where? What would be the next area of roof chosen for treatment? Would the gunman fire at random or to a systematic pattern? It was impossible to guess. Perhaps at that very moment the muzzle of the Schmeisser was only two inches from the middle of his spine. The very thought was enough to galvanise Smith into a quick roll that stretched him out over the line of holes that had just been made. It was unlikely that the gunman would fire in exactly the same place again, but even that was a gamble, the gunman might figure just as Smith was doing and traverse the same area again. But he wasn't figuring the same as Smith, the next burst was three feet away towards the trailing end of the car.

Using the suspension bracket as support, Smith pulled himself to his feet until he was quite vertical, hanging on to the cable itself. This way, the possible target area was lessened by eighty percent. Quickly, soundlessly, sliding his hands along the cable, he moved forward until he was standing at the very front of the car.

The cable car's angle of arc through the sky was increasing with every swing of the pendulum. The purchase for his feet was minimal, all the strain came on his arms, and by far the greater part of that on his sound left arm. There was nothing smoothly progressive about the cable car's sideways motion through the sky, it jumped and jerked and jarred and jolted like a Dervish dancer in the last seconds before total collapse. The strain on the left arm was intolerable, it felt as if the shoulder sinews were being torn apart: but shoulder sinews are reparable whereas the effects of a Schmeisser blast at point-blank range were not. And it seemed, to Smith, highly unlikely that anybody would waste a burst on the particular spot where he was standing, the obvious position for any roof passenger who didn't want to be shaken off into the valley below was flat out on the roof with his arms wrapped for dear life round one of the suspension arm's support brackets.

His reasoning was correct. There were three more bursts, none of which came within feet of him, and then no more. Smith knew that he would have to return to the comparative security of the suspension arm and return there soon. He was nearly gone. The grip of his left hand on the cable was weakening, this forced him to strengthen the grip of his right hand and the resulting agony that travelled like an electric shock from his hand up his arm clear to the right-hand side of his head served only to compound the weakness. He would have to get back, and he would have to get back now. He prayed that the Schmeisser's magazine was empty.

And then, and for another reason, he knew that he had no option but to go now: and he knew his prayer hadn't been answered. The leading door of the cable car opened and a head and a hand appeared. The head was Carraciola's: the hand held the Schmeisser. Carraciola was looking upwards even as he leaned out and he saw Smith immediately: he leaned farther out still, swung the Schmeisser one-handedly until the stock rested on his shoulder and squeezed the trigger.

Under the circumstance accurate aiming was impossible but at a distance of four feet accurate aiming was the last thing that mattered. Smith had already let go of the cable and was flinging himself convulsively backward when the first of the bullets ripped off his left-hand epaulette. The second grazed his left shoulder, a brief burning sensation, but the rest of the burst passed harmlessly over his head. He landed heavily, stretched out blindly, located and grasped one of the suspension arms and scuttled crablike round the base of the suspension arm until he had it and what little pathetic cover it offered between him and Carraciola.

For Carraciola was coming after him and Carraciola was coming to mak' siccar. He had the gun still in his hand and that gun could have very few shells indeed left in the magazine: it would be no part of Carraciola's plan to waste any of those shells. Even as Smith watched, Carraciola seemed to rise effortlessly three feet into the air—a feat of levitation directly attributable to the powerful boost given him by Thomas and Christiansen—jackknifed forward at hip level and flattened his body on top of the cable car roof: his legs still dangled over the leading edge. A suicidal move, Smith thought in brief elation, Carraciola had made a fatal mistake: with neither handhold nor purchase on that ice-coated roof, he must slide helplessly over the edge first jerk or jolt of the cable car. But the elation was brief indeed for Carraciola had made no mistake. He had known what Smith hadn't: where to find a secure lodgment for his hand on the smooth expanse of that roof. Within seconds his scrabbling fingers had found safety —a gash in the cable-car roof that had been torn open by one of the bursts from the Schmeisser. Carraciola's fingers hooked securely and he pulled himself forward until he was in a kneeling position, his toes hooked over the leading edge.

Smith reached up with his wounded hand and clawed desperately for a grenade in the canvas bag slung over his left shoulder, at the same time pushing himself as far back as his anchoring left hand, clutched round a suspension bracket, would permit: at that range a grenade could do almost as much damage to himself as to Carraciola. His legs slid back until his feet projected over the trailing edge and he cried out in pain as a tremendous pressure, a bone-breaking, skin-tearing pressure, was applied to his shins, halfway between knees and feet: someone had him by the ankle and that someone seemed determined to separate his feet from the rest of his body. Smith twisted his head round but all he could see was a pair of hands round his ankles, knuckles bone-white in the faint wash of moonlight. And no one man's weight, Smith realised, could have caused that agonising pain in his shins, his companion must have had him by the waist, whether to increase the pressure or to ensure his safety if Smith did slide over the end. The reasons were immaterial: the effect was the same. He tried to draw up his legs but with a pinning weight of well over 200 lbs., any movement was quite impossible.

Smith risked a quick glance forward, but Carraciola hadn't moved, the cable car was now halfway between the header station and the top pylon, the pendulum swing was at its maximum and Carraciola, still in his kneeling position, was hanging on for his life. Smith abandoned his attempt to reach for a grenade which could now serve no purpose whatsoever, unsheathed his knife, clasped the haft in the three good fingers of his right hand, twisted round and tried to strike at those hands that were causing him such excruciating agony. He couldn't get within fifteen inches of them.

His legs were breaking: his left arm was breaking: and his clenched grip on the support was slowly beginning to open. He had only seconds to go, Smith knew, and so he had nothing in the world to lose. He changed his grip on his knife, caught the tip of the blade between his broken thumb and the rest of his fingers, turned and threw the knife as powerfully and as accurately as his smashed hand and pain-dimmed eyes would permit. The stinging pain in his left ankle and the scream of pain from the trailing door were simultaneous. Immediately, all the pressure on his ankles vanished: a second later, Christiansen, whom Thomas had managed to drag back inside the cable car, was staring stupidly at the knife that transfixed his right wrist.

In that one instant Smith had won and he had lost. Or so it most surely seemed, for he was defenceless now: Carraciola had bided his time, calculated his chances and flung himself forward until he had reached the safety of the suspension bracket. Now he pulled himself slowly to his feet, his left arm round the suspension arm itself, his left leg twined securely round one of the brackets. The Schmeisser pointed into Smith's face.

"Only one bullet left." Carraciola's smile was almost pleasant. "I had to make sure, you see."

Perhaps he hadn't lost, Smith thought, perhaps he hadn't lost after all. Because of the pinioning effect of Christiansen's hands on his ankles he'd been unaware, until now, how much less difficult it had become to maintain position on that ice-sheathed roof, unaware how much the pendulum swaying of the cable car had been reduced. And it seemed that, even now, Carraciola was still unaware of it or, if the change of motion had registered with him, the reason for it had not. With a conscious effort of will Smith shifted his by now half-hypnotised gaze from the staring muzzle of the Schmeisser to a point just over Carraciola's shoulder. The suspension arm of the first pylon was less than twenty feet away.

"Too bad, Smith." Carraciola steadied the barrel of his machine pistol. "Comes to us all. Be seeing you."

"Look behind you," Smith said.

Carraciola half-smiled in weary disbelief that anyone should try that ancient one on him. Smith glanced briefly, a second time, over Carraciola's shoulder, winced and looked away. The disbelief vanished from Carraciola's face as if a light had been switched off. Some sixth sense or instantaneous flash of comprehension or just some sudden certainty of knowledge made him twist round and glance over his shoulder. He cried out in terror, the last sound he ever made. The steel suspension arm of the pylon smashed into his back. Both his back and intertwined leg broke with a simultaneous crack that could have been heard a hundred yards away. One second later he was swept from the roof of the cable car but by that time Carraciola was already dead. From the rear open doorway of the cable car Christiansen and Thomas, their shocked faces mirroring their stunned disbelief, watched the broken body tumbling down into the darkness of the valley below.

Shaking like a man with the ague and moving like an old man in a dream, Smith slowly and painfully hauled himself forward until he was in a sitting position with an arm and leg wound round one of the after arms of the supporting bracket. Still in the same dreamlike slow motion he lifted his head and gazed down the valley. The other cable car, moving up-valley on its reciprocal course, had just passed the lowermost of the three pylons. With luck, his own cable car might be the first to arrive at the central pylon. With luck. Not, of course, that the question of luck entered into it any more: he had no options or alternatives left, he had to do what he had to do and luck was the last factor to be taken into consideration.

From his kit bag Smith extracted two packages of plastic explosives and wedged them firmly between the roof of the car and the two after arms of the suspension bracket, making sure that the tear strip igniters were exposed and ready to hand. Then he braced himself, sitting upright, against the suspension bracket, using both arms and legs to anchor himself and prepared to sit it out once more as the cable car, approaching mid-section of its second lap between the first and central pylons, steadily increased its swaying angle of arc across the night sky.

It was foolish of him, he knew, to sit like that. The snow had momentarily stopped, and the full moon, riding palely in an empty sky, was flooding the valley with a wash of ghostly light. Sitting as he was he must, he realised, be clearly visible from either the castle or the lower station: but apart from the fact that he doubted whether concealment mattered any longer he knew there was nothing he could do about it, there wasn't the strength left in his one good arm to allow him to assume the prone spread-eagled position that he and Schaffer had used on the way up.

He wondered about Schaffer, wondered about him in a vaguely woolly detached way for which exhaustion, loss of blood and the bitter cold were almost equally responsible. He wondered about the others, too, about the elderly man and the girl perched on top of the header station roof, about the two men inside the cable car: but Mary and Carnaby-Jones were helpless to do anything to help and the chances of the unarmed Thomas and Christiansen carrying out another roof-top sortie were remote indeed: Carraciola had carried a Schmeisser, and they had seen what had happened to Carraciola. Schaffer, it was Schaffer who mattered.

Schaffer was feeling even more vague and woolly than Smith, if for different reasons. He was waking, slowly and painfully, from a very bad dream and in this dream he could taste salt in his mouth and hear a soft urgent feminine voice calling his name, calling it over and over again. In normal times Schaffer would have been all for soft feminine voices, urgent or not, but he wished that this one would stop for it was all part of the bad dream and in this bad dream someone had split his head in half and he knew the pain wouldn't go until he woke up. He moaned, put the palms of his hands on the floor and tried to prop himself up. It took a long time, it took an eternity for someone had laid one of the girders from the Forth bridge across his back, but at last he managed it, managed to straighten both his arms, his head hanging down between them. His head didn't feel right, it didn't even feel like his head, for, apart from the fact that there seemed to be a butcher's cleaver stuck in it, it seemed to be stuffed with cotton wool, grey and fuzzy round the edges. He shook his head to clear it and this was a mistake for the top of his head fell off. Or so it felt to Schaffer as the blinding coruscation of the multicoloured lights before his eyes arranged themselves into oddly kaleidoscopic patterns. He opened his eyes and the patterns dimmed and the lights began to fade: gradually, beneath his eyes, the pattern of floorboards began to resolve themselves, and, on the board, the outlines of hands. His own hands.

He was awake, but this was one of those bad dreams which stayed with you even when you were awake. He could still taste salt—the salt of blood—his head still felt as if one incautious shake would have it rolling across the floor and that soft and urgent voice was still calling.

"Lieutenant Schaffer! Lieutenant Schaffer! Wake up, Lieutenant, wake up! Can you hear me?"

He'd heard that voice before, Schaffer decided, but he couldn't place it. It must have been a long time ago. He twisted his head to locate the source of the voice—it seemed to come from above—and the kaleidoscopic whirligig of colours was back in position again, revolving more quickly than ever. Head-shaking and head-twisting, Schaffer decided, were contra-indicated. He returned his head slowly to its original position, managed to get his knees under him, crawled forward in the direction of some dimly seen piece of machinery and hauled himself shakily to his feet.

"Lieutenant! Lieutenant Schaffer! I'm up here."

Schaffer turned and lifted his head in an almost grotesque slow motion and this time the whole universe of brightly dancing stars was reduced to the odd constellation or two. He recognised the voice from the distant past now, it was that of Mary Ellison, he even thought he recognised the pale strained face looking down from above, but he couldn't be sure, his eyes weren't focussing as they should. He wondered dizzily what the hell she was doing up there staring down at him through what appeared to be the bars of a shattered skylight: his mind, he dimly realised, was operating with all the speed and subtle fluency of a man swimming upstream against a river of black molasses.

"Are you—are you all right?" Mary asked.

Schaffer considered this ridiculous question carefully. "I expect I shall be," he said with great restraint. "What happened?"

"They hit you with your own gun."

"That's right." Schaffer nodded and immediately wished he hadn't. He gingerly fingered a bruise on the back of his head. "In the face. I must have struck my head as—" He broke off and turned slowly to face the door. "What was that?"

"A dog. It sounded like a dog barking."

"That's what I thought." His voice slurred and indistinct, he staggered drunkenly across to the lower iron door and put his ear to it. "Dogs," he said. "Lots of dogs. And lots and lots of hammering. Sledge-hammers, like enough." He left the door and walked back to the centre of the floor, still staggering slightly. "They're on to us and they're coming for us. Where's the major?"

"He went after them." The voice was empty of all feeling. "He jumped onto the top of the cable car."

"He did, eh?" Schaffer received the news as if Smith's action had been the most natural and inevitable thing in the world. "How did he make out?"

"How did he make—" There was life back in her voice now, a shocked anger at Schaffer's apparent callousness. She checked herself and said: "There was a fight and I think someone fell off the roof. I don't know who it was."

"It was one of them," Schaffer said positively.

"One of—how can you say that?"

"The Major Smiths of this world don't drive over the edge of a cliff. Quotation from the future Mrs. Schaffer. The Major Smiths of this world don't fall off the roofs of cable cars. Quotation from the future Mrs. Schaffer's future husband."

"You're recovering," Mary said coldly. "But I think you're right. There's still someone sitting on top of the cable car and it wouldn't be one of them, would it?"

"How do you know there's someone sitting—"

"Because I can see him," she said impatiently. "It's bright moonlight. Look for yourself."

Schaffer looked for himself, then rubbed a weary forearm across aching eyes. "I have news, for you, love," he said. "I can't even see the damn cable car."

The cable car was ten yards away from the central pylon. Smith, upright now, stooped, tore off the two friction fuses, straightened and, holding the cable in his left hand, took up position just on the inner side of the car roof. At the last moment he released his grip on the cable and stretched both arms out before him to break the impact of his body against the suspension arm. The ascending car on the other cable was now almost as close to the central pylon as his own. It didn't seem possible that he could make it in time.

The impact of the horizontal suspension arm drove the thought from his mind and all the breath from his body, had it not been for the buffering effect of his outstretched arms, Smith was sure, some of his ribs must have gone. As it was, he was almost completely winded but he forced himself to ignore the pain and his heaving lungs' demand for oxygen, swung his feet up till they rested on the lower cross-girder, hooked his hands round the upper girder and made his way quickly across to the other side. At least, his hands and his feet moved quickly, but the steel was so thickly coated in clear smooth ice that his scrabbling feet could find almost no purchase whatsoever on the lower girder. He had reached no farther than the middle when the ascending car began to pass under its suspension arm. For the first time that night Smith blessed the brightness of the moon. He took two more slipping, sliding steps and launched himself towards the ice-coated cable that glittered so brightly in the pale moonlight.

His left hand caught the cable, his right arm hooked over it and the cable itself caught him high up on the chest. He had made no mistake about the location of his hand and arm, but his sliding take-off had caused his body to fall short and the cable slid up under his chin with a jerk that threatened to decapitate him. His legs swung out far beneath him, swung back and touched the roof as he lowered himself to the full extent of his left arm. He released his grip on the cable, dropped on all fours and reached out blindly but successfully for one of the arms of the suspension bracket. For long seconds he knelt there, retching uncontrollably as he was flooded by the nausea and pain from his throat and still winded lungs: then, by and by, the worst of it passed and he lay face down on the roof as the cable car began to increase its pendulum swing with the increasing distance from the central pylon. He would not have believed that a man could be so totally exhausted and yet still have sufficient residual strength and sufficient self-preservation instinct to hang on to that treacherous and precarious handhold on that ice-coated roof.

Long seconds passed and some little measure of strength began to return to his limbs and body. Wearily, he hauled himself up into a sitting position, twisted round and gazed back down the valley.

The cable car he had so recently abandoned was now hardly more than fifty yards from the lower-most pylon. Thomas and Christiansen sat huddled in the middle, the latter wrapping a makeshift bandage round his injured hand. Both fore and aft doors were still open as they had been when the abortive attack on Smith was made. That neither of the two men had ventured near the extremities of the car to try to close either of the doors was proof enough of the respect, if not fear, in which Smith was now held.

From the roof of the cable car came a brilliant flash of

light, magnesium-blinding in its white intensity: simultaneously there came the sound of two sharp explosions, so close together as to be indistinguishable in time. The two rear supports of the suspension bracket broke and the car, suspended now by only the two front supports, tilted violently, the front going up, the rear down.

Inside, the angle of the floor of the car changed in an instant from the horizontal to at least thirty degrees. Christiansen was flung back towards the still open rear door. He grabbed despairingly at the side—but he grabbed with his wounded hand. Soundlessly, he vanished through the open doorway and as soundlessly fell to the depths of the valley below.

Thomas, with two sound hands and faster reactions, had succeeded in saving himself—for the moment. He glanced up and saw where the roof was beginning to buckle and break as the forward two suspension arm support brackets, now subjected to a wrenching lateral pressure they had never been designed to withstand, began to tear their retaining bolts free. Thomas struggled up the steeply inclined floor till he stood in the front doorway: because of the tilt of the car, now almost 45° as the front supports worked loose, the leading edge of the roof was almost touching the car. Thomas reached up, grabbed the cable with both hands, and had just cleared his legs from the doorway when the two front supports tore free from the roof in a rending screech of metal. The cable car fell away, slowly turning end over end.

Despite the cable's violent buffeting caused by the sudden release of the weight of the car, Thomas had managed to hang on. He twisted round and saw the suspension arm of the lowest pylon only feet away. The sudden numbing of all physical and mental faculties was accurately and shockingly reflected in the frozen fear of his face, the lips drawn back in a snarling rictus of terror. The knuckles of the hands gleamed like burnished ivory. And then, suddenly, there were no hands there, just the suspension arm and the empty wire and a long fading scream in the night.

As his cable car approached the header station, Smith edged well forward to clear the lip of the roof. From where he crouched it was impossible to see the east wing of the Schloss Adler but if the columns of dense smoke now drifting across the valley were anything to go by, the fire seemed to have an unshakeable hold. Clouds were again moving across the moon and this could be both a good thing and a bad thing: a good thing in that it would afford them cover and help obscure those dense clouds of smoke, a bad thing in that it was bound to highlight the flames from the burning castle. It could only be a matter of time, Smith reflected, before the attention of someone in the village or the barracks beyond was caught by the fire or the smoke. Or, he thought grimly, by the increasing number of muffled explosions coming from the castle itself. He wondered what might be the cause of them: Schaffer hadn't had the time to lay all those distractions.

The roof of the cable car cleared the level of the floor of the header station and Smith sagged in relief as he saw the figure standing by the controls of the winch. Schaffer. A rather battered and bent Schaffer, it was true, an unsteady Schaffer, a Schaffer with one side of his face masked in blood, a Schaffer who from his peering and screwed-up expression had obviously some difficulty in focussing his gaze. But undoubtedly Schaffer and as nearly a going concern as made no odds. Smith felt energy flow back into him, he hadn't realised just how heavily he had come to depend on the American: with Schaffer by his side it was going to take a great deal to stop them now.

Smith glanced up as the roof of the header station came into view. Mary and Carnaby-Jones were still there, pressed back against the castle wall. He lifted a hand in greeting but they gave no sign in return. Ghosts returning from the dead, Smith thought wryly, weren't usually greeted by a wave of the hand.

Schaffer, for all the trouble he was having with his eyes and his still obviously dazed condition, seemed to handle the winch controls immaculately. It may have been—and probably was—the veriest fluke, but he put the gear lever in neutral and applied the brake to bring the cable car to rest exactly halfway in under the lip of the roof. First Mary and then Jones came sliding down the nylon rope onto the roof of the car, Jones with his eyes screwed tightly shut. Neither of them spoke a word, not even when Schaffer had brought them up inside and they had slid down onto the floor of the station.

"Hurry! Hurry!" Smith flung open the rear door of the cable car. "Inside, all of you!" He retrieved Schaffer's fallen Luger from the floor, then whirled round as he heard the furious barking of dogs followed by the sound of heavy sledges

180

battering against the iron door leading from the station. The first of the two defences must have been carried away: now the second was under siege.

Mary and a stumbling Schaffer were already inside the cable car. Jones, however, had made no move to go. He stood there, Smith's Schmeisser in his hand, listening to the furious hammering on the door. His face seemed unconcerned. He said, apologetically: "I'm not very good at heights, I'm afraid. But this is different."

"Get inside!" Smith almost hissed the words.

"No." Jones shook his head. "You hear. They'll be through any minute. I'll stay."

"For God's sake!" Smith shouted in exasperation.

"I'm twenty years older than any of you."

"Well, there's that." Smith nodded consideringly, held out his right hand, said, "Mr. Jones. Good luck," brought across his left hand and half-dragged, half-carried the dazed Jones into the cable car. Smith moved quickly across to the controls, engaged gear all the way, released the handbrake and ran after the moving car.

As they moved out from below the roof of the station, the sound of the assault on the inner door seemed to double in its intensity. In the Schloss Adler, Smith reflected, there would be neither pneumatic chisels nor oxyacetylene equipment for there could be no conceivable call for either, but, even so, it didn't seem to matter: with all the best will in the world a couple of iron hasps couldn't for long withstand an attack of that nature. Thoughtfully, Smith closed the rear door. Schaffer was seated, his elbows on his knees, his head in his hands. Mary was kneeling on the floor, Jones's head in her lap, looking down at the handsome silvery-haired face. He couldn't see her expression but was dolefully certain that she was even then preparing a homily about the shortcomings of bullies who went around clobbering elderly and defenceless American actors. Almost two minutes passed in complete silence before Carnaby-Jones stirred, and, when he did, Mary herself stirred and looked up at Smith. To his astonishment, she had a half-smile on her face.

"It's all right," she said. "I've counted ten. In the circumstances, it was the only argument to use." She paused and the smile faded. "I thought you were gone then."

"You weren't the only one. After this I retire. I've used up a lifetime's luck in the past fifteen minutes. You're not looking so bright yourself."

"I'm not feeling so bright." Her face was pale and strained as she braced herself against the wild lurching of the cable car. "If you want to know, I'm seasick. I don't go much on this form of travel."

Smith tapped the roof. "You want to try travelling steerage on one of those," he said feelingly. "You'd never complain about first class travel again. Ah! Pylon number two coming up. Almost halfway."

"*Only* halfway." A pause. "What happens if they break through that door up there?"

"Reverse the gear lever and up we go."

"Like it or not?"

"Like it or not."

Carnaby-Jones struggled slowly to a sitting position, gazed uncomprehendingly around him until he realised where he was, rubbed his jaw tenderly and said to Smith: "That was a dirty trick."

"It was all of that," Smith acknowledged. "I'm sorry."

"I'm not." Jones smiled shakily. "Somehow, I don't really think I'm cut out to be a hero."

"Neither am I, brother, neither am I," Schaffer said mournfully. He lifted his head from his hands and looked slowly around. His eyes were still glassy and only partially focussing but a little colour was returning to his right cheek, the one that wasn't masked in blood. "Our three friends. What became of our three friends?"

"Dead."

"Dead?" Schaffer groaned and shook his head. "Tell me about it sometime. But not now."

"He doesn't know what he's missing," Smith said unsympathetically. "The drama of it all escapes him, which is perhaps just as well. Is the door up above there still standing or are the hinges or padlocks going? Is someone rushing towards the winch controls? Is there—"

"Stop it!" Mary's voice was sharp, high-pitched and carried overtones of hysteria. "Stop talking like that!"

"Sorry," Smith said contritely. He reached out and touched her shoulder. "Just whistling in the dark, that's all. Here comes the last pylon. Another minute or so and we're home and dry."

"Home and dry," Schaffer said bitterly. "Wait till I have that Savoy Grill menu in my hand. *Then* I'll be home and dry."

"Some people are always thinking of their stomachs,"

Smith observed. At that moment he was thinking of his own and it didn't feel any too good. No stomach does when it feels as if it has a solid lead ball, a chilled lead ball lodged in it with an icy hand squeezing from the outside. His heart was thumping slowly, heavily, painfully in his chest and he was having difficulty in speaking for all the saliva seemed to have evaporated from his mouth. He became suddenly aware that he was unconsciously leaning backward, bracing himself for the moment when the cable car jerked to a stand-still then started climbing back up to the Schloss Adler again. I'll count to ten he said to himself, then if we get that far without being checked, I'll count to nine, and then— And then he caught sight of Mary's face, a dead-white, scared and almost haggard face that made her look fifteen years older than she was, and felt suddenly ashamed of himself. He sat on the bench, and squeezed her shoulder. "We'll be all right," he said confidently. All of a sudden he found it easy to speak again. "Uncle John has just said so, hasn't he? You wait and see."

She looked up at him, trying to smile. "Is Uncle John always right?"

"Always," Smith said firmly.

Twenty seconds passed. Smith rose to his feet, walked to the front of the cable car and peered down. Though the moon was obscured he could just dimly discern the shape of the lower station. He turned to look at the others. They were all looking at him.

"Not much more than a hundred feet to go," Smith said. "I'm going to open that door in a minute. Well, a few seconds. By that time we won't be much more than fifteen feet above the ground. Twenty, at the most. If the car stops, we jump. There's two or three feet of snow down there. Should cushion our fall enough to give an even chance of not breaking anything."

Schaffer parted his lips to make some suitable remark, thought better of it and returned head to hands in weary silence. Smith opened the leading door, did his best to ignore the icy blast of wind that gusted in through the opening, and looked vertically downwards, realising that he had been over-optimistic in his assessment of the distance between cable car and ground. The distance was at least fifty feet, a distance sufficient to arouse in even the most optimistic mind dismaying thoughts of fractured femurs and tibias. And then he dismissed the thought, for an even more dismaying factor had now to be taken into consideration: in the far distance could be heard the sound of sirens, in the far distance could be seen the wavering beams of approaching headlamps. Schaffer lifted his head. The muzziness had now left him even if his sore head had not.

"Enter, left, reinforcements," he announced. "This wasn't on the schedule, boss. Radio gone, telephone gone, helicopter gone—"

"Just old-fashioned." Smith pointed towards the rear window. "They're using smoke signals."

"Jeez!" Schaffer stared out the rear windows, his voice awe-struck. "For stone, it sure burns good!"

Schaffer was in no way exaggerating. For stone, it burnt magnificently. The Schloss Adler was well and truly alight, a conflagration in which smoke had suddenly become an inconsiderable and, indeed, a very minor element. It was wreathed in flames, almost lost to sight in flames, towering flames that now reached up almost to the top of the great round tower to the northeast. Perched on its volcanic plug halfway up the mountainside against the dimly seen backdrop of the unseen heights of the Weissspitze, the blazing castle, its effulgence now beginning to light up the entire valley and quite drowning out the pale light of a moon again showing through, was an incredibly fantastic sight from some equally incredible and fantastic fairy tale.

"One trusts that they are well insured," Schaffer said. He was on his feet now, peering down towards the lower station. "How far, boss? And how far down."

"Thirty feet. Maybe twenty-five. And fifteen feet down." The lights of the leading cars were passing the still smouldering embers of the station. "We have it made, Lieutenant Schaffer?"

"We have it made." Schaffer cursed and staggered as the car jerked to a violent and abrupt stop. "Almost, that is."

"All out!" Smith shouted. "All out!"

"There speaks the eternal shop steward," Schaffer said. "Stand back, I've got two good hands." He brushed by Smith, clutched the doorjamb with his left hand, pulled Mary towards him, transferred his grip from waist to wrist and dropped her out through the leading door, lowering her as far as the stretch of his left arm would permit. When he let her go, she had less than three feet to fall. Within three seconds he had done the same with Carnaby-Jones. The cable car jerked and started to move back up the valley. Schaffer practically bundled Smith out of the car, wincing in pain as he momentarily took all of Smith's two-hundred-pound weight, then slid out of the doorway himself, hung momentarily from the doorway at the full stretch of his arms, then dropped six feet into the soft yielding snow. He staggered, but maintained balance.

Smith was beside him. He had fished out a plastic explosive from the bag on his back and torn off the friction fuse. He handed the package to Schaffer and said: "You have a good right arm."

"I have a good right arm. Horses, no. Baseball, yes." Schaffer took aim and lobbed the explosive neatly through the doorway of the disappearing cable car. "Like that?"

"Like that. Come on." Smith turned and, catching Mary by the arm while Schaffer hustled Carnaby-Jones along, ran down the side of the lower station and into the shelter of the nearest house bare seconds before a command car, followed by several trucks crammed with soldiers, slid to a skidding halt below the lower station. Soldiers piled out of the trucks, following an officer, clearly identifiable as Colonel Weissner, up the steps into the lower station.

The castle burned more fiercely than ever, a fire obviously totally out of control. Suddenly, there was the sharp crack of an explosion and the ascending cable car burst into flames. The car, halfway up to the first pylon, swung in great arcs across the valley, its flames fanned by the wind, and climbed steadily upwards into the sky until its flame was lost in the greater flame of the Schloss Adler.

Crouched in the shelter of the house, Schaffer touched Smith's arm. "Sure you wouldn't like to go and burn down the station as well?"

"Come on," Smith said. "The garage."

ELEVEN

COLONEL WYATT-TURNER leaned over in the co-pilot's seat, pressed his face against the side screen and stared down unhappily at the ground. The Mosquito bomber, all engines and plywood, was, he was well aware, the fastest warplane in the world: even so, he hadn't been prepared for anything quite so fast as this.

Normal flying, of course, imparts no sensation of speed, but then, Wing Commander Carpenter wasn't engaged in normal flying, he was engaged in what Wyatt-Turner regarded as highly abnormal flying and flying, moreover, that was liable to bring them to disaster at any second. Carpenter was giving a ground-level performance of some spectacular note, skimming across fields, brushing treetops, skirting small hills that stood in his way, and Wyatt-Turner didn't like any of it one little bit. What he liked even less was the appalling speed of their own moon-shadow flitting over the ground beneath them; and what he liked least of all was the increasing number of occasions on which plane and shadow came within almost touching distance of each other. In an effort to keep his mind off what must inevitably happen when and if the gap were finally closed he withdrew his almost mesmerised stare and glanced at his watch.

"Twenty-five minutes." He looked at the relaxed figure in the pilot's seat, at the world-weary face that contrasted so oddly with the magnificent panache of the red handlebar moustache. "Can you make it in time?"

"I can make it," Carpenter said comfortably. "Point is, will they?"

"God only knows. I don't see how they can. Both the Admiral and I are convinced that they're trapped in the Schloss

Adler. Besides, the whole countryside must be up in arms by this time. What chance *can* they have?"

"And that is why you came?"

"I sent them," Wyatt-Turner said emptily. He glanced through the side screen and recoiled as plane and shadow seemed to touch as they skimmed over the top of a pine forest. He said plaintively: "Must you fly so close to the damned ground?"

"Enemy radar, old chap," Carpenter said soothingly. "We're safer down here among the bushes."

Smith, with Mary and Jones behind him and Schaffer bringing up the rear, skirted the backs of the houses on the east side of the village street and cautiously made their way through the automobile junkyard to the rear double doors of Sulz's garage. Smith had his skeleton keys in his hand and was just reaching for the padlock when one of the doors opened quietly inwards. Heidi stood there. She stared at them as if they were creatures from another world, then up at the burning castle, then wordlessly, questioningly, at Smith.

"All here in black and white." Smith patted his tunic. "Into the bus."

Smith waited till they had filed through the door, closed it, crossed to a small barred window at the front of the garage and peered out cautiously.

The street was packed with a milling crowd of people, most of them soldiers, nearly all unarmed men who had come hurrying out from the various *Weinstuben* to watch the burning Schloss Adler. But there were plenty of armed soldiers nearby—two truckloads not thirty yards from the garage, not to mention three more truckloads even further up the street at the foot of the lower station. Further down the street a motorcycle patrol was parked outside Zum Wilden Hirsch. The one real physical obstacle in the way of their escape was a small command car, manned, parked directly outside the doors of Sulz's garage. Smith looked at the car thoughtfully, decided that this was an obstacle that could be overcome. He withdrew from the window and crossed to the doors to check that the four bolts were still withdrawn.

Mary and Carnaby-Jones had already made their way into the bus. As Heidi went to follow, Schaffer caught her by the shoulders, kissed her briefly and smiled at her. She looked at him in surprise.

"Well, aren't you glad to see me?" Schaffer demanded.

"I've had a *terrible* time up there. Good God, girl, I might have been killed."

"Not as handsome as you were two hours ago." She smiled, gently touched his face where Carraciola's handiwork with the Schmeisser had left its bloody mark, and added over her shoulder as she climbed into the bus: "And that's as long as you've known me."

"Two hours! I've aged twenty years tonight. And that, lady, is one helluva long courtship. Oh, God!" He watched in wearily resigned despair as Smith climbed into the driver's seat and switched on the ignition. "Here we go for another twenty. On the floor, everyone."

"How about you?" Heidi asked.

"Me?" Schaffer's surprise seemed genuine. He smashed the front window with the butt of the Schmeisser, reversed the gun, released the safety catch and knelt on the floor. "I'm the conductor. It's against regulations."

The middle finger of Smith's bloodstained bandaged hand reached for the starter button and the big diesel caught at once. Smith started to back towards the rear of the garage. Two perfectly good cars, a Mercedes and an Opel, lay in his way and by the time that Smith—whose expression betrayed no awareness of their presence—reached the back of the garage neither was fit for anything other than the scrap heap that lay beyond the rear doors. Smith stopped, engaged first gear, revved up the engine and let in the clutch with a bang. The bus jerked forward, gathering speed as it went.

Smith aimed the angled point of the massive snowplough at the junction of the double doors and for all the resistance the doors offered they might have been made of brown paper. With a splintering crash that sent shattered door planks flying through the air like so much confetti, the bus roared out into the street, Smith spinning the wheel violently to the right as they careened into the crowded thoroughfare.

Crowded the thoroughfare might have been, but the pedestrians, the rubber-neckers gazing at the funeral pyre of the Schloss Adler, had had at least sufficient warning given them by the accelerating clamour of the post bus's diesel to fling themselves clear as the bus came crashing through the doors. But the two occupants of the command car had no such opportunity for escape. Before either of the two occupants of the front seat—a sergeant with his hands resting lightly on the wheel, a major with a radio telephone in one hand, a thin cigar with a long ash in the other—were properly aware of what was happening, their car was swept up and carried away on the post bus's snowplough. For fifteen, perhaps even twenty yards, the command car was carried along, precariously balanced, on the broad blade of the snowplough, before dropping off to one side. Miraculously enough, it landed on even keel, all four wheels still on the ground. The dazed major still had the telephone in one hand, the cigar in the other: he hadn't even lost the ash from his cigar.

Further down the street, outside Zum Wilden Hirsch, a group of Alpenkorps motorcyclists standing just outside the door stared incredulously up the street. Their first reaction, their immediate conclusion was either that Zep Salzmann, the highly popular driver of the post bus, had gone mad or that the accelerator had jammed on the floorboards. Disillusionment was rapid. They heard the unmistakable sound of an engine changing up quickly through the gears and caught a brief glimpse of Smith hunched over the steering wheel and of Schaffer crouched behind the Schmeisser sticking out through the right-hand shattered windscreen: then the post bus's headlamps switched on and they could see no more. But they had seen enough. One quick command from their sergeant and the motorcycle patrol leapt for their machines, began to kick them into life.

But Smith also had seen enough. He blew a warning blast on his town horn, twisted the wheel and slewed the bus into the side of the street. His intentions were unmistakable and the motorcycle patrol's decision to elect for discretion in lieu of suicidal valour was as immediate as it was automatic. They frantically abandoned their machines and flung themselves for their lives up the steps of Zum Wilden Hirsch.

There was a thunderous series of metallic bangs interspersed with the eldritch screeches of torn and tortured metal as the snowplough smashed into the motorcycles and swept them along in its giant maw. As Smith straightened out into the middle of the road again several of them slid off the angled blade and crashed with a great splintering of wood and buckling of metal into the boarded sidewalk: the machines were no longer recognisable as motorcycles. Two of them, however, still remained perched on the blade.

The post bus was still accelerating with Smith's accelerator foot flat on the floorboards. The headlamps were flashing rapidly, alternately main beam and dipped, and the streets ahead were clearing with corresponding rapidity: but the moment when the last few straggling pedestrians were galvanised into

189

jumping for safety came when Smith switched on the Alpine horn.

In the mountains, the Alpine post bus has absolute priority over every other vehicle in the road and its penetrating and stentorian three-toned post horn is the symbol of its total authority, of its unquestioned right to complete priority at all times. The sound of that horn—whether the post bus is in sight or not—is the signal for all vehicles or pedestrians to stop or move well into the side of the road, a signal that is immediately and automatically obeyed, for the absolute entitlement to the right of way of the official post bus is deeply ingrained into the minds of all Alpine dwellers, and has been from earliest childhood. A magic wand might have made a better job of clearing that village street, but not all that much better: vehicles and pedestrians alike pressed into the sides of the streets as if some powerful magnetic affinity had just been developed between them and the walls of the houses. The expression on faces ranged from astonishment to blank incomprehension. Hostility there was none: there had been no time for any to develop for events were moving far too swiftly and comprehension hadn't even begun to overtake the events. The bus had now reached the end of the village street and still not one shot had been fired.

At the sharp left-hand corner at the foot of the street the two remaining motorcycles slid off the snowplough and smashed into a low stone wall: two more absolute certainties, Smith thought inconsequentially, for the automobile cemetery behind Sulz's garage. Ahead of him now he could see the road stretch almost arrow-straight alongside the dark waters of the Blau See. He switched off the Alpine horn button, changed his mind and switched it on again: that horn was worth a pair of machine guns any day.

"Don't you know any other tunes?" Schaffer asked irritably. He shivered in the icy blast from the smashed front window, and sat on the floor to get what little shelter he could. "Give me a call when you require my services. A mile from now, I'd say."

"What do you mean, a mile from now?"

"The barrack gates. That guy in the command car had a radio phone."

"He had, had he?" Smith spared him a brief glance. "Why didn't you shoot him?"

"I'm a changed man, boss." Schaffer sighed. "Something splendid has just come into my life."

"Besides, you didn't have a chance."

"Besides, as you say, I didn't have a chance." Schaffer twisted round and looked through the rear windows of the bus for signs of pursuit, but the road behind them was empty but, for all that, Schaffer reflected, the rearward view was one not lacking in interest: the Schloss Adler, by this time completely enveloped in flames, a reddish-white inferno now lighting up for half a mile around the startling incongruity of its snow and ice-covered setting, was clearly beyond saving: arsonist's dream or fireman's nightmare, the castle was finished: before dawn it would be an empty and desolate shell, a gaunt and blackened ruin to haunt and desecrate for generations to come the loveliest fairy-tale valley he had ever seen.

Schaffer shortened his gaze and tried to locate the three others, but all were on the floor, under seats and completely concealed. He cursed as the shaking shuddering bus lurched violently, throwing him against the right-hand front door, straightened and peered at the illuminated dashboard.

"God save us all," he said piously. "Ninety!"

"Kilometres," Smith said patiently.

"Ah!" Schaffer stiffened as he watched Smith's foot move quickly from accelerator to brake, hoisted a wary eye over the lower edge of the shattered windscreen and whistled softly. The barrack gates were barely two hundred yards away: both the area around the guardhouse and the parade ground beyond were brilliantly illuminated by overhead floodlamps: scores of armed soldiers seemed to be running around in purposeless confusion, a totally erroneous impression as Schaffer almost immediately realised. They were running towards and scrambling aboard trucks and command cars and they weren't wasting any time about it either.

"A hive of activity and no mistake," Schaffer observed. "I wonder—" He broke off, his eyes widening. A giant tank came rumbling into view past the guardhouse, turned right on to the road, stopped, swivelled 180° on its tracks, completely blocking the road: the gun turret moved fractionally until it was lined up on the headlights of the approaching bus. "Oh, my gosh!" Schaffer's shocked whisper was just audible over the fading sound of the post bus's diesel. "A Tiger tank. And that's an 88-millimetre cannon, boss."

"It's not a popgun, and that's a fact," Smith agreed. "Flat on the floor." He reached forward, pulled a switch, and the eighteen-inch long semaphore indicator began to wave gently up and down. Smith first dipped his main headlights, then switched them off altogether, covering the last thirty yards on side lamps alone and praying that all those signs of peaceful normality might help to keep nervous fingers away from the firing button of the most lethal tank cannon ever devised.

The fingers, for whatever reason, left the button alone. Smith, slowed to a walking pace, turned right through the guardhouse gates and stopped. Taking care to keep his injured right hand well out of sight, he wound down his window and leaned out, left elbow over the sill as three guards, led by a sergeant and all with machine pistols at the ready, closed in on the driver's cab.

"Quickly!" Smith shouted. "Telephone. Surgeon to the sick bay." He jerked his thumb over his shoulder. "Colonel Weissner. They got him twice. Through the lungs. For God's sake, don't just *stand* there!"

"But—but the post bus!" the sergeant protested. "We had a call from—"

"Drunk, by God!" Smith swore savagely. "He'll be courtmartialled in the morning." His voice dropped menacingly. "And you, if the colonel dies. Move!"

Smith engaged gear and drove off, still at walking pace. The sergeant, reassured by the sight of a major's uniform, the fact that the bus was moving into the barracks, the slow speed with which it was moving, and above all, by the authoritative clamour of the Alpine horn which Smith still had not switched off, ran for the nearest phone.

Still crawling along in first gear, Smith carefully edged the post bus through the press of men and machines, past a column of booted and gauntleted soldiers mounted on motorcycles, past armoured vehicles and trucks, all with engines already running, some already moving towards the gates—but not moving as quickly towards the gates as Smith would have wished. Ahead of the post bus was a group of officers, most of them obviously senior, talking animatedly. Smith slowed down the bus even more and leaned from the window.

"They're trapped!" he called excitedly. "Upstairs in Zum Wilden Hirsch. They've got Colonel Weissner as hostage. Hurry, for God's sake!"

He broke off as he suddenly recognised one of the officers as the Alpenkorps captain to whom, in his temporary capacity of Major Bernd Himmler, he'd spoken in Zum Wilden Hirsch earlier that evening. A second later the recognition was mutual, the captain's mouth fell open in total incredulity and before he had time to close it Smith's foot was flat on the accelerator and the bus heading for the southern gates, soldiers flinging themselves to both sides to avoid the scything sweep of the giant snowplough. Such was the element of surprise that fully thirty yards had been covered before most of the back windows of the bus were holed and broken, the shattering of glass mingling with the sound of the ragged fusillade of shots from behind. And then Smith, wrenching desperately on the wheel, came careering through the southern gates back on to the main road, giving them at least temporary protection from the sharpshooters on the parade ground.

But they had, it seemed, only changed from the frying pan to the fire. Temporary protection they might have obtained from one enemy—but from another and far deadlier enemy they had no protection at all. Smith all but lost control of the bus as something struck a glancing blow low down on his cab door, ricocheted off into the night with a viciously screaming whine and exploded in a white flash of snow-flurried light less than fifty yards ahead.

"The Tiger tank," Schaffer shouted. "That goddamned 88-millimetre—"

"Get down!" Smith jackknifed down and to one side of the wheel until his eyes were only an inch above the foot of the windscreen. "That one was low. The next one—"

The next one came through the top of the back door, traversed the length of the bus and exited through the front of the roof, just above the windscreen. This time there was no explosion.

"A dud?" Schaffer said hopefully. "Or maybe a dummy practise—"

"Dummy nothing!" Upright again, Smith was swinging the bus madly, dangerously, from side to side of the road in an attempt to confuse the tank gunner's aim. "Armour-piercing shells, laddie, designed to go through two inches of steel plate in a tank before they explode." He winced and ducked low as a third shell took out most of the left-hand windows of the bus, showering himself and Schaffer with a flying cloud of shattered glass fragments. "Just let one of those shells strike a chassis member, instead of thin sheet metal, or the engine block, or the snowplough—"

"Don't!" Schaffer begged. "Just let it creep up on me all unbeknownst, like." He paused, then continued: "Taking his time, isn't he? Lining up for the Sunday one."

"No." Smith glanced in the rear-view mirror and steadied

the wildly swaying bus up on a steady course. "Never thought I'd be glad to see a few carloads or truckloads of Alpenkorps coming after me." He changed into top gear and pushed the accelerator to the floor. "I'm happy to make an exception this time."

Schaffer turned and looked through the shattered rear windows. He could count at least three pairs of headlights on the road behind them, with two others swinging out through the southern gates: between them, they effectively blotted the post bus from the view of the tank gunner.

"Happy isn't the word for it. Me, I'm ecstatic. Tiger tanks are one thing but little itsy-bitsy trucks are another." Schaffer strode rapidly down the central aisle, passing by Mary, Heidi and Carnaby-Jones, all of whom were struggling rather shakily to their feet, and looked at the crates stacked in the rear seats.

"Six crates!" he said to Heidi. "And we asked for only two. Honey, you're going to make me the happiest man alive." He opened the rear door and began to empty the contents of the crate onto the road. A few of the bottles just bounced harmlessly on ridges of hard-packed snow, but the speed of the bus was now such that most of them shattered on impact.

The first of the two leading pursuit cars was within three hundred yards of the bus when it ran into the area of broken glass. From Schaffer's point of view it was impossible to tell what exactly happened, but such indications as could be gathered by long-range sight and sound were satisfying enough. The headlights of the leading car suddenly began to slew violently from side to side, the screeching of brakes was clearly audible above the sound of the post bus's diesel, but not nearly as loud as the rending crash of metal as the second car smashed into the rear of the first. For a few seconds both cars seemed locked together, then they skidded wildly out of control, coming to rest with the nose of the first car in the right-hand ditch, the tail of the second in the left-hand ditch. The headlamps of both cars had failed just after the moment of impact but there was more than sufficient illumination from the lamps of the first of the trucks coming up behind them to show that the road was completely blocked.

"Neat," Schaffer said admiringly. "Very neat, Schaffer." He called to Smith: "That'll hold them, boss."

"Sure, it'll hold them," Smith said grimly. "It'll hold them for all of a minute. You can't burst heavy truck tyres that way and it won't take them long to bulldoze those cars out of the way. Heidi?"

Heidi walked forward, shivering in the icy gale now blowing through both the shattered front and side windows. "Yes, Major?"

"How far to the turn-off?"

"A mile."

"And to the wooden bridge—what do you call it, *Zur Alten Brücke?*"

"Another mile."

"Three minutes. At the most, that." He raised his voice. "Three minutes, Lieutenant. Can you do it?"

"I can do it." Schaffer was already lashing together packages of plastic explosive. He used transparent adhesive tape, leaving long streamers dangling from the bound packages. He had just secured the last package in position when he lurched heavily as the post bus, now clear of the Blau See and running through a pine forest, swung abruptly to the left on to a side road.

"Sorry," Smith called. "Almost missed that one. Less than a mile, Lieutenant."

"No panic," Schaffer said cheerfully. He fished out a knife to start cutting the fuses to their shortest possible length, then went very still indeed as he glanced through where the rear windows had once been. In the middle distance were the vertically wavering beams of powerful headlights, closing rapidly. The cheerfulness left Schaffer's voice. "Well, maybe there is a little bit panic, at that. I've got bad news, boss."

"And I have a rear mirror. How far, Heidi?"

"Next corner."

While Schaffer worked quickly on the fuses, Smith concentrated on getting the post bus round the next corner as quickly as possible without leaving the road. And then they were on and round the corner and the bridge was no more than a hundred yards away.

It was not, Smith thought, a bridge he would have chosen to have crossed with a bicycle, much less a six-ton bus. Had it been a bridge crossing some gently meandering stream, then, yes, possibly: but not a bridge such as this one was, a fifty-foot bridge surfaced with untied railway sleepers, spanning a ravine two hundred feet in depth and supported by trestles, very ancient wooden trestles which, from what little he could see of them from his acute angle of approach, he wouldn't have trusted to support the tables at the vicar's garden party.

Smith hit this elderly and decrepit edifice at forty miles per hour. A more cautious and understandable approach might have been to crawl over it at less than walking pace but Smith's conviction that the less time he spent on each ancient sleeper the better was as instantaneous as it was complete. The heavy snow chains on each tyre bit into and dislodged each successive sleeper with a terrifying rumble, the post bus bounced up and down as if on a giant cake walk while the entire structure of the bridge swayed from side to side like the bridge of a destroyer at speed in a heavy cross sea. It had been Smith's original intention to stop in the middle of the bridge but once embarked upon the crossing he would no more have done so than dallied to pick an edelweiss in the path of an Alpine avalanche. Ten feet from the end of the bridge he stamped on the brakes and skidded to a sliding halt, on solid ground again, in less than twenty yards.

Schaffer already had the back door open and the two packages of plastic explosives in his hands before the bus stopped. Five seconds after hitting the road he was back on the bridge again, skipping nimbly over a dozen dislodged sleepers until he had arrived at the main supports of the central trestle. It took him less than twenty seconds to tape one package to the right-hand support, cross the bridge and tape the second package to the left-hand support. He heard the deepening roar of a rapidly approaching engine, glanced up, saw the swathe of unseen headlamp beams shining round the corner they had just passed, tore off the ignition fuse, crossed the bridge, tore off the other and raced back for the bus. Smith already had the bus in gear and was moving away when Schaffer flung himself through the back doorway and was hauled inside by helping hands.

Schaffer twisted round till he was sitting on the passageway, his legs dangling through the open doorway, just in time to see the headlamps of the pursuing car sweep into sight round the corner. It was now less than a hundred yards from the bridge, and accelerating. For a brief, almost panic-stricken moment Schaffer wondered wildly if he had cut the fuses short enough, he hadn't realised the following car had been quite as close as it was: and from the tense and strained expressions on the faces of the two girls and the man beside him, expressions sensed rather than seen, he knew that exactly the same thought was in their minds.

The two loud, flat detonations, each fractionally preceded by the brilliant white flash characteristic of plastic explosive, came within one second of each other. Baulks of timber and railway sleepers were hurled forty feet into the air, spinning lazily around in a curious kind of slow motion, many of them falling back again onto the now tottering support structure with an impact sufficient to carry away the central trestle. One moment, a bridge: the next, an empty ravine with, on the far side of it, the wildly swinging headlamp beams as the driver flung his car from side to side in a nothing-to-be-lost attempt to prevent the car from sliding over the edge of the ravine. It seemed certain that he must fail until the moment when the car, sliding broadside on along the road, struck a large rock, rolled over twice and came to a halt less than six feet from the edge of the ravine.

Schaffer shook his head in wonder, rose, closed the rear door, sat in the back seat, lit a cigarette, tossed the spent match through the smashed rear window and observed: "It's lucky you people have me around."

"All this and modesty, too," Heidi said admiringly.

"A rare combination," Schaffer acknowledged. "You'll find lots of other pleasant surprises in store for you as we grow old together. How far to this airfield now?"

"Five miles. Perhaps eight minutes. But this is the only road in. With the bridge gone, there's no hurry now."

"That's as may be. Schaffer is anxious to be gone. Tell me, honey, were *all* those beer bottles empty?"

"The ones we threw away were."

"I just simply don't deserve you," Schaffer said reverently.

"We're thinking along the same lines at last," Heidi said acidly.

Schaffer grinned, took two beer bottles and went forward to relieve Smith, who moved out only too willingly with the bus still in motion. Smith's right hand, Schaffer saw, hadn't a scrap of bandage left that wasn't wholly saturated in blood and the face was very pale. But he made no comment.

Three minutes later they were out of the forest, running along through open farmland, and five minutes after that, acting on Heidi's directions, Schaffer swung the bus through a narrow gateway on the left-hand side of the road. The headlamps successively illuminated two small hangars, a narrow, cleared runway stretching into the distance and, finally, a bullet-riddled Mosquito bomber with a crumpled undercarriage.

"Ain't that a beautiful sight, now?" Schaffer nodded at the damaged plane. "Carnaby-Jones transport?"

Smith nodded. "It began with a Mosquito and it will end —we hope—in a Mosquito. This is Oberhausen airfield. HQ of the Bavarian Mountain Rescue pilots."

"Three cheers for the Bavarian Mountain Rescue pilots." Schaffer stopped the bus facing up the length of the runway, switched off the lights and turned off the engine. They sat silently in the darkness, waiting.

Colonel Wyatt-Turner glanced through the side screen and breathed with relief as, for the first time that night, the ground fell away sharply beneath the Mosquito. He said sarcastically: "Losing your nerve, Commander?"

"I lost that September 3, 1939," Carpenter said cheerfully. "Got to climb. Can't expect to see any recognition signals down among the bushes there."

"You're sure we're on the right course?"

"No question. That's the Weissspitze there. Three minutes' flying time." Carpenter paused and went on thoughtfully. "Looks uncommon like Guy Fawkes night up there, don't you think."

The wing commander was hardly exaggerating. In the far distance the silhouette of the Weissspitze was but dimly seen, but there was no mistaking the intensity of the great fire blazing halfway up the mountainside. Occasionally, great gouts of red flame and what looked like gigantic fireworks could be seen soaring high above the main body of the fire.

"Explosives or boxes of ammunition going up, I'd say," Carpenter said pensively. "That's the Schloss Adler, of course. Were any of your boys carrying matches?"

"They must have been." Wyatt-Turner stared impassively at the distant blaze. "It's quite a sight."

"It's all of that," Carpenter agreed. He touched Wyatt-Turner's arm and pointed forwards and down. "But there's a sight far finer far, the most beautiful sight I've ever seen."

Wyatt-Turner followed the pointing finger. Less than two miles away, about five hundred feet below, a pair of headlamps were flashing regularly on and off, once every two seconds. With a conscious effort of will he looked away and glanced briefly at Carpenter, but almost at once was back on the flashing headlamps. He stared at them hypnotically and shook his head in slow and total disbelief.

Schaffer had the headlights switched on main beam, illuminating the runway, and the post bus engine running as the black squat shape of the Mosquito, air brakes fully extended, lined up for its approach to the runway and had the bus itself moving, accelerating quickly through the gears, as the Mosquito sunk down over the top of the bus and settled down beautifully without the slightest suspicion of a bounce.

Within a minute Schaffer brought the bus to a skidding halt only yards from the now stationary plane. Half a minute later, with all five of them safely inside the plane, Carpenter had the Mosquito turned through 180° and was standing hard on the brakes as he brought the engines up to maximum revolutions. And then they were on their way, gathering speed so rapidly that they were airborne two hundred yards before the end of the runway. For the first mile of their climb Carpenter kept the plane heading almost directly towards the blazing castle that now redly illuminated the entire valley, then the funeral pyre of the Schloss Adler vanished for the last time as the Mosquito banked and headed for the northwest and home.

TWELVE

WING COMMANDER Carpenter took the Mosquito up to five thousand feet and kept it there. The time for dodging around among the bushes was past, for, on the outward journey, Carpenter had been concerned only that no German station pick him up long enough to form even a rough guess as to where he had been going. But now he didn't care if every radar station in the country knew where he was going: he was going home to England, mission accomplished, and there wasn't a warplane in Europe that could catch him. Wing Commander Carpenter pulled luxuriously at his evil-smelling briar. He was well content.

His five newly acquired passengers, were, perhaps, a fraction less content. They lacked Carpenter's well-upholstered pilot's seat. The interior of the Mosquito made no concessions whatsoever to passenger comfort. It was bleak, icy, cramped —it didn't require much space to carry a 4000 lb. bombload, the Mosquito's maximum—and totally devoid of seating in any form. The three men and the two girls squatted uncomfortably on thin palliasses, the expressions on their faces pretty accurately reflecting their acute discomfort. Colonel Wyatt-Turner, still holding across his knees the Sten gun he'd had at the ready in case any trouble had developed on the ground or that the flashing lights of the truck had been a German ruse, was sitting sideways in the co-pilot's seat so that he could see and talk to the pilot and the passengers at the same time. He had accepted without question or apparent interest Smith's brief explanation of the two girls' presence as being necessary to escape Gestapo vengeance. Colonel Wyatt-Turner had other and weightier matters on his mind.

Smith looked up from the bleeding mangled hand that

200

Mary was rebandaging with the plane's first aid kit and said to the colonel: "It was good of you to come in person to meet us, sir."

"It wasn't good of me at all," Wyatt-Turner said frankly. "I'd have gone mad if I'd stayed another minute in London—I *had* to know. It was I who sent you all out here." He sat without speaking for some time, then went on heavily: "Torrance-Smythe gone, Sergeant Harrod, and now, you say, Carraciola, Christiansen, and Thomas. All dead. A heavy price, Smith, a terrible price. My best men."

"All of them, sir?" Smith asked softly.

"I'm getting old." Wyatt-Turner shook his head wearily and drew a hand across his eyes. "Did you find out who—"

"Carraciola."

"Carraciola! Ted Carraciola? Never! I can't believe it."

"*And* Christiansen." Smith's voice was still quiet, still even. "*And* Thomas."

"And Christiansen? And Thomas?" He looked consideringly at Smith. "You've been through a lot, Major Smith. You're not well."

"I'm not as well as I was," Smith admitted. "But I was well enough when I killed them."

"You—*you* killed them?"

"I've killed a traitor before now. You know that."

"But—but traitors! All three of them. Impossible. I can't believe it! I *won't* believe it!"

"Then maybe you'll believe this, sir." Smith produced one of the notebooks from his tunic and handed it to Wyatt-Turner. "The names and addresses or contacts of every German agent in southern England *and* the names of all British agents in northwest Europe who have been supplanted by German agents. You will recognise Carraciola's writing. He wrote this under duress."

Slowly, like a man in a dream, Wyatt-Turner reached out and took the notebook. For three minutes he examined the contents, leafing slowly, almost reluctantly through the pages, then finally lay the book down with a sigh.

"This is the most important document I have ever seen." Wyatt-Turner sighed. "The nation is deeply in your debt, Major Smith."

"Thank you, sir."

"Or would have been. It's a great pity it will never have the chance to express its gratitude." He lifted the Sten from his knees and pointed it at Smith's heart. "You will do nothing foolish, will you, Major Smith?"

"What in God's name—" Carpenter twisted in his seat and stared at Wyatt-Turner in startled and total disbelief.

"Concentrate on your flying, my dear Wing Commander." Wyatt-Turner waved the Sten gently in Carpenter's direction. "Your course will do for the present. We'll be landing at Lille airport within the hour."

"The guy's gone nuts!" Schaffer's voice was a shocked whisper.

"If he has." Smith said drily, "he went nuts some years ago. Ladies and gentlemen, I give you the most dangerous spy in Europe, the most successful double agent of all time." He paused for reaction, but the silence remained unbroken: the enormity of the revelation of Wyatt-Turner's duplicity was too great for immediate comprehension. Smith continued: "Colonel Wyatt-Turner, you will be court-martialled this afternoon, sentenced, removed to the Tower then taken out, blindfolded and shot at eight o'clock tomorrow morning."

"You knew?" Wyatt-Turner's affable self-confidence had completely deserted him and his voice, low and strained, was barely distinguishable above the clamour of the engine. "You knew about me?"

"I knew about you," Smith nodded. "But we all knew about you, didn't we, Colonel? Three years, you claimed, behind the German lines, served with the Wehrmacht and finally penetrated the Berlin High Command. Sure you did. With the help of the Wehrmacht and the High Command. But when the tide of war turned and you could no longer feed the Allies with false and misleading reports about proposed German advances, then you were allowed to escape back to England to feed the Germans true and accurate reports about Allied plans —and give them all the information they required to round up British agents in northwest Europe. How many million francs do you have in your numbered account in Zurich, Colonel?"

Wing Commander Carpenter stared straight ahead through the windscreen and said very slowly: "Frankly, old chap, this is preposterous."

"Try batting an eyelid and see just how preposterous that Sten gun is," Smith suggested. He looked at Wyatt-Turner again. "You underestimated Admiral Rolland, I'm afraid. He's had his suspicions about you and the four section leaders of Department C for months. But he was wrong about Torrance-Smythe."

"Guess away." Wyatt-Turner had recovered his composure and most of his self-confidence. "It'll pass the time till we get to Lille."

"Unfortunately for you, there is no guesswork. Admiral Rolland recalled me—and Mary—from Italy: he could no longer be sure of anyone in London. You know how corruption spreads? Played it very clever, did the Admiral. He told you he had his suspicions about one of his section leaders, but didn't know which. So, when General Carnaby crashed, he put up to you the idea of sending the section officers to the rescue—and made damn sure that you never once had the opportunity of talking to any of them in private before they took off."

"That—that was why I was called in?" Schaffer looked as if he had been sandbagged. "Because you couldn't trust—"

"For all we knew, M.I.6 was riddled . . . Well, Colonel, you weren't too happy until Rolland asked *you* to pick the leader. So you picked me. Rolland knew you would. You'd only just met me for the first time, but you knew from Kesselring's military intelligence chief, through your pal Admiral Canaris, that I was their top double agent. Or thought you did. Rolland was the only man on either side who knew I wasn't. For you, I was the ideal choice. Rolland made certain that you didn't have the chance of talking to *me* either, but you weren't worried. You knew that I would know what to do." Smith smiled bleakly. "I'm happy to say I did. It must have been quite a shock to your system this afternoon when he told you what I really was."

"You knew that? You knew all that?" Wyatt-Turner's newfound composure had vanished, his voice was quiet and vicious. He lifted the Sten slightly. "What goes on, Smith?"

"All prearranged, to force your hand. We had everything —except proof—about you. I got that proof this evening. Colonel Kramer *knew* that we were coming, *knew* that we were after General Carnaby." He nodded towards Jones. "Incidentally, meet Cartwright Jones, an American actor."

"What?" Wyatt-Turner forced out the word as if a pair of powerful hands were squeezing on his windpipe.

"General Carnaby is spending a quiet weekend at the Admiral's country house in Wiltshire. As a stand-in, Mr. Jones was quite admirable. He had them all as deceived as that faked plane crash—you will have realised by now that it was a deliberate crash landing." Wyatt-Turner tried to speak, but the words failed to come: his mouth was working and the colour had drained from his ruddy face. "And why did Kramer know? He knew because you had informed Berlin as soon as Rolland had put the plan to you. *Nobody else had the chance to. And* he knew that we would be in Zum Wilden Hirsch this evening. He knew because I told you on the radio broadcast this morning and you lost no time in passing the good word on."

"Are you sure?" Heidi asked. "Couldn't the informant have been whichever of the men—Carraciola or Christiansen or Thomas—who killed Torrance-Smythe. There's a phone box just outside the inn."

"I know. No, he didn't have time. I left the inn for exactly seven minutes. Three minutes after I'd left, Torrance-Smythe did the same—to follow one of the three others he'd just seen leaving. Smithy was clever and he knew something was far wrong. He—"

"How did he know?" Schaffer demanded.

"We'll never be sure. I think we'll find that he was a highly skilled lip reader. Anyway, he caught the man he'd seen leaving in the phone booth outside the post office—before he'd had time to get through to either Weissner or Kramer. There was a fight to the death. By the time the killer had dragged Smithy around to the back and returned to the booth, someone else was occupying it. I saw him. So the killer had to go back into the inn. Kramer it was who told Weissner—and the colonel here who told Kramer."

"Very interesting." There was a sneer in Wyatt-Turner's voice, but a sneer belied by the deep unease in his face. "Fascinating, in fact. Quite finished, Major Smith?"

"Finished." Smith sighed. "You just had to come to meet us, hadn't you, Colonel? This was the last door to life left open to you. In my final broadcast I told the admiral 'I have it all.' He told you what that meant—all the names, all the addresses. We could never have got at you through Carraciola, Christiansen or Thomas—they were too close to you in M.I.6, you were too cagey and they never knew who they were working for. You used intermediaries—and all their names are in that book. You *knew* they'd put the finger on you—when it's a choice between taking a walk to the gallows and talking—well, it's not much of a choice, is it?"

Wyatt-Turner didn't answer. He turned to Carpenter and said: "Lay off a course for Lille airport."

"Don't bother," Smith said.

Wyatt-Turner lined his Sten on Smith. "Give me one good reason why I shouldn't shoot you now."

"I can do that." Smith nodded. "Why do you think that Admiral Rolland accompanied you to the airport? He never has before."

"Go on." Wyatt's voice was hard, abrupt, but his eyes were sick, sick with the sudden certainty of defeat and death.

"To make quite certain that you took that Sten and only that Sten with you. Tell me, can you see two parallel scores where the stock meets the barrel?"

Wyatt-Turner stared at him for long moments then glanced down quickly at the Sten. There were two unmistakable parallel scratches exactly where Smith had said they would be. Wyatt-Turner looked up again, his face contorted, desperation replacing the sickness in his eyes.

"That's right," Smith said. "I personally filed off the firing pin exactly thirty-six hours ago." With his left hand Smith reached awkwardly under his tunic flap and brought out Schaffer's silenced Luger. Wyatt-Turner, with his Sten lined up on Smith's head and the muzzle less than three feet from Smith's face, squeezed the trigger time and again, and each convulsive contraction of his forefinger was rewarded by a dry and empty click. With a stunned, almost uncomprehending expression on his face, Wyatt-Turner slowly lowered the Sten to the floor, then quickly whirled in his seat, jerked open the door and threw the notebook out into the night. He turned and smiled bleakly at Smith.

"The most important document in Europe, I believe I called it."

"So you did." Smith handed his gun to Schaffer, reached under hs tunic and brought out two more books. "Duplicates."

"Duplicates!" The smile slowly faded from the heavily jowled face, leaving it frozen in defeat. "Duplicates," he whispered. He looked slowly around them all and then finally back at Smith, who had retrieved his gun from Schaffer. He said: "Are you going to shoot me?"

"No."

Wyatt-Turner nodded, slid back the door to its widest extent and said: "Can you really see me in the Tower?" He stepped forward into the doorway.

"No." Smith shook his head. "No, I can't see that."

"Mind the step," said Schaffer. His voice was cold and empty, his face was carved from stone.

"Well, now, time to make a call." Smith slid shut the door, scrambled painfully into the co-pilot's seat and looked at Mary. "The Admiral must be getting worried by this time."

"Time to make a call," Mary repeated mechanically. She stared at him as if seeing a ghost. "How can you sit there—just after—how can you be so *calm?*"

"Because it's no shock to me, silly. I *knew* he was going to die."

"You knew—of course, of course," she murmured.

"Now then," Smith went on, deliberately brisk-voiced as he took her hand. "You realise what this means, don't you?"

"Do I realise what what means?" She was still ashen-faced.

"You and I are all washed up," Smith explained patiently. "Finished. In Italy, in northwest Europe. I won't even be allowed to fight as a soldier because if I were captured I'd still be shot as a spy."

"So?"

"So, for us, the war is over. For the first time we can think of ourselves. O.K.?" He squeezed her hand and she smiled shakily in reply. "O.K. Wing Commander, may I use your radio?"

"So that's the way he went." Admiral Rolland, telephone in hand and standing by the big transceiver in his London Operations HQ, looked old and very very tired. "Maybe it's all for the best, Smith. And you have all the information you want?"

Smith's voice crackled over the earphone. "Everything, sir."

"Magnificent, magnificent! I have all the police forces in the country alerted. As soon as we get that book . . . There's a car waiting for you at the airport. See you in an hour."

"Yes, sir. There's one thing, sir, a small thing. I want to get married this morning."

"You what?" Grey bushy eyebrows lifted towards the mane of white hair.

"I want to get married," Smith explained slowly and patiently. "To Miss Mary Ellison."

"But you can't," Rolland protested. "This morning! Impossible! There are such things as banns, permits, the registrar's office will be shut today—"

"After all I've done for you," Smith interrupted reproachfully.

"Blackmail, sir! You play on an old man's gratitude. Downright blackmail!" Rolland banged down the phone, smiled tiredly and picked up another phone. "Operator? Put me through to the Forgery Section."

Wing Commander Carpenter, his pipe well alight and by his elbow a cup of coffee newly poured from a vacuum flask, was his old imperturbable self again. Smith talked quietly to Mary while Jones had his eyes closed and appeared to be asleep. Further aft in the fuselage, Schaffer had his arm around Heidi, who was making no attempt to fight him off.

"Right," Schaffer said. "So we go to this pub tonight, see—"

"You said the Savoy Grill," Heidi reminded him.

"A rose by any other name . . . So we go to this pub, and we'll have paté, smoked trout, sirloin of Aberdeen Angus—"

"Aberdeen Angus!" Heidi looked at him in amusement. "Forgotten the war, haven't you? Forgotten rationing? More like a sirloin of horse meat."

"Honey." Schaffer took her hands and spoke severely and earnestly. "Honey, don't ever again mention that word to me. I'm allergic to horses."

"You eat them?" Heidi gazed at him in astonishment. "In Montana?"

"I fall off them," Schaffer said moodily. "Everywhere."